Snuggled under the soft gray comforter, his pretty guest looked like an angel, and a wave of affection swept over Aengus. It charmed him to note that she was wearing one of his plaid flannel shirts as an impromptu nightgown. The colors suited her—red like her flushed cheeks, dark green like her laughing eyes. Of course the shirt was huge on her. It would probably hang all the way to her knees. He could almost picture her shapely body beneath the loose fabric, and as he did his thoughts focused on her bare legs and the soft warm reaches to which they might lead a lonely man.

Slowly, the scene was no longer charming and innocent. This was not a child in his bed. Nor was it the sturdy, humorless bedmate he'd been expecting through the mail. This was a luscious, golden-haired, soft-skinned, half-naked female—

"Aengus?"

His guilty gaze shifted to her face. "Good morning."

Suzannah smiled shyly. "I almost thought I dreamed you." She seemed to notice his interest in her makeshift nightgown and began to finger the top button. "I hope you don't mind."

"It suits you." Aengus grinned. "Are you wearing anything else under there?"

"I didn't need anything else," she began, then her green eyes flashed with annoyance, and she grabbed the coverlet up to her neck. "Aengus Yates!"

He chuckled, completely unrepentant. "When a girl sleeps in a man's bed, she needs to expect a little attention. . . ."

Praise for the novels of Kate Donovan:

"Wow! An enchanting and unusual story. Delectable."
—*Rendezvous* on A DREAM APART

"Keeps you turning the pages as fast as you can."
—*Romantic Times* on A DREAM EMBRACED

"Unforgettable, riveting."
—*Rendezvous* on TIME WEAVER

Dear Reader,

In July, we launched the Ballad line with four new series, and each month we'll present both new and continuing stories set everywhere from medieval England to the American West—the kind of passionate, romantic stories you love best, written by the most gifted authors. At the back of each book, we'll tell you when you can find subsequent books in the series that have captured your heart.

The pageantry of medieval England will sweep you away in **A Knight's Vow,** the first book in *The Kinsmen* series. In newcomer Candice Kohl's story, a dashing knight in search of vengeance finds a spirited woman instead—and passion in her embrace. Next, Gabrielle Anderson takes us back to early nineteenth century Boston with **A Matter of Convenience,** the first in a series in which three very special women find the men of their hearts' desire with the help of *The Destiny Coin.*

Mail-order brides don't expect romance—but that's what they'll find when they sign up with *The Happily Ever After Co.!* In Kate Donovan's first Ballad book, **Game of Hearts,** a woman dreaming of a better future will discover that a man from her past has the key to her heart. Finally, the second installment of Maria Greene's *Midnight Mask* series offers the magic of **A Lover's Kiss** when the infamous Midnight Bandit is unmasked by a woman who has nothing left to lose—and only love to gain in his arms. Enjoy!

Kate Duffy
Editorial Director

The Happily Ever After Co.

GAME OF HEARTS

Kate Donovan

ZEBRA BOOKS

KENSINGTON PUBLISHING CORP.

http://www.zebrabooks.com

To Irish men, for having such a way about them.

ZEBRA BOOKS are published by

Kensington Publishing Corp.
850 Third Avenue
New York, NY 10022

Zebra and the Z logo Reg. U.S. Pat. & TM Off.

First Printing: September 2000
10 9 8 7 6 5 4 3 2 1

Printed in the United States of America

Prologue

February, 1866

"Suzannah, I love you like a daughter, and I've enjoyed your visit more than I can say, but if you don't choose one of these candidates to be your husband soon . . ." Russell Braddock, matchmaker extraordinaire and proprietor of the Happily Ever After marriage brokerage, took a deep breath before admitting ruefully, "You're the greatest challenge of my career, do you know that, Miss Hennessy?"

Sitting in a pile of letters on the floor at his feet, his golden-haired guest grinned up at him with unrepentant delight. *"You're* the only man on earth I trust, so I suppose you'll just have to marry me yourself."

"Suzannah!" Megan Braddock's soft gray eyes were laughing as she too looked up toward her uncle. "Didn't I warn you about her, Uncle Russ? She'll be a spinster for sure. And I'll be one too, because of my silly promise not to get married before her.''

"There'll be no spinsters on my watch,'' Braddock assured them, surveying the pair with amused affection. These two young women had been best friends—almost sisters, in fact—since childhood, yet differed from one another in so many ways. Suzannah with her spirited, irreverent playfulness. Megan with her earnest sweetness and desire to please. Each of them was priceless in Braddock's eyes, and he was determined to find them perfect mates. It was his business, after all. And in this case, also his privilege.

"These files are bursting with orders from lonely men willing to pay handsomely for brides. I won't rest until I find one for each of you.''

"They have to live nearby one another, so our children can play together,'' Suzannah reminded him sharply. "And no city men—we especially don't trust *them*. Right, Meg?''

"Uncle Russ is a city man,'' Megan countered her friend wearily. "Other than him, I don't know many, although the ones we've met during this visit have seemed decent enough.''

Braddock nodded, encouraged. "Reconsider, then, and allow me to find you both husbands here in Chicago. Noelle and I would love to have you nearby.''

"We'll miss you awfully when we go,'' Megan agreed. "And we'll miss Noelle too.''

"She'll be old enough for marriage herself soon, and I guarantee you *she* won't be willing to allow me to choose her husband. If you two were in Chicago, you could counsel her—''

"I can't stay,'' Suzannah interrupted. "Noelle is darling, and you're the closest thing to a father I've ever had the pleasure to know, but sometimes . . ." She looked from one to the other, her green eyes pleading for understanding. "Some people were born for city life. They thrive on the bustling crowds and magnificent architecture. And this house! It's practically a mansion. But I yearn for something else. Green meadows, not gray buildings. The sound of songbirds, not of whistles and horns. I can't explain it—"

"I think you just did, sweetheart," Braddock said. "It's a pity, though. I've made many a successful match through the mail, but I much prefer to interview prospective bridegrooms, face to face. I met a gentleman last night in fact who—"

"A city man?"

He chuckled in defeat. "Yes, Suzannah."

"Then he simply won't do. For either of us. Isn't that so, Meg?"

The dark-haired girl shrugged. "You're giving Uncle Russ an impossible task. Finding two men in his files who meet your high standards, and both must live in the same small town? What are the odds of that? Wouldn't it make more sense to include small cities like Denver? They can't have many tall buildings or crowded streets, can they?"

"Denver?" Suzannah arched an eyebrow. "Please don't tell me you're going to mention that schoolteacher again! We decided against him hours ago."

"*You* decided, not me."

"And I was correct. The man's pompous and humorless. That was plain to see from his letter. Three pages, all about himself."

"All about how he started a school for poor boys," Megan countered stubbornly. "That's generous, not pompous."

"And what about poor girls?" Suzannah demanded. "Don't you see, Meg? Men like him want to keep women ignorant and dependent and helpless, so they can walk all over us, and then disappear without warning, just like my father did. Just like Aengus Yates did. It's despicable."

"Your father didn't disappear, he died," Megan reminded her quietly. "And I'm sure Aengus had reasons for leaving his family, too. We'll just never know them."

"Aengus Yates?" The name teased at Russell Braddock's memory. "Who is that?"

Suzannah's eyes flashed with disgust. "Meg and I refer to him whenever we need an example of the depths men can sink to."

"That's not true." Megan smiled wistfully. "It's to remind ourselves that no one is perfect. That was Aengus's greatest sin," she explained to her uncle. "He seemed so perfect, and then he disappointed us so thoroughly. And he broke Suzannah's heart. Twice."

Intrigued, the marriage broker leaned forward in his soft leather chair. If his recollection was accurate, they were referring to a young wrangler he'd met at his brother's funeral years earlier. The earnest, soft-spoken, yet imposing young immigrant had made an indelible impression on the matchmaker despite the brevity of the meeting. Was this the type of man who caught Suzannah's fancy? If so, Braddock had his work cut out for him. "Go on. This sounds like useful information."

The two friends exchanged glances, then Suzannah spoke up. "Yes, he broke my heart. Just as Megan says. You'll laugh at me, I suppose, but—"

"A broken heart is never a laughing matter."

She nodded gratefully. "I loved Aengus Yates from the first time I laid eyes on him. I was just a child, but in my heart, I was certain he was the man I would marry one day. Remember, Meg? I watched him by day, and dreamed of him by night, and adored him through and through. He worked on a large ranch outside town, and he had a reputation for being able to gentle any horse, no matter how ornery or wild. And you'd believe it when you saw him, because he was so strong, and calm, and he had the most beautiful face—all tanned, with deep windburns on his cheekbones, and this slow, soft smile . . ."

Megan sighed and picked up the story. "Aengus must have been fourteen or so when he started working for the Monroes, and we couldn't have been seven or eight years old at the most. But he caught her eye for sure. She thought they had a destiny, but as time went by, she began to worry that he'd marry someone else before he got a chance to see her full grown. So on her eleventh birthday, she marched right up to him and told him straight out that he'd better wait. She told him she was growing as fast as she could, and she was determined to be worth waiting for."

"That must have been quite a picture."

Suzannah nodded. "Aengus was tall and strong. I must have seemed like a little pest, but still . . ." Almost to herself, she added, "He should have waited for me. Maybe things wouldn't have gone so wrong if he had."

Braddock cocked his head. "He married?"

"That same year," Megan said, her tone almost mournful. "That's the first time he broke her heart. The Monroes had a houseguest named Katherine. A thin, haughty girl from Boston. The next thing any of us knew, she and Aengus were married. It was a shock, especially to poor Suzannah. Then Katherine had a baby boy. Two years later, she had another one."

"And two years after that, Aengus deserted them." Suzannah spoke the words in a quiet voice laced with anger and betrayal. "I thought he was the finest man on earth, but he walked away from those babies and never came back."

"That was the second time he broke your heart?" Braddock leaned down to pat his houseguest's arm. "It explains so much to me, Suzannah. Here you are, full of energy and enthusiasm and love, but you won't trust a man with any of it. I see now why that is."

Suzannah flushed. "I'd gladly be alone until the day I died if I didn't adore children so awfully much, but I do. You should have seen Aengus's sons! He had something so wonderful, yet he walked away. If I can have children of my own one day, I'll never ask for anything else."

"Suzannah grew close to the Yates boys after Aengus abandoned them," Megan explained to her uncle. "Katherine took good care of them in her own way, but she was not a warm woman by any standard. Suzannah was like a big sister to them."

Suzannah bit her lip, as though to keep it from quivering. "Losing Aengus was something I had in common with his sons. They needed me, and I needed them. To tell you the truth," she added sheepishly, "it's one of the reasons I let Meg talk me into coming here after my mother died. I was growing too attached to Luke and Johnny for anyone's good."

"It was a wise thing to do," Braddock agreed. "Otherwise, you might have had your heart broken a third time. I'm determined not to let that happen, by the way. I'll find you a good husband—"

"No!" Suzannah flushed. "I've changed my mind about that. Find one for Meg. I'll make the trip with her, to wherever her fiancé lives, and I'll find myself a husband there. It shouldn't be too hard," she added with a disdainful sniff. "All I need do is pretend to be ignorant and weak, and I imagine someone will find me irresistible."

"A pretty girl with sparkling green eyes and golden curls?" Braddock nodded pensively. "I'm sure you won't have trouble finding prospective grooms. The worry is you'll try to choose someone who is different in every way from this Aengus Yates."

Suzannah studied him cautiously. "Why is that a worry?"

"Because you clearly want a man who is—how did you describe him?—tall and strong, and calm. Tanned by the sun. A soft, slow smile."

She stared in delighted amazement. "You remember every word?"

"I built this business by paying close attention to customers' words—both expressed and unexpressed. What you need is someone very like your Aengus, but who deserves the love of a good woman. Someone you can trust enough to fall in love with."

"Someone I can trust enough to be the father of my children," Suzannah corrected. "That's all I ask."

"Consider it done. He must be in my files somewhere."

"Just find a good man for Megan," Suzannah advised firmly. "Someone she can trust. I'll take care of myself somehow."

The matchmaker had learned better than to argue with his pretty guest, who had proven to be every bit as stubborn as his own daughter Noelle had become. Grateful to have at least one levelheaded female in his life, he turned his gaze, and his attention, to Megan. "I'll find someone for you who lives in a newly settled area. A mining town, perhaps. There will almost certainly be a lack of available women in such a place. If Suzannah goes along with you, she'll have her choice of men, I'm sure."

"But, Uncle Russ!" Megan's gray eyes had widened with concern. "Suzannah couldn't find an acceptable husband in all your files! What chance is there she'll find someone in a dusty old mining town?"

"Don't worry, Meg. We'll have our double wedding," Suzannah promised her friend. "We'll live out our lives in a mining town. We'll raise our children together. And if either of our men tries to leave," she added impishly, "I'll shoot him dead. What could be simpler?"

"Read it again, Meggie," seventeen-year-old Noelle Braddock pleaded. "Just once more? Father never allows me to read the men's letters, and this one is *sooo* romantic. *Please?*"

"Go to sleep," Suzannah groaned. If it hadn't been so dark in Noelle's bedroom, she would have glared at her precocious young hostess. "Do you want Megan to have dark circles under her eyes when she meets Mr. Riordain?"

"She can sleep on the ship. I wish I could go too. I'm old enough, and I *need* a husband too, but Father is *sooo* blind."

"Go to sleep," Suzannah grumbled.

Megan giggled in the darkness. "Suzannah doesn't like Mr. Riordain's letter, Noelle. Because he reminds her of a man from her past."

"You had a man in your past, Suzannah?" Noelle

seemed completely impressed. "Who was he? Please tell me!"

"If you don't go to sleep, I'm moving back to the guest room," Suzannah warned. "And I'm sure Mr. Riordain is nothing like Aengus Yates."

"You can practically hear Aengus's brogue in the letter," Megan teased. "Are you certain you don't want him for yourself, Suzannah? If that's what's made you so cross, why don't you talk to my uncle? You could have Mr. Riordain, and I'll take the school-teacher—"

"And I'll take anyone," Noelle interrupted. "As long as he's rich and handsome. Do you suppose Mr. Riordain is handsome, Meggie?"

"No, I don't suppose he is," Megan sighed. "Why would a handsome man resort to ordering a woman through the mail? Fortunately, I don't measure a man by his appearance. I measure him by his words. And Mr. Riordain's words are music to my soul."

"Read it!"

Megan turned up the lamp, adopted a rhythmic brogue, and began: "Dear Mr. Braddock, I've heard you've a talent for making a match, and so I'm writing you this letter asking for your help. Not so much for myself, but for the two motherless children I have in my care. In the short time since my wife's unexpected death, the poor boys' lives have gone from bad to worse, and I'm desperate beyond words to find some source of love and hope to share with them.

"I'm twenty-six years in age, strong in body, and steadfast in character. I've a small horse ranch outside Bent Creek, a proper and growing town in the Sierra Nevada mountains. I cannot offer luxuries, but a woman of modest tastes and needs will be treated with the respect and gratitude she shows herself to deserve. And if it's the love of a child she needs, she'll earn herself twice that and more if she does me the great honor of becoming my bride.''

There was a short, awe-filled silence before Noelle gushed, "I love the way he sounds! It makes me tingle all over.''

"That's silly," Suzannah protested, although she too found the rancher's words seductive. Aching loneliness, combined with a strong sense of responsibility—in Suzannah's mind, those might just be the perfect ingredients for a husband. Of course, Riordain might be nothing like he sounded. Perhaps he was even illiterate, and had had someone else write the letter for him! And what if his wife's "untimely death" had been due to being overworked by a brutish beast? Had Megan thought of *that*?

No. Instead, Megan kept insisting Riordain was like Aengus, of all people! And based on what? The fact that he worked with horses and had an Irish name? Those things meant nothing. And the fact that each man had fathered two sons—well, that meant something, but certainly not that the men were similar. It wasn't the act of fathering a son that mattered, it was the way a man behaved in the years thereafter. In that sense, Dennis Riordain was far superior to Aengus Yates.

Suzannah sighed. This idea of allowing Megan to marry a stranger was seeming less and less wise, yet at this point she knew her friend would not be dissuaded. The girl had insisted for years that, when the time came, she would place her fate in her uncle's famous hands, confident that he would find her just the right mate. For reasons that Suzannah knew full well, Megan Braddock didn't trust herself to choose a man.

"He sounds so manly and sweet," Noelle was insisting. "Did Aengus sound like that?"

"I suppose he did."

"Did he have an accent?"

Suzannah sighed in the darkness. "Just the hint of where he'd come from. Like my mother's, if you must know the truth. It made me trust him more, I suppose. One of my many mistakes where Aengus Yates was concerned."

"Did you let him kiss you?"

"He never wanted to. But I often dreamed of the day he would. What a fool I was," she added, mostly to herself.

"Now it's Meggie who'll kiss an Irish horseman first," the young hostess said impishly.

When Megan giggled at the impudent observation, Suzannah had to smile. Perhaps this arranged marriage was for the best after all. Mr. Riordain would be respectful and kind, and perhaps Megan might abandon her fears and self-doubts once and for all. If the "Irish horseman" could accomplish that, Suzannah would be forever in his debt. It might even restore her own faith in men, and allow her to find a husband for herself. In Bent Creek. "A proper and growing town in the Sierra Nevada mountains . . ."

Chapter One

Ben Steele played games for a living. Playing games, devising strategies, distracting opponents—his effectiveness at such pursuits could not be denied. But he was beginning to think he'd met his match in Suzannah Hennessy, who seemed to have a counter for his every move, an insight into his every bluff, and a determination to win that equaled his own in every way. She was pretty too. Under other circumstances, she might have figured in this contest as both opponent *and* prize. But in this particular game, it was a beautiful creature named Megan Braddock he was determined to win.

The dark-haired beauty made the gambler's usually untouchable heart pound in his chest, to the point where she was in his every thought and dream. Her long, graceful neck; her soft, melodious voice; the perfectly manicured hands that nested in her lap, so prim and proper, waiting patiently to be introduced to the feel of a man. Ben Steele was determined to be that man.

During the five days since he'd first met the pretty pair and offered to serve as their escort on the long voyage from New York to San Francisco, his interest in Megan had shifted from admiration to lust to pure yearning, then back to lust, again and again. If only he could be alone with her for just a few moments. Or the rest of his life. Or anything in between.

But the only thing "in between" was Suzannah Hennessy. And of course, the mysterious "Mr. Riordain" of whom they spoke in guarded whispers. And the even more mysterious "Aengus Yates," who was apparently someone from their past who had earned Suzannah's undying wrath. It was all very intriguing. Not to mention frustrating.

"What exactly did he do to you?" Ben demanded finally in mock exasperation as their ship sailed into the royal blue waters of the Caribbean.

"I beg your pardon?" Suzannah shot him a haughty glance. "Was our conversation disturbing you, Mr. Steele?"

"Completely, Miss Hennessy." Ben winked toward Megan. "You've mentioned a scoundrel named Aengus so often I almost feel as though he's riding along with us."

To Ben's delight, his true love's soft gray eyes began to twinkle. "Aengus is always with us, Mr. Steele, because Suzannah carries such strong feelings for him in her heart. Would you like to hear the story?"

Before Ben could respond, Suzannah frowned and insisted, "It's the story of an irresponsible man. I'm certain that, in *your* profession, you meet dozens of such men every year."

"Suzannah!" Megan blanched. "Forgive her, Mr. Steele."

"Call me Ben," he reminded her. "And don't apologize. I wasn't at all offended." Leaning forward, he dared to up the ante. "May I call you Megan?"

"You may not!" Suzannah scolded. "We've tolerated your attentions on this voyage, Mr. Steele. But you would be mistaken to feel encouraged in any way."

Megan's eyes clouded. "You've been a wonderful escort, Mr. Steele. And a perfect gentleman. We don't mean to seem ungrateful, but—"

"But we'll be in Panama City in just a few days, boarding the steamship for San Francisco," Suzannah reminded her friend firmly. "Mr. Steele will be heading to his fancy hotel. And you wiil be only weeks away from marrying Dennis Riordain."

"Marrying?" Ben almost choked on the word. "Is that so, Miss Braddock?" When Megan's gaze dropped from his, he groaned aloud. "I had no idea. Forgive me. You just didn't seem . . ."

"Didn't seem what, Mr. Steele?" Suzannah taunted. "Didn't seem engaged to be married? Well, I'm afraid she is."

Ben placed his hand tenderly over Megan's. "You didn't seem like a girl in love, Miss Braddock. You seemed like a girl *falling* in love."

Megan gasped and pulled free of him just as Suzannah's huge emerald eyes flashed in warning. "You've insulted my closest friend, Mr. Steele, and now I must insist you find other company to keep for the remainder of this trip."

"No, wait!" Megan wailed. "I have something to say first."

Ben and Suzannah stared, united for once in disbelief at the gentle girl's strident tone.

"Miss Braddock?" he asked cautiously. "Are you angry?"

Megan moistened her lips. "Suzannah? Could you give me just a moment alone with Mr. Steele?"

"Pardon?"

"Please? Just . . . well, ten minutes?"

"Ten?"

It was all Ben could do to keep from grinning victoriously in the flabbergasted chaperon's direction, but he wisely adopted a humble tone instead. "I assure you I'll behave, Miss Hennessy."

Suzannah was quick to rally. "I wouldn't be so smug, Mr. Steele. I'm quite certain she simply wants to say good-bye." With a haughty glare, the golden-haired passenger slipped out of her deck chair, smoothed the skirt of her finely tailored traveling outfit, and hurried away.

Ben waited, patient and hopeful, while Megan visibly gathered her thoughts. Finally she blurted, "I'm flattered by your attention, Mr. Steele. But honestly, I don't understand it! I can only imagine the adventures you've had and the women you've known . . ." She blushed frantically. "In any case, I have apparently misled you, and so you are entitled to an explanation, and so . . . Well, I'm not in love with Mr. Riordain yet. I can't imagine how you guessed that. I suppose your experience—"

"I've had little experience with true love," Ben interrupted gently. "But they say that when it happens, one knows. By the racing of the pulse, and the tightening of the throat, and the yearning of the heart. You feel it too, don't you, Megan darling?"

"Mr. Steele, please. Don't say such things."

He grasped her hand and knelt quickly before her. "I'm sure you have your reasons for admiring this Dennis Riordain fellow. Perhaps he's been kind to you in the past, and has promised to care for you. I appreciate that, but . . ." He caught the flicker of something—confusion? embarrassment? guilt?—in her dove gray eyes, and prodded warily, "What is it, Megan?"

"It's . . . it's just . . . you wouldn't understand. You're being so patient, though. I thank you for that. But I assure you, the situation is hopeless."

Her smile, so hesitant and vulnerable, made Ben yearn to gather her into his arms. Instead, he murmured, "You can tell me anything, darling. I promise I won't judge you."

Megan tilted her head, as though seeing him for the first time, and he thought for an instant he had managed to find the only words that could unlock the mysteries of her heart. Then she reached into her satchel and pulled out a fold of paper, which she proffered shyly.

It was a letter. A love letter? Ben struggled against a surge of jealousy and forced himself to read it. At first it made no sense, and then . . .

"He's a stranger?"

Megan nodded.

"You've never even *met* him?"

"No."

"This has been arranged?"

"By my uncle. It is his business, and his talent. I'm sorry, Mr. Steele."

"Megan . . ." He was almost giddy with relief. "Darling, our obnoxious chaperon will be back at any moment." Cupping her chin in his hand, he whispered, "May I kiss you?"

"But—"

"Shh." He smiled, completely confident at last. "Just one kiss. Mr. Riordain won't mind, I assure you."

"Mr. Steele!" Megan pulled free in dismay. "You mustn't joke about it. I've made a promise—"

"To a stranger—a man who wants someone to cook and clean and wipe his sons' noses. Any woman can do that. An angel like you would be wasted on him, don't you see?"

"An angel? Is that how you see me?"

"Yes, darling."

"Good grief, Megan!" Suzannah had reappeared from nowhere. "Are you going to send this interloper away, or do I have to do it for you?"

Ben jumped to his feet and pulled the startled newcomer into his arms. "I have wonderful news, Miss Hennessy."

Suzannah stared, clearly fascinated. "News?"

"You care about Megan, don't you?"

"Of course."

"Then you'll be relieved to hear she's not going to marry some lackluster stranger and spend her days slaving away to raise another woman's children."

"Let me guess," Suzannah drawled. "She's going to become a pompous ass's mistress, and die in an alley of some dreadful foreign disease?"

"Stop it! Both of you!" Megan pleaded. "Mr. Steele, *please* go away. Go smoke a cigar, or have a brandy. I need to talk to Suzannah now."

"Of course, darling," he grinned. "Explain it all to our wonderful friend here, won't you? I'll be back in a short while and we'll all celebrate together."

Before either woman could protest, he grabbed Megan's hand and kissed it, then strode away toward the upper deck, confident at last that Megan Braddock was his, whether she knew it yet or not.

Suzannah watched until the cocky gambler had disappeared, then spun on her friend and eyed her sternly. "What on earth did you say to him?"

Megan shrugged in helpless confusion. "I told him I've made a commitment to Mr. Riordain. I showed him the letter. I thought he'd understand, but somehow, it encouraged him!" Lowering her voice, she added unhappily, "He almost kissed me, Suzannah. It doesn't make sense? Why me?"

"Because you're pretty, and you're too polite to slap his face." Suzannah smiled in spite of her annoyance. "You should see how you look at him, Meg. Are you really falling in love?"

"I don't know! I'm so confused."

Suzannah's smile became a sympathetic grin. "Let's sort it out together then, shall we? Mr. Steele is a smooth-talking city man. You're a small-town girl. He's known hundreds of women. You're naive and inexperienced. He wants a mistress. You want a husband. In fact, you have one waiting for you in Bent Creek. A husband who'll love you forever, not just for a week or a month."

Megan buried her face in her hands. "You're right, of course. What was I thinking?"

"You were thinking Ben Steele is a handsome specimen of manly perfection, and you're right," Suzannah explained gleefully. "Those heavenly brown eyes. I'd kill for his lashes! And that naughty voice, and thick black hair. Any girl would weaken under Ben Steele's attentions."

Megan looked up in hopeful disbelief. "Really?"

"Absolutely." Suzannah stretched out in the deck chair Ben had recently vacated. "It's the way of the world, you know. We want the bad ones. The Bens and the Aenguses. They dazzle us, and then, if we're not careful, we get our hearts broken. And Ben Steele is a heartbreaker if I ever saw one.''

"But you noticed his eyes? Aren't they amazing?"

Suzannah nodded. "Amazing and dangerous."

"When he looks at me, I feel as though he can see right through to . . . well, to—"

"To your soul?"

"No." Megan flushed. "To my naked body."

Suzannah burst into laughter. "Megan Braddock! For a virtuous girl, you're having some very naughty thoughts. Should I worry?"

"You mean, because of my mother?"

"Of course not, silly. You don't still think about all that, do you?"

"No. At least, not until . . . well, until I met Mr. Steele." Megan shook her head unhappily. "I just want to forget all about him. I'm going to marry Mr. Riordain, and that's all that matters. Isn't that so?"

Suzannah studied her with quiet concern. "You seem tired, Meg. Why don't you try to nap. I'll make sure no one disturbs you."

The dark-haired girl smiled gratefully and curled up in her chair. "Thanks, Suzannah. I can always count on you."

When her friend had drifted into sleep, Suzannah sighed and rubbed her own eyes, suddenly exhausted. After all these years, it was so unfair that Megan still wrestled with her childhood demons. It had been so long since either of them mentioned it, she had dared to believe the doubts had faded. Instead, they seemed in some ways stronger than ever. Somehow Ben Steele, with his silken voice and satin eyes, had reawakened them. But to be fair, Suzannah could not put all the blame on the handsome gambler. This particular tragedy had begun in quite a different way.

Suzannah thought back to the day, ten years earlier, when Megan's parents had been found—shot to death—in the living quarters over her father's newspaper office. Blessedly, Megan had been visiting the Hennessy home that evening, and thus had not fallen victim to the intruder.

Intruder? Or had Megan's father himself committed a heinous murder/suicide? That had been the not-so-subtle speculation among the townsfolk, some of whom chose to believe that a confrontation over the wife's past affairs had taken a deadly turn. Or perhaps, these same gossips had speculated, one of her old lovers had come to town and murdered the couple in a jealous rage.

The stories were nonsense. Even as a child, Suzannah had known that in her heart. But the sheriff had added fuel to the fire by announcing that the evidence was "inconclusive." It suited his purposes, of course, since he was loyal to a judge who had been the subject of blistering editorials over the weeks preceding the murders. Fair-minded persons knew that the murderer had most likely been motivated by a desire to silence the newspaper publisher rather than by an alleged affair from years earlier.

The truth was simple and heart-wrenching. Megan's parents had been passionately in love, right up to their last, shared breath. But a story began to circulate, and it was apparently true, up to a point. Prior to the time Russell Braddock had matched his only brother with a winsome beauty named Eliza, the bride had been employed at a dance hall, as both a dancer and a singer. A talented one, by all reports—a fact that seemed to further convince the town gossips that she must have led a life of wanton alliances.

Suzannah's mother had taken a brokenhearted Megan into their home immediately, reassuring the girls that, as awful as it was, the disaster had not been the fault of anyone they loved. Russell Braddock had rushed to his niece's side, and had offered to take her to Chicago, but the still-shocked child had chosen to stay in Indiana with the Hennessys, an arrangement that even the matchmaker admitted seemed best under the circumstances. He visited often thereafter, sometimes bringing the precocious Noelle to see her cousin, but Megan always chose to stay behind when he left.

It had taken months for the orphan to begin to recover from her loss, and she might have healed completely had the stories of her mother's past not continued to plague her. The child took those stories to heart, not only because the physical resemblance between herself and her mother had been so strong, but because Megan had had the singing voice of an angel and the grace of a ballerina from early childhood, talents that had been nourished by both of her proud parents. The parallel was strong, and there were those in the town who took delight in discussing it at length. Before long, Megan had become self-conscious and withdrawn, and anxious to prove that she was a "good girl."

Suzannah and her mother had done their best to reassure her. While the widow Hennessy did so by praising Megan's homemaking skills and sweet disposition, Suzannah's tactics were more mischievous as she half dragged her best friend into all of her silly fantasies and schemes. Despite Megan's protests, the two spent countless daylight hours spying on Aengus

Yates as he worked the Monroe horses or bathed in a secluded pond, and endless hours at night imagining how it would be when Suzannah became the handsome horse trainer's bride. The second prong of the fantasy was Megan's future, which revolved around her uncle's legendary matchmaking prowess. The girls had heard stories, mostly from Megan's father, about Russell Braddock's uncanny ability to make dreams come true. Surely he would find the man who would see Megan for the angel she so desperately wished to be.

"Pardon me, Suzannah. May I sit with you?"

Startled out of her reverie, she scowled slightly in Ben Steele's direction. "My friend needs her rest, sir. Your constant unwelcome attentions have exhausted her."

"She's beautiful when she's sleeping," Ben murmured.

His lovesick expression made Suzannah smile despite herself. "I've never met an incorrigible man before, Mr. Steele. Do you honestly intend to pursue her in spite of her engagement?"

"I have no choice." He spoke in a husky whisper, as though disturbing Megan's sleep would have been the most despicable of crimes.

Disarmed, Suzannah pointed to a neighboring chair in invitation. When the gambler had joined her, she took a moment to study him. "Do you know what Meg and I have decided?"

He winced but held her gaze. "I'd like to know."

"We've decided you're the most handsome man we've ever met."

Guarded now, he cleared his throat. "Oh?"

"It's your eyes, as you well know. I imagine women compliment them endlessly."

"Almost never," he countered carefully. "It's my money that usually causes hearts to flutter."

Suzannah laughed lightly. "Money doesn't matter to Megan."

"Does it matter to you?"

"I don't know. I've never had any." She bit her lip. "How much do you have?"

"It varies."

"Depending on whether you've been winning or losing?"

"Exactly."

The honest answer surprised her. "Do you cheat? At cards, I mean. I know you cheat on your mistresses."

"I don't cheat," he smiled. "But I bluff extremely well. I suspect that's something you and I have in common."

Suzannah fought an urge to smile again. "Pardon?"

"You pretend not to like me, but you do. That's bluffing. You pretend you want your dearest friend to enter into a loveless marriage. *That's* bluffing. You pretend you're immune to love because of one bad experience—"

"Two bad experiences," she corrected, amused by his audacity.

"Oh? I know there was the infamous Aengus. Who was the other one?"

"It was Aengus both times, if you must know."

"Then he was a fool twice, to turn his back on such an amazing female."

"The first time, I was a scrawny child. The second time, he was a married man." She laughed at his obvious confusion. "Do you really think I'm an amazing female?"

"Yes."

"And Megan?"

His gaze shifted to the sleeping beauty. "I adore her."

"But for how long?" The question hung in the air a trifle too long, and Suzannah's patience snapped. "I thought so. Go away, Mr. Steele."

He cocked his head to the side. "Would you like some advice?"

"Not particularly." Weakening, she nodded. "What is it?"

"I know you have enough influence over her to make her send me away, but don't. Let Megan decide for herself. Otherwise, she'll never forgive you."

It was true, and Suzannah knew it. Even if Mr. Dennis Riordain proved to be a saint, there would be a corner of Megan's heart that would always remember Ben Steele. That was the way love worked, at least for females. Just as Aengus could own a bit of Suzannah despite his bad behavior, Ben Steele had won a place for himself forever. It could be a fond memory or a bitter one. And the last thing Suzannah wanted for her friend was the wonder of what might have been had love's course not been thwarted by a third party, no matter how pure that person's intentions had been.

And Suzannah was confident that Megan would in fact send Ben away. He was a gambler who had regaled them with tales of his travels from one thriving city to the next. Although he claimed he was considering settling down, now that he had won title to a hotel that he intended to turn into a showplace, that hotel was in San Francisco. Megan would never consider settling there, even if Ben offered to make her his wife rather than just his mistress.

Most importantly, Megan had made a commitment to Dennis Riordain, and while Suzannah might have encouraged her to break it for a more dependable suitor, Megan would never consider such an act. It could be perceived as flighty and dishonorable. Exactly the kind of conduct engaged in by showgirls and stage actresses and other wanton women. Exactly the kind of symptom Megan feared she might one day manifest.

"Will you go and arrange dinner for us, Mr. Steele? We'll let Meg sleep a while longer; then we'll all have a nice meal and get to know one another a little better."

He stood and bowed respectfully. "Just for the record, Miss Hennessy, I meant what I said earlier. Aengus Yates was a fool. Twice." With an impish smile he took her hand and kissed it. Twice.

As Ben courted cautiously and Megan resisted half-heartedly, their reluctant chaperon hovered nearby, confused over how best to be a friend. *At least,* she consoled herself, *Meg will have this blissfully romantic memory of sunsets and moonlit seas to warm her throughout the rest of her days.*

If they had taken the long, harrowing voyage around Cape Horn at the tip of South America, Ben might even have had enough time and opportunity to seduce Megan and thereby change the course of her life. But Russell Braddock had augmented the funds sent by Dennis Riordain for his bride's passage, ensuring that both Megan and Suzannah could travel in first-class luxury to Panama, where they then saved more than a month off their trip by taking the four-hour train trip across the isthmus to Panama City. At that point, they had boarded a steamship bound for San Francisco.

While Ben's stateroom on the sailing ship had been right beside that of Suzannah and Megan, his accommodations on the steamship were half a deck away. Still, it seemed to Suzannah that he was never out of sight.

At times, her heart ached for the love-struck couple. But more often, she was simply pleased to see that they were slowly and painfully coming to the only rational decision—that Megan needed to marry Dennis Riordain, and Ben needed to let her go.

But the gambler wasn't one to admit defeat easily. His strategy, as far as Suzannah could tell, was to learn every fact he could about his "darling." And for the most part, Megan seemed willing to share certain details—of how they had hidden in the bushes and watched Aengus Yates; of the twice-broken heart; of the early days, when her father ran the newspaper; and of course, of Russell Braddock and his daughter Noelle, the only blood relatives Megan had in the world.

Still, Suzannah was acutely aware of the tales her friend *didn't* tell. The murders; the cruel gossip; the singing and dancing that had filled her life until the moment when those joys had been banished forever from Megan's existence.

Even Ben noticed the absence of certain stories, and finally asked directly. "Tell me about your mother."

"They say I am very like her."

"Then she must have been beautiful."

"She was a loving mother."

He glanced toward Suzannah, who struggled to keep her face expressionless. This was doubly rocky terrain for her, and she wasn't about to make a mistake. "I have fond memories of her, too. She and my mother were close friends for many years."

Ben's instincts had clearly been activated, and he seemed about to probe further when he instead shrugged and completely changed the subject, offering to teach the girls another in the endless series of card games he'd shared with them on the trip. Suzannah knew he was curious to learn how Megan's parents had died, or why she had never had childhood sweethearts or dreams beyond those entrusted to Russell Braddock, but he never raised the subject of Megan's past again.

Ben could learn a lot about people by playing cards with them. Suzannah Hennessy was competitive, daring, intuitive, and mischievous; if she'd been born a man, she would have made a consummate gambler. Suzannah was also innocent and sweet, and he grew fonder of her by the minute, even though he knew she did not approve of him.

Megan, too, was sweet and innocent, and so determined to be ladylike that Ben almost worried for her. It occurred to him that that might be the reason she rarely mentioned her parents. They must have been overly strict, he speculated. Quick to criticize their daughter, when they should have lavished her with praise and love. He intended to make up for their mistakes, if only the girl would abandon herself to the passion that was growing between them.

Sometimes he suspected Megan could read his mind and knew how he ached to have her. If so, she never once frowned or objected. From a girl like Megan, he had a feeling that was the closest thing to encouragement a rogue could expect. Still, he didn't dare make physical advances just yet. Not that Suzannah would have allowed such a thing even if he decided to try!

He was content to watch the beautiful Megan as she played the role she somehow felt obligated to play: studiously reading her book of poetry; gently laughing at Suzannah's outrageous observations; listening politely to Ben's stories; and, all in all, acting in so perfect and controlled a manner that it made him want to scoop her up and carry her off to the nearest bed, so he could teach her the real reason she'd been brought into this world.

Although the specter of Megan's upcoming marriage to Dennis Riordain hung always in the air, Ben never believed it would come to pass. At least, not until the day their steamship sailed into San Francisco Bay. Suzannah had blessedly left them unchaperoned for a moment, and he took the opportunity to pull Megan aside and win her heart once and for all.

Predictably, she reminded him that she was promised to another, at which he scoffed, "A commercial transaction, nothing more. I'll refund his money to him—doubled!—and he'll be no worse off than before."

Megan bit her lip. "In your world, money may well have that sort of power. But Mr. Riordain wants a wife, not dollars. If you had taken the time to really read his letter, you'd know that. He wants a mother for his sons, and a companion for himself."

"A companion," Ben agreed. "*Any* companion. Don't make it sound romantic, darling."

"Read his letter," she repeated softly. "It was as though he placed his heart and his soul in my uncle's hands. He trusted him to find just the right girl—"

"Or he's too lazy, or ugly, or uncivilized to go into the nearest city and find her himself." He grinned when Megan pouted. "Don't scold me, darling. I take it all back. Mr. Riordain is a wonderful, loving man. He deserves a wonderful bride. So I won't offend him by offering him money. I'll offer him Suzannah instead."

To his delight, Megan giggled. "I dare you to say such a thing to her face."

"She'd strangle me," he admitted. "But you must admit, Mr. Riordain would be content with the match."

Megan glanced about herself, then dared to stroke Ben's cheek. "Try to understand, won't you? My uncle has a talent. Directly from God, I believe. To make a match between lonely hearts. He matched me with Mr. Riordain, and I intend to honor it."

"I'm lonely too, darling. I ache for you. If your uncle were here—"

"Hush," she interrupted softly. "This may be our only chance, Mr. Steele. Shouldn't you kiss me, just this once?"

A wave of longing swept over him—longing to sweep her into his arms and carry her off forever—but he knew she would never allow it. The fact that she would allow even one innocent kiss was a miracle in its way, and so he placed his hands on her waist and drew her against himself as he lowered his lips to hers.

To his amazement, she immediately curled her arms around his neck, moistened her lips, and welcomed him with such genuine need that he felt a jolt clear through his loins. He hadn't expected—hadn't dared hope!—that she would want him as completely as he wanted her, but it was true! Sliding one hand into the small of her back, he laced the other into her thick, luxurious hair, working frantically to free the locks from the countless pins she'd used to imprison them. It was as though they were suddenly the only two persons on board the ship, placed there for only one purpose—to make love to one another forever.

"Megan Braddock!"

Suzannah's words ripped through them, and he could feel Megan trying to wrench away, but he held her tightly and growled, "Stay out of this. It's her choice—"

"My choice," Megan agreed, pulling herself free and blushing frantically. "My choice to kiss you good-bye, Mr. Steele. Please understand."

"Good-bye?"

"I know you hoped we would stay in San Francisco for a while, but we intend to travel immediately to Sacramento, and from there to Bent Creek. My uncle's friend will telegraph Mr. Riordain, who is awaiting our arrival. I have no intention of keeping my future husband waiting for one more minute than is necessary."

"What are you saying?" He stared in abject dismay. "You can't kiss me like that and then say good-bye. You can't leave that taste on my lips and then go to another man's bed—"

"Ben, don't," Suzannah warned softly.

That was the final blow. That voice, filled with pity and concern. Pity for him! As though Suzannah knew in her heart that it was over.

If only she had scolded. If only she had believed he had a chance. But her voice told him otherwise, as did the tears sparkling in Megan's dove gray eyes.

"I'm sorry, Mr. Steele. Please excuse us." Megan started to walk away, then paused, confused. "Suzannah? Are you coming?"

"In a minute, sweetie. I want to say good-bye too."

Megan nodded, the tears now streaming down her cheeks, and she stumbled away toward their cabin.

Suzannah sandwiched Ben's face between her hands. "Poor darling, I'm so sorry. It's for the best, but still, I'm so sorry."

"She kissed me—"

"It was a good-bye kiss."

"It was not!"

Suzannah winced. "You mustn't pursue her anymore, Ben. You're breaking her heart. Can't you see that?"

"I need your help, Suzannah."

"And so does Megan. I have to take care of her now. I have to help her get ready to meet . . . to meet Mr. Riordain."

When Suzannah choked back a sob, Ben realized for the first time that she had been his secret ally all along. Despite her protests to the contrary, she had hoped love would triumph over reason; over commitment; over everything. Touched, he embraced her tenderly. "Don't worry, Suzannah. I won't let her marry Riordain. I promise."

"You're incorrigible," she reminded him softly. "Good-bye, Mr. Steele. Good luck with your hotel and your games. We'll remember you fondly."

He stared after her, grateful for the knowledge that Suzannah had only pretended to support the match with Riordain, all the while believing, as Ben had believed, that when the time was right, Megan herself would free them all from the fiction and take her rightful place at Ben's side.

In his heart, Ben believed it still.

* * *

"Are you thinking about Ben?" Suzannah murmured, struggling, as she'd done for the entire trip, to find a way to best assist her friend. Megan had been blinking back tears for two days straight, first during the lackluster train trip to Sacramento, and now during this bumpy yet breathtaking introduction to the pine-covered Sierra Nevada mountains in springtime.

"For the tenth time, no. I'm thinking about Mr. Riordain."

Mindful of their three stagecoach companions—all men! all headed for Virginia City—Suzannah lowered her voice to a whisper. "Tell me the truth, Megan. If you feel you've made a mistake and you can't go through with it—"

"I'm fine."

"If you're worried about keeping your commitment to Mr. Riordain—I mean, if that's all that's keeping you from marrying Ben"—Suzannah took a deep breath—"perhaps I could take your place?"

"Suzannah Hennessy!" Megan's tears disappeared, replaced by a flash of anger that made her gray eyes seem almost silver. "My uncle matched me with Mr. Riordain. You're as bad as Ben Steele! Acting as though it's just a game. Do you suppose I traveled all this way for nothing? And do you really believe Mr. Riordain wants just any girl?"

"Since when am I just any girl?" Suzannah complained.

Megan's fury subsided. "You aren't, of course. And Mr. Riordain would be thrilled to have you as his bride. But Uncle Russ matched him to me—"

"Oh, for heaven's sake, marry him then! I approve wholeheartedly of the match."

"Then why are you so cross with me?"

"Because you're crying over Ben."

Megan dabbed at her eyes with a lace handkerchief. "I feel so guilty over the way I misled him. That's all. I shouldn't have kissed him good-bye."

Suzannah wanted to remind her that it had been somewhat elaborate for a good-bye kiss, but knew it would just aggravate the situation. "Are you telling me the truth, Meg? You don't want to marry Ben?"

"Marry *him*?" Megan stared. "He's a gambler! A smooth-talking city man. He claims to love me now, but as you've said so often, he's been with hundreds of women. He's not anyone's lifelong mate. For that, I need a man like Dennis Riordain. Remember, Suzannah? We want to spend our days raising our children in this crisp, clear mountain air. It was a good, sensible plan when we left Chicago, and it's a good plan now."

"I agree."

When the driver shouted down to them, one of their male companions stuck his head out of the window and confirmed, "Looks like there's a way station coming up. That's where you ladies are headed, isn't it?"

"Oh, dear," Megan winced. "So soon?"

"Do you want me to take a peek?" Suzannah smiled sympathetically. "It might be more romantic if you were the first to see him, though."

Megan nodded, squared her shoulders, and moved to the window, poking her head out as far as safety and gentility would allow.

"Do you see him, Meg?"

"I see three men, I think. We're still too far away to see their faces, but . . . Oh, my goodness!"

"Tell me." Suzannah felt her pulse begin to race. "Is there something dreadfully wrong with him? Because if there is, you needn't marry him. You know that, don't you?"

Megan settled back into the seat and explained nervously, "Do you remember how Mr. Riordain reminded us of Aengus?"

"Reminded *you* of Aengus."

She nodded. "There are three men, and it's too soon to see their faces, but one reminded me of Aengus. Wouldn't it be odd if that were Mr. Riordain?"

"Oh, for heaven's sake, let *me* look." Suzannah leaned across her friend and stuck her head out the window far enough to see the upcoming station. The sight of Ben Steele, pacing in the distance, made her laugh with delight. "Are you blind, Meg? That's Ben! He rode ahead to meet you! If it weren't so romantic, I'd strangle him for his audacity."

"Ben?" Megan edged Suzannah aside and craned her neck. "Where? Oh, dear, you're right. What shall I say to him?"

"I imagine Mr. Riordain will do the talking for you," Suzannah predicted. "He paid for you, after all. Assuming he even shows up."

Megan eyed her friend impatiently. "You're not paying attention, Suzannah! He's there. Leaning on the corral fence."

Suzannah stuck her head out of the window again and gasped at the sight of a tall, lean, suntanned figure lounging against a fence post in a way that evoked memories of a love long since lost. The man *could* be Aengus Yates's double! Even in the shadows, his hair appeared to be an all-too-familiar golden brown, worn shaggy, almost to his shoulders, as Aengus had worn his. "It's incredible, Meg."

"I know. He shouldn't have followed me here."

"No. I mean, the resemblance is incredible. It's almost as though . . ." A wave of dizziness swept over her as the man came into sharper focus. "Good grief, I think it really *is* Aengus!"

"But how can it be? *Your* Aengus, in the same part of the country as *my* Mr. Riordain?"

"I think it's even worse than that," Suzannah warned her friend in dazed disbelief. "I think my Aengus Yates *is* your Mr. Riordain."

Chapter Two

Ben's glance shifted uneasily from the approaching stage to the bronzed, Thor-like fellow who was patiently awaiting its arrival. Although the gambler still believed Megan would make the right choice when she stepped back into his life, he couldn't help but notice that the matter had become somewhat more complicated than expected.

As Megan's unseen but still diligent escort, Ben had trailed the stage through the mountains on horseback, riding ahead only when the final destination had become the next stop. He hadn't had much of a plan, other than to size up Riordain in hopes that the man would be so seriously flawed, in appearance or otherwise, that Megan herself would take care of the rest. If not Megan, then hopefully Suzannah could be counted upon to intercede to prevent a truly gruesome match.

To his elation, he had no sooner arrived at the

way station than he had spied a crusty, toothless gentleman who was old enough to be Megan's great-grandfather. His heart had jumped with joyful relief, knowing that Suzannah Hennessy would never allow so extreme a mismatch to go forward.

Unfortunately, the buzzard had turned out to be the stationmaster. Still, Ben had felt encouraged. There was no sign of anyone else, which raised the possibility that Riordain had come to his senses and decided not to go through with the arranged match. Megan would be crushed, Ben knew. And Suzannah would take it as more proof that all men were like the infamous Aengus Yates. And Ben would be there to comfort and reassure them both. Then he'd take them back to San Francisco, find a randy, romantic friend to take Suzannah off his hands, and live happily ever after with the girl of his dreams.

Those dreams had been interrupted by the unmistakable grind of wagon wheels, coming not from the west along the stage route, but from the south. It was a simple wagon, driven by a simply dressed man, and Ben immediately began to recalculate the odds. From the looks of things, this Dennis Riordain probably needed money as much as he needed a bride. He might take eagerly to Ben's offer, knowing that, with money, he could go to Virginia City or Sacramento and choose a woman for himself in person. Of course, Megan would be furious, and so that tactic should be left as a last resort. Better for the moment to strike up a conversation with the newcomer, discover his vices and weaknesses, and then decide what to do.

The stranger had pulled his wagon into the yard, jumped down to consult briefly with the old stationmaster, and then proceeded to unhitch his team of nicely matched chestnut workhorses. Without a glance toward the west, he'd then watered the animals, checked their legs and hooves, and patted their necks as though they were the finest horseflesh on earth. Then he'd moved to Ben's newly purchased black stallion, stroking it while evaluating it with a casual but practiced eye. And with the stranger's every move, Ben had grown more and more alarmed.

He'd seen fellows like this one before. To put it quite simply, women were instinctively attracted to this type. Ben had witnessed the phenomenon half a dozen times. And despite his own history of success with women, he had always envied these competitors because of the ease of their victories. Ben's own successes had been built on charm, seduction, and games. All this Riordain fellow needed to do, however, was exist. To walk into a room, stand apart, and wait. The women would be perfectly willing to do all the work.

Didn't Riordain know it? Had he lived so far out of civilization his whole life that he'd never walked into a bar, or a church social, or a barn dance, and had pretty girls competing to hang on his arm? It didn't seem possible. There had to be another reason a man like this would arrange for a bride through the mail.

Once Riordain had finished catering to the horses, he had leaned on the top rail of the paddock, finally turning his gaze westward. There was no hint of nervousness. No spark of anticipation. No doubt, yet also no hope. Either the man was completely unreadable or he was a true Stoic. Either way, Ben found his rival's attitude frustrating. This man, he suspected, was not interested in selling his contract. He would want Megan Braddock, and no amount of money would dissuade him. And Megan would want to honor her "commitment." Which meant it would come to blows, and Thor would make mincemeat out of Ben.

Reminding himself that Megan loved him—the kiss, if nothing else, had been proof of that!—Ben nevertheless imagined how she'd react when she caught sight of her "intended." After all her speculation as to what Riordain's attributes and flaws might be, he had a feeling she had never expected a particularly good-looking bridegroom. Good-hearted, yes. But lean, tanned limbs of steel? A mane of wheat-colored hair to his shoulders? High cheekbones and clear, steady cobalt eyes? Probably not.

The telltale cloud of dust in the distance was growing larger, and Ben decided he had to do something. To find something wrong with this man, and fast. There had to be a reason Riordain was choosing so unconventional and unnecessary a route toward matrimony. Ben had all of ninety seconds to learn exactly what that reason was.

Striding over to his competitor, he announced cheerfully, "Looks like we're both waiting for the stage. Expecting someone special?"

The stranger sized him up for a second, then shrugged. "Hard to say. Is that your stallion over there?"

"I bought him three days ago in San Francisco," Ben explained, annoyed by the hint of a brogue in the man's steady voice. Megan was just enough of a romantic to be seduced by subtle touches such as that, and Suzannah disarmed as well. "He's a fast horse, but skittish."

"He's a beauty," the prospective bridegroom corrected. "If you're interested in getting something tamer, we might be able to make a deal. I have a ranch a few miles from here. Quality stock, and well broke."

Resisting a desperate temptation to offer the horse in exchange for Megan, Ben gave a casual shrug. "He's definitely for sale, for the right price. Depending on what happens in the next few minutes, I'll either be on the stage when it leaves, or the next one through. Either way, I don't plan on keeping the stallion."

"Depending on what happens in the next few minutes?" For the first time, the rancher smiled. "Sounds like you're planning on robbing the stage. Mind if I get my bride off safely before you start waving that pistol around?"

Ben grinned wryly. "The only thing worth stealing on that stage *is* your bride."

The cobalt blue eyes narrowed. "What's that supposed to mean?"

The gambler could almost feel Riordain's strong hands clench and unclench at his sides, as though readying themselves for his adversary's neck. Reminding himself that he couldn't realistically hope to win a physical confrontation, he explained quietly, "It means things have gotten complicated, my friend. But we're men of reason, and we'll work it out." Extending his hand, he said, "My name's Ben Steele. Nice to meet you."

The rancher hesitated, then admitted, "I don't like complications, Steele. But like you said, we're men of reason. So . . ." He grabbed Ben's hand and almost broke it with his grip. Then he grinned and announced, "My name's Aengus Yates. Welcome to the Sierras."

Ben stared, believing for a moment that the pain

in his hand had caused him to hallucinate. Aengus Yates? *Suzannah's* Aengus Yates?

Then the stage was there, roaring to a stop, and Ben knew, from the expression on Suzannah Hennessy's face as she burst open the door and jumped to the ground, heedless of the driver's entreaties that she wait for assistance, that it was true.

More importantly, he knew at that moment that Megan was his, and the knowledge made him grin with sympathetic relief when his former rival murmured, in dazed disbelief, "The little Hennessy lass?"

Ben slapped him on the back. "The stallion's all yours, friend. Consider it a gift. If you're smart, you'll jump on its back and get the hell out of here before that wildcat scratches your eyes out." Without waiting for a reply, he hurried to the stagecoach in time to help Megan make a more graceful exit than her companion had. Pulling her into an immediate warm embrace, he whispered, "Darling, are you glad to see me?"

"Wait!" Megan wriggled free quickly. "You won't believe who that man over there is, Ben."

He chuckled in defeat. "I suppose our reunion will have to wait until Suzannah has extracted her pound of flesh. Let's go and watch, then, shall we?"

"*Aengus Yates!*" Suzannah gestured contemptuously toward the handsome beast she'd once loved so dearly. "How *dare* you show your face around here!"

"Around here?" He seemed completely disoriented. "I *live* around here, Suzy. What are *you* doing here?"

"That's none of your business!" She took a deep

breath, then accused sharply, "Did you or did you not order a bride from Megan's uncle?"

He blanched visibly. "Don't tell me he sent *you?*"

"Don't be ridiculous! Do you suppose I'd consider marrying an Irishman, or a rancher, or anyone else for that matter, after what you did to me?"

Aengus winced. "I don't remember doing anything to you—"

"Did you order a wife?" Before he could reply, she snapped, "You already *have* a wife! It's bad enough you turned your back on her, and your two darling sons, but *this?* Is *this* what you've been doing since you left town? Marrying woman after woman, just to leave them, alone with their babies?"

"Katherine is dead."

Suzannah's hand flew to her mouth, stifling the gasp his announcement had wrenched from deep within her. Katherine? Dead? Could it be true? She and Megan had heard nothing about it. "The boys . . . ?"

"They're with me now."

Megan stepped up at that moment to touch the rancher's cheek, as though comforting him and verifying his existence in one soft motion. "We're so sorry, Aengus. We hadn't heard."

He smiled warily. "Megan? You're here too?" Then he blanched again. "Your uncle sent *you* to marry me?"

She flushed and nodded. "We had no idea, of course. You used a different name. Why?"

"I remembered—" He stopped himself and grinned reluctantly. "It's good to see you, Megan."

"It's wonderful to see you too, Aengus, despite the circumstances."

He nodded. "Dennis Riordain was my grandfather's name. I used it because I thought your uncle might remember mine. I met him once, did you know?''

"No. When was that?"

"At your parents' funeral. We spoke for a while. And even before that, I'd heard stories about his matchmaking abilities from your father." He took a deep breath. "When I decided to contact him, I didn't want to admit . . . no, that's not right. I just wanted to keep things simple. But as your Mr. Steele says, it's gotten complicated anyway."

"He isn't *my* Mr. Steele." Megan giggled nervously. "But it's clear you're not my Mr. Riordain, either. I suppose all we can do is write to my uncle—"

"I want to see Luke and Johnny," Suzannah interrupted impatiently. "We can work out the details of Aengus's many marriages later. Those poor babies must be devastated, and of course"—she fixed Aengus with an imperious stare—"here *you* are, miles away from them again. Just when they need you most. And ordering them a mother through the mail, as though they're not worth any more effort than that?"

"Suzannah!" Megan scolded. "You're being too rude. It's obvious Aengus is doing his best—"

"His best?" she scoffed. "That's not saying much." Before Megan could protest again, she repeated, "I want to see Luke and Johnny. Now!"

Megan touched Aengus's shoulder. "After you left town, Suzannah and the boys grew very close. You probably didn't know that—"

"How would he know? He never wrote—"

"That's *enough!*" Aengus interrupted sharply.

Suzannah stepped back, intimidated by the growl in his voice, and the unfamiliar look on his face. In all the years she'd known him, she'd never seen him cross, much less angry. Somehow, despite all her criticisms of him, she had managed to cling to one last fantasy. The calm, steady manner. The cool, clear gaze. *The slow smile,* she mocked herself silently. *You never really knew the beast at all, Suzannah Hennessy. You're such a goose.*

Having reestablished order, Aengus announced quietly, "You're all welcome to come to Bent Creek with me. The boys are waiting there for me, at the home of a friend. There's a small hotel, or you can stay at the ranch. Or"—he stared coolly at Suzannah—"you can go back to San Francisco. It's your choice."

Suzannah forced herself to meet his gaze. "I really do want to see the boys. Please, Aengus? It must be so awful for them, losing their mother, and then moving to a strange place. Let me offer them some comfort."

"Suzannah lost her own mother not ten months ago," Megan interceded softly. "That's why we went to stay with Uncle Russ in Chicago."

The last tinge of anger left the rancher's cobalt eyes. "I'm sorry, Suzy. Your mother was a good woman." He gestured toward the station yard. "I'll hitch up the wagon. If we start now, we'll be in Bent Creek before dark." To Suzannah's dismay, he then grabbed her by the shoulders and stared down at her sternly. "There'll be no more of your nagging, young lady. Agreed?"

Before she could retort, he smiled, and to her confused delight, it was the same slow, warm, deadly smile that had turned her insides to mush for so many years. For a moment, she almost thought he was going to kiss her, but instead he observed cheerfully, "You were always a brat of a girl. Nice to know some things don't change." Then he *did* kiss her, but it wasn't the kind of kiss a man bestows on a woman. Definitely not the kind of kiss of which she'd dreamed so often. Instead, it was an affectionate but meaningless gesture, from a man to a child. A bratty child, no less.

"She's a pest," Ben was agreeing. "She's been making my life miserable since we sailed from New York. Her friend here, on the other hand, is an angel." He slipped his arm around Megan's shoulder. "What was she like as a child, Yates?"

"Little Megan Braddock?" Aengus smiled. "The loveliest child you'd ever want to see. Of course, our Suzy here lured her into mischief from time to time, but on her own, this one was a blessing through and through." He touched Megan's chin, encouraging her to tip her face up toward his own. "Her mother was the most beautiful woman I ever laid eyes on. And here she stands, every bit as lovely. What were you thinking, Megan?"

Megan's cheeks had gone from pink to crimson. "Thinking?"

"Selling yourself through the mail to a stranger. Do you not know how foolish that was?"

"She ended up with me, so no harm done," Ben interrupted. "Shouldn't we be getting into town before it gets dark, like you said?"

The annoyance in Ben's tone made Suzannah almost smile for the first time since Aengus had come into view. It was irrational for the gambler to be bothered by the compliments Aengus was heaping on Megan, but Suzannah could sympathize, since she herself had felt a twinge of jealousy. Not that she wanted Aengus to praise *her*, of course. But somehow, the idea that he saw Suzannah as a brat and Megan as a beauty seemed unfair.

Aengus was studying Ben directly. "I told you before, I don't like complications. And it looks to me like you're full of them."

Suzannah's pulse quickened, and she glanced slyly at Megan, wondering if the girl realized that two virile, experienced men were about to come to blows over her. It was so exciting! Even if one of the men was Aengus.

"Let me simplify things for you," Ben drawled. "I'm in love with Megan. She's in love with me. Once Suzannah is convinced you're not beating your sons, the three of us will be taking the next stage for San Francisco. Is that clear enough?"

Aengus glanced at Megan. "Is that how it is?"

"No," she flushed. "I mean, not exactly. It's more complicated than that. But not for you, Aengus. You needn't worry—"

"That's right," Suzannah agreed. "It's none of your business. Ben is our escort, and we trust him. Or at least, we trust him more than we trust *you*."

Ben chuckled reluctantly. "If hell hath no fury like a woman scorned, you're in a world of danger, my friend. You should never have broken her heart once, let alone twice."

"Twice?" To Suzannah's dismay, Aengus seemed amused by the reference. "I remember the pint-sized marriage proposal, but when was the other offense?"

"Never mind!" Suzannah eyed him haughtily. "Are we going to Bent Creek or not?"

Aengus put his hand on Ben's shoulder. "You escorted these lasses from New York, and I'm grateful for that. It's an amazement to me that Russell Braddock allowed them to come all this way alone. Still, I feel obliged to make certain your intentions are honorable. They may have been pests when I knew them last, but I've a fondness for them. So?''

Ben smiled. "My intentions toward Suzannah are to resist any and all urges to gag her. As for Megan, I intend to marry her."

"For how long?" Suzannah mocked. "That's the real question, isn't it, Aengus?"

The rancher's eyes darkened, and for a moment Suzannah thought he was going to raise his voice to her again, but instead he muttered, "I'll ready the wagon," then turned and strode toward the paddock.

"Really, Suzannah." Megan shook her head sadly. "Why are you treating Aengus this way? He's doing his best—"

"Stop saying that."

"You really are a brat," Ben assured her. "Any other man would have told you to shut up long before this. If nothing else, I credit him with restraint."

"He knows I'm right." Suzannah watched as Aengus began to hitch up the team without a backward glance. "He left his wife and children, and only took responsibility for his sons when there was no other choice. And even then . . ." Her voice broke, but she recovered quickly. "Even then, he couldn't be bothered to find a proper stepmother for them. Anyone would do, so long as she eased *his* burden."

Ben slipped his arm around Suzannah's shoulders. "Speaking of burdens, you're not going to interfere with my courtship of Megan now, are you? I promise I'll find you a good man in San Francisco. One who will stay married to you forever no matter how obnoxious you are. And"—his brown eyes twinkled impishly—"maybe even one who thinks you're as beautiful as Megan and her mother."

Suzannah responded gratefully to his teasing.

"Wasn't that annoying? You'd think Aengus never saw a pretty girl before. What will you do if he decides to hold Meg to the marriage contract after all?"

"Then I'll just have to marry you instead."

"You're both being terrible," Megan complained. "Look at poor Aengus over there. Ben, go and help him. And Suzannah? I want your word you won't criticize him anymore."

"I don't plan on speaking to him at all," Suzannah assured her.

"I'll give him the good news," Ben grinned. "Maybe then he'll stop treating me like some sort of scoundrel."

"Don't be too nice to him, Ben. He doesn't deserve it."

Ben grinned again, bowed, and then ambled over to the corral.

"I'm surprised at you, Suzannah." Megan arched an eyebrow critically. "You treat Aengus as though he's a murderer, and Mr. Steele as though he's your long-lost brother."

"I'll behave from here on out." Suzannah stared into the distance, weary suddenly of the turn the day had taken. "I've finally had a chance to tell Aengus Yates what I think of him. I believe I can put my feelings for him to rest now."

Megan was clearly stifling a smile. "It wasn't very gallant of him to call your marriage proposal 'pint-sized.' "

"Nor to call me a brat. But you, at least, seem to have made a wonderful impression on him."

"He was being kind," Megan assured her. "He was always kind, especially after my parents died. Remember? I always knew in my heart that Katherine drove him away with her cold, nasty disposition. Now that she's dead, he's taken the boys back, and he'll be a wonderful father. Please don't scold him anymore.''

Suzannah wanted to remind Megan that, no matter how awful Katherine was as a wife, Aengus never should have left the way he did. At the very least, he should have taken the boys with him! But what did it matter now? The boys were with their father, and perhaps he would find a way to make it up to them. That would truly be a happy ending. ''I won't scold him anymore, I promise. All I want to do is visit the boys; then we'll be on our way.''

Megan studied her warily. ''To San Francisco?''

''Of course. I know a handsome gentleman who owns a hotel there.'' She eyed her friend impishly. ''Are you going to kiss him again soon?''

''Don't tease me,'' Megan pleaded. ''I need your advice more than ever now.''

Suzannah shrugged. ''It's your decision, Meg. Do you want to spend the rest of your life with him?''

''No.''

The quickness of the reply surprised Suzannah, and she cautiously balanced her loyalty to Megan against her growing fondness for Ben Steele. His heart would be broken! He would recover, of course. He was a man, and a fairly resilient one at that, so she doubted he'd pine forever. Still, it had all seemed to be working out so well.

''There's no Mr. Riordain now, Meg—''

''There's a Mr. Riordain somewhere,'' Megan interrupted firmly. ''Uncle Russ will find him for me. I can't marry a man like Ben, and you know it. He's a city man—''

''I've changed my mind about them.''

Megan frowned. ''He's a gambler.''

"That's only a vice if one loses. And I can tell Ben wins all the time. So in a way, it's almost a virtue."

"Don't be ridiculous." Megan touched her friend's arm. "I don't want to marry him, Suzannah. I don't even trust him. Please help me? I know you're fond of him—"

"I adore him. But I adore you a thousand times more. If you're certain—truly certain—that he's not the man you want, I'll help you send him away. Just promise me you're not allowing that . . . that business about your mother to cloud your judgment."

"My mother?"

Suzannah groaned in defeat. "You know exactly what I mean, Megan Braddock. Ben obviously frequents saloons and dance halls—"

"Suzannah! It has nothing to do with that, I swear!" Megan flushed but continued valiantly. "I simply don't want to marry a vagabond. And I don't trust Ben to love me forever. To him I'm a prize to be won."

"You kissed him—"

"Because I wanted to see how it felt!" Megan flushed and lowered her voice quickly. "For once, I wanted to do something naughty, just to see how it felt. And it felt wonderful. *That's* my mother's legacy, I suppose. I kissed a man I didn't love and it felt wonderful." Covering her face with her hands, she pleaded, "I don't want to talk about it anymore."

Suzannah pulled her friend's hands into her own and grasped them tightly. "We won't talk about it anymore. We'll go to San Francisco, because it would be insane to come all this way and not spend a few weeks in so beautiful a city. But we'll write to your uncle, and he'll tell us what to do next. And we'll follow our original plan to find husbands in the same place. How does that sound?"

"And you'll help me explain it all to Ben?"

"He'll know," Suzannah assured her quietly. "Until now, he could hope that it was only your commitment to Dennis Riordain that stood in his way. Now, when you turn him down, he'll know you really don't want to marry him. Just don't kiss him again," she added wryly. "If you want to kiss a man you don't love, try Aengus. He apparently finds you very attractive."

Megan giggled through her tears. "I knew that bothered you. If you want him to notice what a pretty woman *you've* become, you should try smiling at him. Or at least stop berating him. Men don't find that particularly attractive."

"Do you suppose I care what Aengus Yates thinks?" Suzannah began, then grimaced in defeat. "The sooner we put both these men behind us, the better off we'll be. At least now you'll know."

Megan cocked her head inquiringly. "At least now I'll know what?"

"How it feels to want the wrong man," Suzannah sighed. "They say it's better to have loved and lost than never to have loved at all, but I don't believe that's true, do you?"

"No." Megan's gaze shifted to Ben, who was cheerfully loading the women's luggage into the back of Aengus's wagon. "No, I don't think it's better at all."

To Suzannah's relief, Aengus didn't ride in the wagon with them on the bumpy trail to Bent Creek. Instead, he rode Ben's black stallion, while Suzannah positioned herself between the gambler and the object of his affections, trying her best to make the ride more bearable for the lovelorn suitor. She knew he was confused and discouraged by Megan's aloof attitude. Suzannah was a bit confused herself, but had vowed to respect Megan's decision in this matter, and Megan's decision was clearly to decline Ben's offer to live happily ever after.

As the April sunlight streamed through pine branches to warm the crisp mountain air, Suzannah took more than a moment to surreptitiously study the man who had once owned her heart. Aengus dressed differently these days, she noted wistfully. In place of the boyish brown dungarees and threadbare jacket of his days in Adamsville, he wore a loose-fitting white muslin shirt, a sturdy black leather vest, blue denim waist overalls, and thick-heeled black leather boots. Practical and unpretentious as always, but with a different sort of style. She could see that, even in the way he sat in his saddle. He had always been at ease there, but seemed now to exude a more mature sort of confidence and independence than she'd remembered from before.

And he had been skinnier in Adamsville, despite the gargantuan meals he had consumed in the kitchen of the Adamsville Inn, courtesy of housekeeper and cook Mary Hennessy. Suzannah's mother had loved feeding Aengus, almost as much as Suzannah had loved staring at him while he ate. He had visited often, after the paying guests had left, to reminisce with Mary, mostly about Ireland. Suzannah had never been to their native land herself, but could picture it clearly because of their stories, and she smiled now at the thought that her mother might at that very moment be somewhere as beautiful and magical as the land she and Aengus had described so long ago.

And in its way, Aengus's new home was every bit as magical, although there was a different, harsher aspect to the pureness of nature here in the mountains. It differed from Indiana too, and Suzannah wondered how Aengus had managed to find enough flat land to actually establish a horse ranch here. And where on earth did his horses graze? Surely they didn't eat pine needles!

Aengus was taking them to Bent Creek proper, rather than to his ranch, but perhaps she could convince Luke to take her for a ride, just for a quick peek at the place where the father would be raising the sons.

They arrived in town late in the afternoon, only to find that Luke and Johnny were not at the home of Judge and Mrs. Avery Winston. Judge Winston explained that the boys had gone out to the ranch to do their chores, and might not be back for hours, despite the fact that dinner would be served promptly at six.

"I'll send them back as soon as I'm home, and you can have a nice long visit with them over dinner," Aengus offered to Suzannah. "Why don't you rest for a while? And be sure to drink plenty of water. This altitude will dry your throat surer than anything."

Suzannah grabbed his arm. "Take me with you, please, Aengus? I won't nag you, I promise. I just want to see them right away. And I'm sure they'll want to sleep in their own little beds. I could fix dinner at your ranch," she added quickly. "And I'm sure I can find my way back here——"

"Luke can bring you back." He hesitated, then asked cautiously, "Do you cook as well as your mother did?"

Suzannah smiled easily at that. "No one cooks as

well as my mother did, but she taught me a trick or two. We're agreed, then?''

He nodded, turning his attention to Megan. "Will you be coming with us?''

"If you don't mind, I'd like to rest,'' she murmured. "You said there was a hotel?''

But the Winstons would have none of that, and once it was decided that Ben and Megan would dine with them, and that the two guest rooms would be made up for the travelers, Aengus took Suzannah's arm and helped her up onto the wagon's smooth wooden bench.

They rode in silence for almost half an hour, but to Suzannah's surprise, there was none of the tension she had expected between them. Perhaps it was as she'd said. She now felt at peace with Aengus's flaws and her own misplaced affections. And Luke and Johnny were together with their father, just as they should be. In a remote, untamed, yet idyllic location. The perfect place to raise two young boys to manhood.

"I want to apologize, Aengus,'' she ventured finally. "I was so harsh with you, back at the way station. I see now that everything may have happened for a reason. It's so beautiful here . . .''

"Isn't it?'' He smiled easily. "You were always happiest out of doors, weren't you? I remember the first time I saw you. Twenty feet above the ground in a sycamore tree, with a wreath of daisies in your hair. Like a little wood sprite.''

Suzannah stared in open-mouthed delight. "I don't remember that at all.''

"You had your sights on a chipmunk, as I recall,'' he teased. "It was only later that you turned your affections to myself.''

She winced but nodded. "I guess you thought all that was silly."

"Did I?" He seemed to consider it, then shook his head. "I didn't know what to make of it, truth be told. If you'd had a father, I imagine I would have gone to him, if only to protect myself from misunderstandings." His blue eyes began to twinkle. "Especially when you and Megan began watching me in the lake."

Suzannah's cheeks warmed rapidly as the image of a naked and majestic young Aengus sprang vividly out of her memory. "You knew about that? We only did it once or twice. Just to see if—well, to see whether—well, not to see anything at all, of course."

He grinned at her confusion. "It was bold on your part. And once I realized you were there, I made the necessary adjustments."

She nodded, daring to be a brat one last time. "You started wearing your trousers right into the lake."

Aengus threw back his head and roared with laughter until it seemed as though the Sierras themselves might begin to rumble from the sound. "It's a fond memory, Suzannah, and I thank you for it."

She had forgotten all about that laugh. Rare, unexpected, unrestrained. The sound was like a pull on a trigger, exploding her senses with a heady combination of childhood memories and womanly anticipation, and she mentally gulped for air, hoping he wouldn't see how completely disoriented she had become.

But Aengus seemed oblivious to her. It was only the memory that interested him, and in a way, she didn't blame him. It had been a good time in both their lives. For all his eventual faults, the Aengus Yates of those bygone days had been poor, hardworking, and honest. Alex Monroe had brought him to Adams-ville from Boston because Aengus's talent with horses had meshed with Alex's desire to be a gentleman rancher rather than a farmer like his wealthy father-in-law. Alex—or rather, Alex's wife, Elaine—had pro-vided the capital, while Aengus had provided the brawn, the skills, the instinct, and the soul.

Unfortunately, it had also been Alex Monroe who had introduced Aengus to Katherine, who had been a houseguest at the Monroe ranch during a month-long celebration of a niece's wedding. Only six weeks after the infamous "pint-sized marriage proposal"! Before another month was over, a second wedding had taken place on the Monroe premises, and Suzan-nah's heart had been broken for the first time.

"Aengus?"

He turned to her, nodding for her to continue.

"How did Katherine die?"

There was no pain in his expression, and she didn't know whether to be relieved or annoyed. He seemed only to be considering how to phrase his answer, and so she prompted, "I won't scold you, no matter what you say."

He chuckled softly. "After this morning's tongue-lashing, that's a welcome guarantee." Sobering slightly, he added, "It was unexpected. And over quickly. At least, that's what I'm told. The symptoms of consumption, but progressing so rapidly, the doc-tor didn't know what to make of it."

"Were either of the boys sick?"

"Not a day. They went to stay with Monroe at the end. He's the one who contacted me."

"That was good of him."

Aengus shrugged. "We're almost there. On the other side of that rise."

"Is that Bent Creek, over there in the distance?" she asked, hearing, more than seeing, the thunderous waterway.

"That's the river," Aengus corrected. "If we had time, I'd show it to you. It's a spectacular sight this time of year, with the snow melt feeding it. Like one long, ferocious waterfall, cascading down the mountainside."

"It sounds like thunder."

Aengus nodded. "The creek's not much to see. They only named the town after it because of the Bent Creek mine, up there along that ridge."

"A gold mine?"

Aengus nodded. "Ten years ago it was still producing well, but now it's all boarded up. There's only the occasional nugget in the creekbed to remind folks how the town got its start."

"There are riches more than gold here," Suzannah sighed, taking in the sights, from the snowcaps to the rugged granite outcroppings that punctuated the landscape. Every tree seemed greener and straighter and taller than the last, with a scent so pungent and delicious that she wished she could capture it and take it with her back to Chicago.

Aengus was studying the view also, but with a different purpose. "I don't like the look of those clouds, Suzy. There's been the feel of a storm in the air, but I didn't expect it this soon. Maybe we should turn back—"

"No! I want to see Luke and Johnny. And I *don't* want them to be all alone when some awful storm hits."

"They'll be fine," Aengus began, then seemed to think better of it. "It'll be a quick visit, then. And the three of us will bring you back to town. How's that?"

She smiled sweetly. "That's just what I wanted to hear. That way, the boys can see Megan too. And you can have a long talk with Ben."

He eyed her warily. "Why would I be wanting to do that?"

"Megan doesn't want to marry him."

"Then she won't. I'll see to that."

"I want you to help me explain it to Ben. I want to let him down gently."

"He'll be fine," Aengus assured her coolly. "I'll make it clear, man to man."

"I want you to let him down gently," she repeated. "I'm afraid it's going to crush him."

"He doesn't seem like the marrying kind. Of course," Aengus added mockingly, "I suppose I'm not one to talk, having been such a bad husband and all myself."

Suzannah bit her lip, then asked cautiously, "What about that?"

"What?"

"You sent for a bride. It's a little awkward, I know, but"—she took a deep breath—"are you hoping you and Megan might go through with the marriage contract?" When he stared in disbelief, she explained quickly, "You said yourself she's the most beautiful woman you've ever seen. And you sent for a bride, so you must want one."

"If I'd wanted a child bride, I would have married *you* when I had the chance," Aengus reminded her with a chuckle.

"She's not a child anymore, and neither am I," Suzannah complained. "Are you blind, Aengus Yates? We're full-grown women."

He pulled firmly on the reins, urging the team to a halt, then turned and locked eyes with her. "Are you asking me to look at you that way, Suzannah Hennessy? The way a man looks at a woman?"

"*No*," she gasped. "Of course not."

"Are you asking me to look at little Megan Braddock that way?"

"Don't you dare!"

Aengus threw back his head and roared again, as though the whole concept had been a hilarious one, and she realized he'd been teasing her. Refusing to take her seriously! Enjoying her company, perhaps, but only as the pesky "brat" he remembered so fondly.

Folding her arms across her chest, she looked away in haughty rebuke. "There's a storm coming, remember? If you don't start driving this stupid wagon, I will."

"Are you afraid of a little rain, Suzy? I remember when you used to run wild in all sorts of weather."

"Be quiet."

The wagon began to move again, and while she kept her eyes turned away from the driver, she was sure he was grinning from ear to ear. It was almost more than she could bear! Was it possible she was a joke to him? After all he'd been to her, both in terms of love and in terms of anguish and betrayal? Had the whole dramatic episode been reduced to this?

"Suzy?"

"Be quiet."

"I'm sorry I teased you. I want to talk seriously for a while, before we get to the ranch." When she continued to ignore him, he persisted doggedly. "I don't think it's wise for you and Megan to spend too much time in San Francisco."

She turned to glare at him. "I beg your pardon?"

Aengus was shaking his head. "It'll encourage the gambler. And it's not a safe place for two young women alone. I'd take you myself, but I can't spare the time."

"We appreciate your concern, Aengus, but we'll be fine. We can stay with a friend of Mr. Braddock's. The same man who sent word to you that our stage would be arriving today."

"It's been a long trip for the two of you," he continued stubbornly. "And a misguided one. You should go back to Chicago as soon as possible, and—"

"We're spending time in San Francisco, and that's final. Ben is a wonderful man, and he'd never allow any harm to come to us. And we don't need advice from the likes of you."

"Fine."

"And don't talk to Ben either. I've changed my mind about that."

"I'll be talking to him," Aengus countered firmly. "He needs to know there'll be consequences to his health if anything happens to you girls."

"You make us sound like children . . ." She broke off as a low split-rail fence came into view. Beyond it, on a gently inclining slope that ended abruptly against a tall wall of rock, stood a graceful ranch house with a porch the size of a parlor. "Oh, Aengus, it's so pretty. Did you build it yourself?"

"The house was there when I bought the place. I added the porch and stable. And the fences. It was a home to a miner and his family back then, not a horse ranch, so I had to do some clearing, but all in all, it was a great spot from the start."

"How did you find it?"

"I have an old friend from my Boston days, name

of Tom Whalen. He moved out here right about the time I left Adamsville. He wrote me that this was a good place to start a new life. He was right.''

"I don't see the boys yet. You don't suppose they've wandered off, do you? With a storm coming?''

"Luke knows better than that. They're probably settling the stock down. There,'' he added, pointing to the stable. "You can see Johnny there in the doorway.''

Suzannah's eyes widened, not only with delight, but with amazement at how much the little one had grown in less than a year. He'd be just under five years old now, she calculated quickly. And Luke would be seven. How tall was *he* going to be?

Then the older boy stepped out of the stable, dusting off his clothes as he walked, and Suzannah gasped. "Look at Luke! He's grown a foot! Oh, Aengus, I can't believe my eyes.'' Without thinking, she threw her arms around the rancher and hugged him fiercely. "I'm so glad they're with you. I know it's a terrible thing to say, but if it took Katherine's dying to put those boys with their father, then I'm glad she's dead.''

Reining the horses to a stop, Aengus cupped her chin in a huge, rough hand and tilted her face toward his. "You won't be talking that way in front of those little lads, will you?''

"Of course not.''

"Then I'll say it too,'' he murmured. "Just this one time. I'm glad she's dead and gone. I only wish she'd never been born in the first place.''

Stunned by the pain that radiated from his deep blue eyes, Suzannah sandwiched his face between her palms. "Forgive me for judging you, Aengus. I see now she broke your heart, and I know all too well how that feels.''

''You don't know anything about it,'' he corrected. ''And I hope you never do.''

A chorus of young voices shouting her name interrupted, and she spun to see the two boys stumbling through the underbrush and waving their arms in frantic greeting, as though they feared she might ignore them forever if they didn't take action immediately. *"Suzannah! Suzannah!"*

A wave of love rushed toward her, and she was suddenly desperate to be inundated—to be swept away by the joy and the need and the memories that were shining in the children's hazel eyes. Pulling free from Aengus, she jumped down from the wagon, gathered up her skirts with one hand, and raced toward the boys with her free arm stretched out before her.

Chapter Three

"Luke! Johnny! Look at you two!"

They were on her in an instant, tackling her to the ground and hugging her with unrestrained adoration. "You're here! You're here!" Johnny cried. "Why are you here, Suzannah?"

"I'm here because I missed you two so much. But I barely recognize you! You're almost as tall as I am, Luke Yates."

"Me too," Johnny interrupted.

"Stand where I can see you, then, John Dennis. I want to see just how big you've gotten."

The little boy wriggled to his feet and stood, his arms stretched out to the side. "See?"

"You're practically full grown," she nodded.

Luke had stood also, and to Suzannah's amusement now offered her his hand and assisted her to her feet. "Thank you, Mr. Yates. You're quite a perfect gentleman these days." Stooping slightly, she pulled them both into another quick embrace. "I can't believe we're together again. Here of all places." Lowering her voice, she added gently, "Your father told me about your mother. I'm so sorry, darlings. It's so terribly, terribly unfair."

Luke's hazel eyes clouded. "It was real bad, Suzannah. She coughed a lot, and every time she coughed, it hurt her and made her sicker. She didn't even look like herself."

"I'm so sorry, sweetie."

"She coughed a lot," Johnny echoed. "And we weren't supposed to bother her, 'cause she was so tired."

"I'm sure you were never a bother," Suzannah cooed. "Did Dr. Langham come to the house every day to take care of her?"

"He came all the times. Even after we moved to Uncle Alex's house."

Suzannah felt a rush of gratitude toward the neighbors who had stepped in so unselfishly. "It was good of the Monroes to help like that."

"Yeah." Johnny nodded. "Their house is big enough to run in. But you're not supposed to."

"Well, you certainly have room to run here, don't you? You boys must have been very surprised when you saw this wonderful ranch for the first time."

"Yeah, we were." The little boy smiled uncertainly. "Suzannah?"

She rumpled his dark, shaggy hair. "Yes, sweetie?"

"Are you our new ma?"

"What? Oh, dear . . ." She bit her lip, then tried to smile. "I see why you might think that, but—"

"Pa said he was bringing a new ma, and he brought *you*," the little one insisted firmly. "So you must be her."

"Pa said she was bringing a stranger," Luke reminded his brother sharply. "Suzannah's not a stranger."

"Luke's right." Suzannah gave Johnny a sympathetic smile. "I'm just here for a short visit. Your father's new bride has been delayed for a while, but she'll be here before summer's over. And she'll be worth waiting for, I promise you."

"We don't want her," Luke shrugged.

"We want you," Johnny added, throwing his arms around Suzannah. "Please stay?"

"I can't, sweetie. Let's just try to make the best of this visit, shall we?"

"Suzannah?"

"Yes, Luke?"

"Can we go with you when you leave?"

She studied the older boy warily. "This is your home now, Luke. Once you get used to it—"

"We don't want to get used to it. We want to go with you. We won't be any bother, I promise. I can work—"

"That's enough," a gruff voice interrupted, and Suzannah turned sheepishly to face Aengus. She hadn't noticed his approach, and didn't blame him for being annoyed at the way she'd bungled things.

"I'm sorry, Aengus. It didn't occur to me they'd think I was the new bride."

"Suzannah is here for a visit," Aengus informed the boys tersely. "She was going to cook for us, but the storm's coming quicker than I thought, so we'll go into town now instead. All of us. The judge's wife offered us dinner—"

"I don't want to eat at the judge's house again," Johnny complained. "Their food is too salty. And I don't want to sleep there neither, cause their beds are lumpy. Can't we just keep Suzannah?"

"Look at Pa's face," Luke advised his brother dryly, jerking his thumb toward Aengus as he spoke. "He doesn't even *want* her to stay."

"That's enough," Aengus growled again. "Go and get cleaned up so we can leave. Both of you."

Suzannah could see that Luke was about to talk back, so she intervened quickly. "Do you know who else is in town, dying to see you again? Megan Braddock! Won't it be fun to see her again?"

Johnny's eyes began to sparkle. "Did she bring her dog?"

"Copper? No, sweetie, he was too old to make the trip, so we left him with her uncle in Chicago."

"Dang!"

"I don't want to hear that kind of talk, John Dennis," she pretended to scold; then she pulled him into a playful embrace. "Go and get cleaned up, like your father told you, and then we'll have a nice long visit in the wagon."

Turning to Luke, she stroked his cheek, anxious to erase the sullen expression that Aengus's barking had caused. "You'll like seeing Megan again, won't you?"

He nodded without meeting her gaze.

"Will you go and get cleaned up, then?"

He nodded again, then grabbed his brother's arm. "We'll do it for *you*, Suzannah. Not *him*." With that, the two raced away as though they were certain Aengus would take a switch to them for their insolence.

Straightening slowly, Suzannah placed her hands on her hips and turned to confront her host. "Well?"

"Don't interfere."

"Don't tell *me* what to do."

"Fine. Do you want to see the house or not?"

"I came to see your sons, not your house."

He nodded. "All the more reason for them to hurry."

Suzannah stepped closer, her voice softening a bit. "You were harsh with them, Aengus. Why?"

"It's my way. Don't interfere."

"It's not your way," she countered stubbornly. "Were you surprised to see how close they feel to me? Is that what annoyed you?"

"I'm not annoyed."

"Well, then, I suppose you're just a bully." She waved a hand to ward off any retort. "I'll see the house now, please."

He nodded and took her arm. "Step carefully here. The ground's uneven."

She walked at his side, silent and confused over what might have made him so gruff. It simply wasn't Aengus Yates's way, despite what he said. An even temper and soothing voice had been the very things, beyond his good looks, that had won her heart so many years ago. And his success at horse training, she knew, had been based on those same reassuring qualities. To see such phenomenal strength of body and of character, and to know that you could rely on it without fear it would ever be abused—that was the very essence of the man's attractiveness.

They stepped onto the porch, and she paused to survey his land, impressed again, despite the darkening of the sky, with the vibrancy of the surroundings. A kind of rough, untamed paradise, she decided wistfully. The kind of place any child, especially a boy, would love to explore. But Aengus's sons wanted to leave. Why? Homesickness, of course. And missing their mother, which was natural. Hopefully, that was all there was to it.

When Aengus took her arm again and ushered her through the door, she felt instantly reassured. It was clean and well built, but so devoid of a woman's touch that it undoubtedly contributed to the boys' sense of loss. No wonder they wanted to cling to Suzannah.

And this is why Aengus is so moody, she assured herself wistfully. *He expected to bring home a bride tonight. To warm this house. Not to mention his bed. This is not exactly the evening he had planned. Instead of a compliant bride, he's saddled with a nosy critic from his past.*

"Suzannah?" He was proffering a cup of cool water.

"Mmm, just what I wanted." She drank deeply, then smiled at her host. "I see now why you're so disappointed, Aengus. But do you know what I think? I think this all happened for the best. Now that we know exactly what you need, Megan and I can help Russell Braddock find the perfect woman for this household. She'll be worth the wait, I promise you."

A rueful grin spread over his handsome features. "Eight years later, and you're still telling me who to marry?"

Suzannah laughed lightly. "You seem incapable of making a good choice on your own, sir, so you oughtn't complain."

"I suppose that's true."

She studied him fondly. "You may be hopeless when it comes to choosing brides, but I'll admit one thing. Your letter to Mr. Braddock was charming. It touched our hearts, Aengus."

"I was drunk when I wrote that."

She grimaced, suspecting he was teasing her again. "Don't ever tell Megan that. She considers you almost a poet because of it."

"Nice to know someone appreciates me."

A crack of thunder split through the conversation, and Aengus excused himself, stepping back onto the porch to study the sky with growing concern. Over his shoulder he called to Suzannah, "Looks like you might be cooking for us after all."

Luke hurried past the guest to join Aengus. "Pa? Should I check on the horses?"

"Go and see that everything's secure," Aengus nodded. "I'll help you when I'm finished putting the team away. We won't be needing them tonight after all, it seems."

"Wait!" Suzannah ordered. "Are you saying we won't go back to Bent Creek tonight?"

Aengus turned to grin at her. "Does that make you nervous, you being a full-grown woman and all?"

"Stop teasing me, Aengus Yates," she warned. Turning to Luke, she suggested, "Go and do what your father asked, but don't put the wagon away until I've talked to him a bit more." When the boy had sprinted toward the stable, she explained to Aengus, "I'm worried about Megan, not myself. I don't want her alone with Ben all night."

"There'll be two guest rooms and two chaperons— the judge and his wife. She'll be fine."

"You don't know Ben Steele. He's tricky. And very determined. And he has plans for Megan."

"Plans?" Aengus grinned again. "I had plans for tonight myself, as I recall."

"Spare me the details. You'll take me back after supper, won't you?"

"You'll stay, and I'll go. I'll see to it the gambler doesn't misbehave. Will you feel safe here with just the boys?"

"Of course. Thank you, Aengus."

When he reached for a rain slicker, she grabbed his arm in protest. "Won't you eat with us first?"

He seemed pleased by the invitation. "I wasn't looking forward to salty food. Will Megan be safe for a few hours longer?"

"I'm sure of it."

"I'll go help Luke, then. Johnny can show you where everything is. And, Suzannah?"

"Yes?"

"It's good to have you here." Stepping close to her, he admitted, "I said I had plans for tonight, but truth be told, I was dreading the prospect of a stranger here in the house. It had all the makings of another mistake."

"I can imagine," she murmured. "I think the boys were worried too."

Aengus nodded. "But instead of a stranger, here you are. Little Suzy Hennessy. And cooking for us, no less. It's enough to make a man believe in miracles."

She wanted to remind him that she wasn't "little" Suzy Hennessy any more, but knew he'd tease her if she did. For some reason, Aengus didn't want to acknowledge that she'd grown up. Maybe seeing her as a child made him remember a nicer period in his life. The uncomplicated times, before he met Katherine.

In a way, she knew she was doing the same thing.

Remembering the Aengus of her childhood. The strapping young man with a calm yet lilting voice, whose dark blue eyes could turn a girl's insides to warm jelly. Strong and intelligent, quiet and dependable. A man who would never turn his back on his wife, or his sons, or his town. Or Suzannah.

"I suppose little Suzy Hennessy had better get started cooking." She smiled shyly, backing away from Aengus as she spoke. "Go on and help your son now, Mr. Yates. Be sure to work up an appetite, because I intend to make my mother's biscuits for you."

"Is that a fact?" His blue eyes twinkled. "I remember how she'd save some for me, knowing I'd come by the inn late on a Sunday afternoon."

"She spoiled us all, bless her heart."

Aengus nodded. "She worked hard, running that place for Monroe all those years." He seemed about to say more, but a clap of thunder redirected his thoughts and he turned quickly toward the door. "If you need anything, send Johnny out to fetch me."

As she watched him disappear into the stormy shadows, she vowed to make this evening a perfect one—filled with warm memories—not only for herself and Aengus, but for Luke and Johnny as well. For one night, at least, the boys wouldn't be brokenhearted orphans, living among strangers in a strange place, waiting for yet another stranger to come and be their stepmother. And Aengus and Suzannah could be children too, recapturing the days before Katherine had come and ruined everything. They could tell familiar stories and eat familiar foods and pretend, just for a while, that nothing had ever really changed.

* * *

"Tell us the truth, Suzannah," Johnny Yates was insisting as he stuffed half a biscuit into his mouth. "How many dolls were there, really?"

"At least five hundred. Row after row after row. Noelle Braddock has more dolls than any other girl alive. In the daytime, they're all just as pretty as can be. But at night"—Suzannah lowered her voice to a playful whisper—"I could feel them staring at me in the dark."

The child's gold-flecked eyes had widened with alarm. "Really?"

"Yes, really. I tried to sleep, but all I could think about was what would I do if they decided to *grab me!*" Her hand shot out to tickle the boy between his ribs.

Johnny jumped half out of his skin, while Luke and Aengus laughed heartily.

"You're scared of dolls," Luke teased his brother. "Even girls aren't *that* scared."

Johnny's chin rose in childlike defiance. "I'm only scared of dolls that can stare at you in the dark. So are you too, and you're a liar if you say you aren't."

Luke grinned. "Scare him again, Suzannah. It's funny."

"Later," she promised. "I'm saving my best story for bedtime. And don't be so cocky, Luke Yates. It may be you who jumps then."

"I'm too old for bedtime stories. Tell it now, please?"

"Let her eat," Aengus advised. "She made all this good food for us. She should have a chance to enjoy it."

Although the father had spoken in an even voice,

Luke reacted as though he'd been lambasted, muttering under his breath as his eyes narrowed ominously.

Aengus didn't seem to notice, but Suzannah saw it. She also saw the joy fade from little Johnny's eyes, and wondered what she could do to help. Probably nothing. It was clearer by the moment that the problem ran deeper than just one emotional day.

After that, they finished the meal quickly and in silence. Then Johnny asked, "Can I go see if the new stallion's still kicking his stall, Pa?"

Aengus nodded, adding to Luke, "Go and watch out for your brother."

"But hurry back," Suzannah dared to add. "I'll miss you both."

When the boys had left, Aengus smiled. "It was a grand dinner, Suzannah. Thank you."

"Johnny seemed to like the biscuits almost as much as you used to," she smiled in return. "He's so adorable, Aengus."

"He's a fine boy."

"I agree. Luke's a fine boy too."

Aengus nodded. "I suppose I'd better be heading into town. The storm's only going to get worse. Are you sure you feel safe here with just the boys?"

"I'll be safe and warm here. It's you I'm worried about."

"I'll probably be struck by lightning," he agreed cheerfully as he shrugged to his feet and ambled toward the door. "Will you miss me, at least?"

"Of course." Joining him, she raised herself onto her tiptoes and pecked his cheek. "Remember not to take your eyes off Ben Steele. And hurry back in the morning. Your sons will miss you, and so will I."

He grinned down at her. "I'll not miss your nagging, I can tell you that. Sleep tight, Suzannah. I'll be back as quick as I'm able."

When he'd left, she moved across the room and sat herself before the huge stone fireplace, enjoying the warmth from the blaze almost as much as the taste of Aengus on her lips. The good-bye kiss—innocent and gentle, like the children they'd been together—had been a fitting end to their imaginary love affair, and she would be eternally grateful for it.

"Suzannah?"

"Oh! Johnny, I didn't even hear you come in." Noting his troubled eyes, she murmured softly, "Is something wrong?"

"You sent Pa away?"

"What a thought!" she scolded. "He's gone to check on Megan, silly. To be certain the judge doesn't feed her salt and put her in a lumpy bed."

Johnny smiled, clearly relieved. "Luke said you made him leave because he's such a grouch."

She hesitated, then pulled the child into her lap. "He has a lot on his mind." Noticing Luke in the shadows, she motioned for him to join them. "I asked your father to go into town to check on Megan."

"I heard you tell Johnny." He crossed the room and sat on the raised hearth across from them. "I'm glad he left, aren't you?"

She cocked her head and studied him fondly. "Do you know what he said while you two were in the stables? He said you're both fine boys."

"Well, he's not a fine pa. He's a bad one."

Suzannah eyed him sympathetically. "He's been living alone all these years. Maybe he needs time to learn to be a father."

"He used to know how." Luke locked eyes with Suzannah. "I remember him."

"So do I," she sighed.

"Me too," Johnny agreed, but Suzannah knew it wasn't true. Johnny had been a toddler when Aengus had left. But Luke had been a son, forging memories with his father that were meant to guide him into adulthood.

In those days, the whole town had enjoyed the sight of little Luke Yates riding on the back of a stallion with his father, or being carried proudly on Aengus's strong shoulders. The child had imitated his hero's every move, to the point where he stood, slouched, frowned, and smiled just like the man he worshiped so completely.

And now Luke Yates was waiting for Suzannah to explain this nightmare to him. Losing a father. Then losing a mother. Then regaining the father, only to find that he was a stranger.

She touched the older boy's cheek. "Why don't you two go and get ready for bed? Once you're all snuggled under your covers, I'll come in and we'll try to make sense of all this together."

Luke shrugged to his feet and nodded, as though relieved to have someone to help shoulder the burden. Johnny, however, still seemed troubled. "Suzannah?"

"Yes, sweetie?"

"Do we still get the bedtime story, like you promised?"

"Hmmm . . . Why do you suppose they call it a *bed*time story?"

The little boy's hazel eyes began to twinkle. "Because you gotta be in bed to hear it?"

"That's right. So run!"

* * *

She told the story first. The one about the thump-thump-thump that a little boy thought was a stallion kicking a stall. He was wrong. It was a pirate's peg leg, thumping on the porch, coming for vengeance against the person who had dared eat the last biscuit at dinner.

When the laughter had faded, she stared into the two fresh-scrubbed, adoring faces and wished she knew what to say. Tucked here, in their large and lump-free bed in Aengus Yates's cozy little ranch house, they seemed as pampered and protected as Noelle Braddock in Chicago. But Suzannah knew it wasn't so.

She kissed each boy's cheek. "I love you both, you know."

"We love you too," Johnny assured her groggily; then to her wistful delight, he nestled under the quilt and began to breathe the shallow, even breaths of a child already asleep.

Tearing her gaze from him, she stood and walked around the bed to sit by Luke, who was waiting patiently. "I've known your father since I was your age," she began carefully. "Even then, I could see the value in him. He didn't talk much, or socialize often. He was a serious boy who loved horses. And horses minded him. I always took that as a sign. Horses trusted him, and I trusted him too."

Luke nodded. "Horses still trust him."

"Do they?" Suzannah paused to savor the reassuring fact. "While I was still a child, your father became a man. He was still quiet and serious, but he was also strong and brave and inspiring. Like a hero from a storybook."

Luke was nodding vigorously. "Like a hero. I remember that."

"But even though he was serious, he would tease me sometimes. And his eyes would twinkle, just like Johnny's do now. And if something really funny happened, he'd roar with the most unexpected laugh. I used to love that."

"Me too."

"I think that's why I was so close to you and Johnny, right from the start. Johnny has his smile. And you have his laugh."

"I *do*?"

"Absolutely. I haven't heard as much of it tonight as I'd like, though. That's what we really need to talk about, isn't it?"

Luke nodded.

"Tell me how it was, after your mother passed away. Do you know how your father heard the news?"

"Uncle Alex knew where he was. It was a secret, but after Ma died, he sent for him."

So Aengus hadn't walked away without a thought to the boys after all, Suzannah realized belatedly. He'd made certain he could be contacted in an emergency. *Look out for my boys,* he must have told his friend Alex. *Here's how to reach me if the need arises.*

"And so your father came back to Adamsville. I wish I'd been there for that."

"Me too. Why did you leave, Suzannah?"

"I suppose, after my mother died, I needed to find a new family."

"But you had us."

"That's true." Suzannah bit her lip, amazed and humbled by the tears that were welling in the boy's eyes. Had she hurt him so much?

"First Pa left. Then you left. Then Ma."

"Oh, Luke, I'm so sorry."

"Then Pa came back, but he's not the same. And you're back, but you're leaving again. And Ma's not never coming back. And me and Johnny, we just wait."

She almost didn't dare ask. "Wait for what?"

"For someone to stay." He wiped his eyes with his bedshirt sleeve.

"Come here." Hugging him unhappily, she explained, "I know it doesn't make sense. I could tell you stories from my own life too. My father dying before I ever met him. The man I loved marrying someone else. My mother dying in the night, without ever having been sick a day in her life. Megan was like a sister, so that helped, but still, I felt alone sometimes."

"But you had us," Luke repeated stubbornly.

"No, I didn't. You were another woman's sons. I didn't know how to be a part of your life. I know you don't believe it, but if I'd stayed, and your mother had lived, the day would have come when you would have had to choose between us. And you would have chosen her. And that would have been right."

Luke nodded. "I guess that's so. But she's gone now. So you could stay if you really wanted to."

"It's not that simple, sweetie. Your father—"

"I hate him!" Luke interrupted, then he grabbed Suzannah's arm. "You don't need to stay. Just take us with you when you go! We'll all three go back to Adamsville, and live in my old house. I'll work for Uncle Alex, and it won't be bad. I promise."

Suzannah took a deep breath. "Can I ask you something?"

Luke nodded.

"Do you trust me?"

He nodded again.

"Really and truly?"

"Yeah."

"Then believe this, because you have my word on it. There's a man in Chicago, and his name is Russell Braddock. Have you heard of him?"

"Braddock?" Luke mused. "That's Megan's name."

"That's right. He's Megan's uncle. But he's something much more amazing. He's a legend. Do you know what that is?"

Luke frowned. "He's not real?"

"Some legends aren't real," Suzannah agreed. "But Mr. Braddock is very real. I stayed in his house in Chicago."

"In the doll room?"

"Right. He seems ordinary, but he has a special power. A gift. Almost like magic."

The boy's eyes widened. "Magic?"

"He's a matchmaker. He can tell instinctively when one person will make another person happy. He matches a man with a woman, and even though they're strangers when he makes the match, they discover they were made for each other. The woman," Suzannah added carefully, "brings out the best in the man."

"That's good."

"Isn't it? And Mr. Braddock takes special care when he's making a match for one of Megan's friends. And do you know who he's matching next?"

"Who?"

"Your father."

The glow disappeared. "That's where the new ma is coming from?"

"Yes, Luke."

"But I don't want her, Suzannah. I want you."

Suzannah took a deep breath, knowing that she had to do this just right. "Suppose you had a choice. You could have me. Or you could have your pa back the way he was before he left. The way you and I remember him from Adamsville."

Tears flooded the boy's eyes again, and he seemed unable to speak.

"That's what the right lady can do, Luke. She can make your father happy again. Russell Braddock will find the right match, and soon, like magic, your pa will begin to change back to the old Aengus. It will take time, but it will happen. You have my most solemn promise."

The boy chewed his lip but still didn't speak, and so Suzannah added quietly, "One year from today, if nothing has changed, you can write to me at Mr. Braddock's house in Chicago. And wherever I live, I'll get the message, and I'll come back here and take you and Johnny away with me."

His mouth fell open in amazement. "You promise?"

"Yes, Luke. I promise."

An angelic smile lit his weary face. "A year's not so long."

"That's right." She kissed his cheek and pulled the covers up to his neck. "Go to sleep now, won't you?"

"Yeah. Thanks, Suzannah. I love you."

"I love you too." She kissed his forehead again, then did the same for Johnny before tiptoeing out of the children's room and into the master bedroom.

More tired than she could remember having been in her life, she stripped off her clothes, slipped into one of Aengus's soft flannel shirts, and climbed up into his bed. As she snuggled under a thick down comforter, she realized ruefully that this day had given her almost everything she'd ever wanted. She'd kissed Aengus Yates. She was nestling in his bed. And it all meant nothing, because he was a misguided disappointment of a man. A man who could hurt and neglect the two most angelic children in the entire world. What had she ever seen in him?

A board creaked at the foot of the bed and she sat up, alarmed that her beastly host may have returned. But it was Johnny, announcing sheepishly, "I had a bad dream."

"Come here and tell me about it."

The boy climbed up beside her. "It was scary."

"I'm sure it was."

"Luke was asleep, and I tried to go back to sleep, too. Then I heard a noise on the porch. I think it was him."

"Him? Your father?"

"No. The pirate."

"The—? Good grief, Johnny Yates!" She covered his little face with kisses. "Would you like to sleep in here tonight?"

The child beamed and nodded.

"Close your eyes, then." She helped him under the coverlet and cuddled him close, intent on protecting him, at least for one night, from the disappointments, and fears, and pirates and Aenguses that life had so unfairly heaped upon him.

Aengus was fairly certain that, when Suzannah Hennessy appointed him chaperon, she hadn't intended for him to stay up half the night drinking and playing poker with the man he was supposed to be watching. Still, she couldn't complain, could she? Little Megan Braddock was presumably still a virgin, and as he strode up to the ranch house from the stable and stepped carefully onto the porch, a beautiful new day was dawning.

Continuing to step quietly, he made his way to his bedroom and was touched to see little Johnny snuggled in Suzannah's arms. It had undoubtedly been the first blissful night the child had spent since Katherine's death, and Aengus was surprised the older boy hadn't followed suit. But of course, Luke would probably consider it a sign of weakness. And *that* boy *never* showed weakness.

Wandering back to the kitchen, he began to make coffee for Suzannah, to go with the scones the judge's wife had sent back with him. It was such a peaceful scene, so different from the one he'd been dreading all week.

He smiled as he remembered his image of his new "bride." Some strange, homely, bossy female with a tawdry, perhaps even criminal, past. Had he honestly considered so drastic a solution? What a narrow escape he'd had!

Of course, the bride would have solved the problem of the two Monroe boys, and in that sense, he was still in something of a predicament. Had the bride arrived as scheduled, Aengus could have turned all responsibility for them over to her. *That* would have been a relief. For everyone, including the boys. *Especially* the boys. Luke in particular.

Crossing to the small bedroom, he studied the older boy wistfully. Luke looked like a tyke again, the way he'd looked just before Aengus left home. Memories of those days were daggers in Aengus's chest. The early days of fatherhood . . .

But of course, it hadn't been fatherhood at all. At least, not for Aengus. Alex Monroe had been the father. Aengus had merely been the dupe. Bragging about his incredible "sons"; hoisting them onto his shoulders to display them to the townsfolk; anxious to teach them to fish and ride.

His memories of Johnny were warm and sweet. A perfect baby, gurgling and innocent. Luke, on the other hand, had been a boy, through and through. Cautious and serious, striving to emulate the man he worshipped because of a lie. Aengus had loved that child so fiercely. And the child had returned that love a millionfold.

Moving to within inches of the boy, he felt a familiar ache. This was the reason he rarely stepped into this room, or to within thinking distance of either boy. Hundreds of miles had been better, but any distance helped.

But now he'd drawn too near, and a memory—*the* memory—came into focus. Luke, age four, sitting with his feet dangling in Monroe's pond. Johnny, age two, toddling nearby. Aengus had left that morning to travel to an auction, but at the last minute had changed his mind. The stock hadn't sounded promising, and little Johnny had had a fever the night before. Katherine hadn't gotten much rest. Perhaps she'd be pleased to know he'd decided to stay nearby. At least, Aengus would know he'd tried, again, to inject some warmth and caring into their strained, uncomfortable relationship.

And so he'd been surprised to see the boys so far from home without their mother. Luke had explained that "Mama said to stay here and watch Johnny. We can't go to the house till she says so."

"Is she baking a surprise?" Aengus had guessed.

"No." The boy had hesitated. "She's telling secrets."

It had made Aengus smile. "You mean, gossiping? Is Mrs. Langham visiting?"

"Not Mrs. Langham. Uncle Alex."

"Alex?"

"They always tell secrets when you go to auctions."

Aengus had heard the words, but had been unable, or unwilling, to make sense of them. "Secrets?"

"That's what Mama calls them."

Thoroughly confused, Aengus had made his way to his house. In his heart, he had half known what he'd find. Katherine had seemed more bored and distant than ever these last few weeks. And Alex Monroe was a weak, greedy man. The impossible seemed ominously possible.

But his suspicions, vivid as they were, hadn't prepared him for what he'd found. Katherine in bed with Alex—that might have been bearable. But Katherine hadn't been "in bed" with him, she'd been astride him, riding him in a hedonistic display of unrestrained sexual voracity that had almost blinded her young husband.

Alex had been predictably cowardly, grabbing his trousers and fleeing without any thought to Katherine's predicament. Katherine, on the other hand, had been eerily calm in the face of Aengus's bitter accusations.

"I want you out of here," Aengus had seethed. "Get dressed and go. I'll pack up your things and send them to you later."

"I'm not going anywhere, Aengus," she had said quietly. "I'm sorry you had to find out this way, but it's a relief, too. You and I were never in love—"

"You should have thought of that before you

climbed into my bed the night we met," he had growled. "I did the honorable thing and married you, and this is the thanks I get? Don't talk to me about love, Katherine. You don't have the right." Sinking onto the foot of the bed, he had buried his head in his hands and added softly, "I won't speak of this to our sons. You have my word on that. Just go, and go quickly. I'll find the words to explain your disappearance somehow."

"Don't you wonder how long I've been in love with Alex?"

"Why should I care?"

"What if I told you I was in love with him before I ever even met you?"

It hadn't made sense, and Aengus had looked up at her in confused disbelief. "All these years . . . ?"

"Right from the start," Katherine had taunted. "In fact, my marriage to you was Alex's idea."

"What?"

"Alex and I fell in love, but he wouldn't leave Elaine, or rather, he wouldn't leave her money. When I discovered I was pregnant, I came here to confront him. I was sure he'd leave her then. But he doesn't have the strong paternal urge you have." She had pulled on a robe and seated herself beside him at the foot of the bed. "Didn't you ever wonder why Luke was born so early? Barely seven months after the night I seduced you in the bunkhouse."

"It happens," Aengus had croaked, dizzy with denial. "It happens all the time, Katherine. He looks just like me—"

"He looks nothing like you," she had sighed. "Fortunately, he resembles me more than Alex, so—"

"Stop it!" Aengus had grabbed her shoulders and

shaken her roughly. "I don't want to hear any more of this. He's my son!"

"He's not!" she had retorted; then her expression had softened. "You've been a good father to him, Aengus. Alex and I appreciate that. And you've been a good husband. Better than I deserved. I'm the first to admit that." Slipping her hand inside his shirt, she had cooed, "It hasn't been perfect, but we've had our moments, haven't we? I know you've longed for romance and love, but now that it's all out in the open, maybe I can give you something better."

"Are you insane?" he'd whispered. "Do you suppose I'd ever touch you again?"

"Give it time," she pleaded seductively. "I adore you as a lover, Aengus. And I admire you as a father. You're twice the man Alex Monroe is. It's my curse that I fell in love with him and not you. But we can still make a life together. The same life we've always had. Can't you see that?"

He had barely been listening to her. All he could hear was a mournful whisper, again and again, echoing in his heart. *Luke . . . Luke . . . Luke . . .*

Then a new wave of panic had assaulted him and he'd demanded, "What about Johnny?"

Katherine had shrugged. "He has Alex's smile, don't you think?"

His hands had ached to strangle her, but instead he had bolted out of the cabin and into the cool spring air. She couldn't know! Even if it was so about Luke, she couldn't know for certain about Johnny. True, the baby didn't look like Aengus, but that didn't mean anything. He didn't look like Alex Monroe either. Neither did Luke, for that matter. Still, neither child had Aengus's vivid blue eyes. Or his hair color. Or even his skin tone. They had hazel eyes, like Katherine's. Alex Monroe's eyes were golden brown, and there was a hint of that in Luke's.

And both boys had dark brown hair. Like Katherine. *And* Alex. They could never know for certain . . .

Katherine was correct about one thing, though. Luke had been born early, but hadn't been a small or struggling infant. If anything, he had been remarkably robust. The women in the town had remarked on it often, and now Aengus knew why.

Katherine had come up behind him and spoken his name. "What are you going to do? It will break Luke's heart if you tell him you're not his father. He adores you."

Aengus had turned to stare at her. "Pardon?"

"I'm willing to allow the boys, and everyone else, to believe you're the father. Poor Alex would be distraught if Elaine ever learned the truth."

"Alex believes they're his boys?"

"Of course."

"He barely spends a moment with them—"

"He doesn't dare. For fear someone will see the resemblance."

"Damn you, Katherine."

"I suppose I already am," she had sighed. "Are you leaving or staying? It's all the same to me. Alex will provide for us if you go. You needn't worry. Just don't try to take my sons from me. Don't force me to tell them the truth."

He had wanted to kill her. Not from rage, but expediency. He could kill her and take the boys, and the secret would be safe forever. Alex Monroe would never jeopardize his status by admitting his infidelity to his wealthy wife. They could go far away from Adamsville, and no one would ever know.

But Aengus would know. He'd look at them and

see Alex Monroe in them. And it might just make a difference.

And one day, Elaine Monroe would die, and Alex would find the boys and tell them the good news—that they were heirs to a ranching dynasty. Luke Monroe—the child was already so smart and skillful. Combine that with the Monroe name and influence and he could be governor someday!

And little Johnny Monroe. What would he be? What did it matter? With his sweet disposition and his father's help, he'd be successful at anything he tried. The last thing in the world that child needed was Aengus Yates as a surrogate father.

"Pa?"

Jolted back to the present, Aengus stared down at the child he'd once cherished. " 'Morning, Luke. Did you sleep well?"

The boy rubbed his eyes and sat up slowly. "Where's Johnny?"

"With Suzannah."

"Really?" The boy smiled weakly. "I thought I dreamed her."

"I know what you mean," Aengus said. "Go and wake your brother. But do it quietly, so our guest can sleep."

"We'll be quiet, Pa."

"Luke?"

"Yeah?"

"Once you finish your chores, you can go into town and visit with Megan Braddock. She's anxious to see you."

"We will, Pa." He seemed about to say more, then rolled out of bed and walked quickly past Aengus. Then with unceremonious efficiency, he fetched his little brother from Suzannah's bed, and in no time the two had grabbed scones from the table and headed outside to begin their chores.

Banishing bad memories, Aengus turned his attention to the pesky houseguest still nestled so sweetly in his huge, warm bed.

Chapter Four

Snuggled under the soft gray comforter, his pretty guest looked like an angel, and a wave of affection swept over Aengus Yates. This girl had been one of the simple pleasures of his early days in Adamsville. Playful little Suzy, pestering him; watching him; spinning her childlike fantasies about him. As a fifteen-year-old boy, he had been embarrassed by her silly attentions. At sixteen, they had bewildered him. But by the time he'd reached eighteen—the year of the infamous marriage proposal—the child's interest had begun to amuse him. More importantly, it had provided a comforting link between the quiet young immigrant and the community in which he'd chosen to make his home.

It charmed him now to note that she was wearing one of his collarless, plaid flannel shirts as an impromptu nightgown. The colors suited her—red like her flushed cheeks, dark green like her laughing eyes. Of course, the shirt was huge on her. It would probably hang all the way to her knees should she decide to scamper about in it. He could almost picture her shapely little body swimming in the loose fabric, and as he did, his thoughts focused on her bare legs, and the soft, warm reaches to which they might lead a lonely man.

And slowly the scene was no longer charming and innocent. This was not a child in his bed. Nor was it the sturdy, humorless bedmate he'd been expecting through the mail. It was a luscious, golden-haired, soft-skinned, half-naked female—the kind that made a man want to close the door, strip off his clothes, and enjoy himself for the rest of the day.

For the first time, he noticed her traveling outfit draped carelessly at the foot of the bed, along with various lacy undergarments and stockings. Further confirmation of what awaited him under that coverlet. Then she shifted slightly, and the movement sent a stab of carnal need through him so strong he was actually tempted to slip his hand under the blanket and surreptitiously enjoy the feel of her. Not that he would, of course, but—

"Aengus?"

His guilty gaze shifted immediately to her face. "Good morning."

Suzannah smiled shyly. "I almost thought I'd dreamed you."

"That's what Luke said about *you*."

"Luke?" She repeated the boy's name with husky affection, then added with a frown, "Where did Johnny go? You didn't scold him for sleeping here, did you?"

"No, ma'am."

Suzannah smiled at the title, then patted the bed

beside her. "Come and sit. Tell me about Megan and Ben."

Aengus grinned as he accepted the invitation. "I'm pleased to report that Miss Braddock's honor is as safe as your own."

"Good. It was sweet of you to ride to her assistance through that awful storm."

"My pleasure."

She seemed to notice his continued interest in her makeshift nightgown, and began to finger the top button apologetically. "I hope you don't mind. I borrowed this."

"It suits you. You can wear it all morning if you'd like."

"Don't be silly," she smiled. "I need to get dressed and back into town."

"Are you wearing anything else under there?"

"I didn't need anything else," she began; then her green eyes flashed with annoyance and she grabbed the coverlet up to her neck as she hissed, "Aengus Yates! What are you staring at?"

He chuckled, completely unrepentant. "When a girl sleeps in a man's bed, she needs to expect a little attention."

"Get out of here this instant!"

He threw his head back and laughed, and for some reason it felt like the first time he'd laughed in years. And it felt damned good, too.

"Get out!"

Shrugging to his feet, he bowed in mock apology, then ambled toward the kitchen, pulling the door closed behind him. He could hear her scurrying about, and imagined that she was almost frantic to be properly attired lest he should have the audacity to return to the scene of his crime.

When she finally joined him in the kitchen, her every button was scrupulously fastened, her hair was pulled into a tight, no-nonsense bun, and her expression was prim and proper. But it was too late. He now saw only breasts and arms and legs, all of them firm and fine, fresh from his bed. He wondered if she knew how errant his thoughts had become. Given her inexperience with men, probably not.

"Take me into town this instant."

"Have something to eat first."

"I'm not hungry. And even if I were, I wouldn't eat with the likes of you."

He stepped closer before murmuring, "I couldn't resist teasing you, Suzy. Don't be angry. I'll not do it anymore."

She hesitated, as though about to scold him, then sighed instead. "You've been such a disappointment to me, Aengus Yates."

"And to myself."

The admission seemed to disarm her, and she touched his cheek with her fingertips. "It doesn't have to be that way. You've been given a second chance, don't you see?"

The statement surprised him, and he asked cautiously, "With you?"

"You promised not to tease anymore," she reminded him tersely. "You know full well what I'm talking about. You've been too strict with your sons—"

"More nagging?" he interrupted. "I thought I put an end to that yesterday."

"I don't take orders from you, Aengus Yates. And even if I did . . . Oh, never mind." She crossed to the stove and poured two cups of hot coffee. "I wasn't nagging you, I was just offering advice. From one friend to another." Setting the coffee on the table, she gestured for him to join her. "I had a long talk with Luke last night, and I think I figured something out."

"This should be interesting," Aengus muttered.

Suzannah sent him a disapproving glance, took a long sip of coffee, then observed, "You're rude, and I know why. That's what I figured out last night. You're cross because you need a woman."

Aengus laughed again, and again it felt good. "The thought occurred to me too. Just now, seeing you in my bed—"

"Aengus! Stop teasing me about that this instant. I'm serious."

Still grinning, he joined her at the table and uncovered the basket of scones he'd brought from town. "The judge's wife sent these for your breakfast."

She took one and studied it critically. "Salty and lumpy?"

"Taste for yourself."

"Mmm . . ." She savored the buttery goodness. "Did the boys eat too?"

Aengus nodded.

"Well, then . . ." She sipped her coffee pensively. "You must admit, Aengus, you and the boys have made a bad start of this. But the right bride can change all that. And now that I've studied the situation, I can describe it all to Mr. Braddock, and he can use the information to select the perfect woman. Not just a mother for the boys," she added firmly. "A companion for yourself too. Someone to bring out the best in you."

Her green eyes were shining as she added, "I've seen you at your best, although not lately. I know in my heart you can be that man again."

"It's not that simple, Suzannah."

"Simple or not, it's what must be done. As soon as Meg and I return to Chicago—"

"I'm not sure I want Mr. Braddock's services anymore," Aengus interrupted.

"Pardon?"

He shrugged his shoulders and explained. "The whole notion never set that well with me. I was drunk when I wrote that letter, and almost sick to my stomach waiting for that stage."

"But, Aengus—"

"I don't trust easily, Suzannah. The notion of letting a stranger into my house. My life. My bed. I need to give all that a bit more thought."

"I see," she sniffed. "You've decided to put yourself first, as usual."

"That's how you see it?" he growled. "Fine. Think what you will. I don't explain myself to anyone. That's part of who I am."

"Those boys are part of who you are, too. Have you no heart at all?"

"Apparently not."

He could see she was struggling, but could honestly think of no way to help her with this. He was a disappointment to her, just as she'd said. She'd get over it, as she'd done before, and one day soon he and the Monroe boys would fade in her memory. Better to let it go now, before the quarrel grew any more harsh.

"I'd best get you into town."

She brushed an invisible crumb from her lips and nodded, completely deflated.

"I know you mean well, Suzy, but—"

"Don't worry. I won't interfere again. May I have a few minutes with your sons, to say good-bye?"

"Actually, I told them they could come into town with us. To see Megan."

"Well, then . . ." A single tear escaped its emerald prison and meandered down her cheek. "In that case, you needn't come. Luke knows the way, does he not?"

Aengus nodded. "I've things to do here. Because of the storm. But I'll come in later, if you don't mind. To say one last good-bye to you and Megan."

"She'd like that, I'm sure." Sliding back her chair, she gathered up the coffee mugs and wandered toward the sink. With her back to him, she admitted, "You've been a disappointment to me, just as I said. But you've also been a sort of friend, from time to time. We shouldn't allow that memory to be destroyed by all this."

"I agree."

"And you'll consider allowing Mr. Braddock to find someone for you?"

He groaned in defeat. "I'll consider it, if you'll consider minding your business for five minutes. Go now and tell the boys I'll finish up for them. You should head into town before Ben Steele wakes up and has another go at Megan."

"You think he's still asleep?"

Aengus grinned. "He doesn't strike me as an early riser. And he was up until dawn, trying to take my money from me."

"Aengus Yates!" A pretty smile lit her lips. "I should have known better than to send an irresponsible man to guard an incorrigible one." Her eyes twinkled fondly. "You'll join us in town before long?"

"I'll be quick as I can. And, Suzy?"

"Yes?"

He stepped to within inches of her and insisted,

"I thank you for coming here. My home is a better one for having had you as its guest."

His parting words had been music to Suzannah's ears, telling her that he finally understood how much the Yates ranch needed a woman's presence. Now he would reconsider his objection to the mail-order-bride notion, and soon the boys *and* Aengus would be happy and well cared for.

She could already see the change in Luke, whose mood had lightened considerably since the previous day. And Johnny, always cheerful, was almost buoyant as the wagon ground its way toward the town of Bent Creek.

"Will Megan remember us?"

"Of course. She's very fond of you."

"She never visited much. Not like you."

"Just the same, she has lovely memories of you," Suzannah assured him. "You'll see."

"I liked her dog."

"You boys should get a dog. A big red one, like Copper."

Johnny's hazel eyes sparkled at the thought. "Do you think Pa would let us?"

"Why wouldn't he?"

" 'Cause he's mean," the boy reminded her. "All he cares about is chores, chores, chores."

"A ranch is a big responsibility, especially here, where nothing is flat," Suzannah reminded him. "I'm sure he's glad to have two strong sons to help him."

"He doesn't seem glad," Johnny countered.

"Well," she sighed. "Perhaps all that will change when his new wife arrives."

"Tell Johnny about *that*," Luke interrupted. "Tell him about your promise."

Suzannah bit her lip, remembering that rash promise, and wondering what she'd do if stubborn Aengus Yates decided not to allow Russell Braddock to help them live happily ever after.

What if that does happen? she challenged herself suddenly. *If Aengus doesn't find a woman, and these poor boys are still being raised by a heartless grouch a year from now, are you just going to stand by and allow it?*

Of course not! She'd keep her promise, come back to Bent Creek, collect the Yates boys, and bring them back to Adamsville. She'd convince Alex Monroe to allow her to clean and cook at the inn, just as her mother had done when she'd found herself widowed and raising a baby daughter. And if by then Suzannah had somehow found herself a husband, all the better. He could help her raise the boys. If not, she'd do it alone. Either way, Luke and Johnny would be better off with her than with a bully as a father.

According to Judge Winston and his wife, Miss Braddock and Mr. Steele had left on a carriage ride right after breakfast. "They're such a charming couple," Dorothy Winston enthused. "It's as though they were made for one another."

"They're barely acquaintances," Suzannah corrected, cursing Aengus silently for having misjudged Ben's need for sleep. Still, in the cool morning air, Megan was more likely to be sensible than in the dark of night, so at least Aengus had been useful to a point.

"Do you want us to go find them, Suzannah?" Luke offered.

Mrs. Winston protested that the couple wouldn't

appreciate the intrusion, but Suzannah kissed both boys' cheeks gratefully and sent them on their way with instructions to insist that Megan return to town immediately, with or without Ben Steele.

The Winstons, Suzannah was discovering, loved entertaining, and were rarely given the opportunity since they'd moved from San Francisco. Their parlor was lavishly furnished in rich blue brocade and velvet, and they served Suzannah tea, along with another scone, on delicate Wedgwood porcelain, as they shared with her the history of the town and their decision to become its permanent residents.

They seemed to admire Aengus greatly, although they were clearly confused as to why he'd chosen to order a bride through the mail. "We've offered time and again to introduce him to lovely women of quality," Dorothy Winston lamented. "He insists he needs a bride who doesn't expect anything of him. Can you imagine? Him? His bride would have that lovely ranch, those charming sons, and the strongest, handsomest man for miles around—present company excepted of course, dear. But he made it sound as though marriage to him would be like a jail sentence."

"He doesn't trust women," Judge Winston interrupted. "I've met men like that before. The prettier the female, the less he'll trust her. I imagine," he added gallantly, "that he's positively terrified of *you*, Miss Hennessy."

"If he's not, he should be," Suzannah grinned. "I've no patience at all with his moods. Did he tell you much about his past?"

"He and Tom Whalen shared stories about army life," the judge said. "But Aengus never talked about the years before that, other than to say he came over from Ireland when he was twelve.''

"He lived in Boston for a few years," Suzannah nodded. "Then he came to work on a ranch outside my hometown, Adamsville, in Indiana. That's where he met Megan and myself. And his wife, Katherine.''

Dorothy leaned forward eagerly. "A troubled marriage?''

"She wasn't the bride I'd always imagined Aengus with," Suzannah hedged. "But between them, they produced two darling sons, and so in that sense, their marriage was a blessing.''

"Mr. Steele mentioned that you once had eyes for Aengus.''

Suzannah frowned. "I was nine years old at the time. Did Mr. Steele mention *that*?"

Judge Winston chuckled. "I hear their carriage returning. This is your chance to reprimand him in person.''

Suzannah jumped to her feet and ran to the window in time to see Ben helping Megan out of the carriage. She had forgotten how darling the gambler was, and wanted to race outside and rescue her friend from his seductive charms, but something held her back. Something in Megan's eyes . . .

Those eyes, huge and gray, were brimming with love and happiness, in a way Suzannah had never seen them. It was as though Megan were alive for the first time in her life, and happy—*truly* happy—for the first time since her parents' murder.

Had Ben Steele actually managed to accomplish that?

And if Megan's expression was angelic, Ben Steele's was actually sublime. Adoration, respect, and yearning—each in a healthy dose—radiated from his love-stricken gaze. He clearly wanted to devour her, yet just as clearly, felt unworthy, humble, and vulnerable.

As Suzannah watched, the gambler steadied Megan on her feet, then lowered his mouth to hers for a kiss every bit as powerful, but infinitely more tender, than anything Suzannah had ever witnessed. Megan's slender arms wrapped around her lover's neck as though never to let go, and her whole body seemed to merge with his, so closely did they embrace. It was quite simply the most perfect sight Suzannah had ever had the privilege of witnessing, and she now knew for certain that these two were destined to spend the rest of their lives in one another's arms.

Then Megan pulled free, and to Suzannah's horror, the girl began to shake her head, as she'd done when she'd sent Ben away the last time. Was she insane enough to do so again? Was she honestly willing to turn her back on true love and true happiness?

Worst of all, was there any possibility she was doing it out of misguided loyalty to her friendship with Suzannah?

Rushing out into the courtyard, Suzannah brushed past Ben, ignoring his stricken expression, and grabbed her friend by the elbow, propelling her through a vine-covered archway that led to the carefully tended rose garden behind the Winston home. The bushes were just beginning to bud, and on any other day Suzannah would have been amazed to see such exquisite results in so cold a climate, but she had other things on her mind.

"Megan Elizabeth Braddock, what on earth do you think you're doing? And *don't* tell me you're not in love, because it's a lie and you know it."

Megan stared at Suzannah as though she'd lost her mind. "What are you talking about?"

"Are you going to marry Ben Steele?"

"Certainly not."

"*That's* what I'm talking about," Suzannah wailed. "What are you doing? How can you turn your back on that darling man when you love him as much as you do?"

Megan moistened her lips, then primly smoothed the skirt of her dark brown dress. "I don't wish to discuss it. Please respect that."

"No."

"You want to talk about Mr. Steele, and I want to talk about Aengus's sons."

"Pardon?"

The girl's gray eyes softened. "I saw the boys. Luke has grown a foot, and Johnny has lost all his baby fat. Has it really been that long since we've seen them?"

"Six months," Suzannah confirmed. "So much can change so quickly."

"Tell me about Aengus. Please? He and I visited for a short while last evening, and he seemed as noble and reliable as ever. Have we misjudged him?"

Suzannah winced. "I don't know what you mean."

"He wants to do what's best for the boys. I admire that, Suzannah. Don't you?"

"I don't want to talk about Aengus. I want to talk about Ben."

Megan blushed. "What is there to say? He's a fine man, and we were fortunate to have him as our escort."

"I agree." Suzannah's eyes narrowed. "Tell me about your carriage ride."

"There's little to tell. He chose a lovely spot. Fresh and clear, because of the storm. It's beautiful here, don't you think?"

Suzannah felt her patience snap. "Do you deny that you're in love with Ben Steele?"

"I deny it completely." Megan's chin rose up in ladylike defiance. "I barely know the man."

The silly response amused Suzannah. "He seems to know *you*. In fact, he seems hopelessly smitten."

"As you said, he has experience with women," Megan sniffed. "I imagine he's been smitten dozens of times."

"Is that what he says?"

"He says so many things. I try not to pay attention. He knows how to charm and flatter," she added meaningfully. "You were absolutely right about him, Suzannah."

"And what if I was absolutely wrong?"

"What do you mean?"

"What if I misjudged him? Honestly, Meg, I can't forget the look on his face when he helped you out of the carriage. It was as though he'd never seen a girl before! As though you were the only female in the world, or at least in *his* world."

Megan tried to square her shoulders, failed, and sank onto a brick bench, covering her face with her hands. "You're confusing me, Suzannah. Ben's been doing that too, and we mustn't allow it. Our best course is to see him as a flirt. An attractive, charming flirt who will never settle down."

Suzannah eyed her with amused sympathy. "Why is that best?"

"Because of who he is," Megan explained tearfully.

"A gambler?"

"Yes."

"But he's ready to settle down and be a hotel proprietor," Suzannah reminded her gently. "That's fairly respectable, don't you think?"

"A hotel in San Francisco," Megan nodded. "He has so many plans, Suzannah. So many dreams. But I'm not sure we fit into them very well."

"We?"

Megan dried her eyes with a lace handkerchief before explaining, "I know you, Suzannah. You'd be miserable in a city. Even a city as beautiful as San Francisco." Sweeping her arms to encompass an unseen horizon, she insisted, "You love all this. Land, not buildings. Remember how miserable you were in Chicago?"

"And as I recall, *you* rather enjoyed Chicago," Suzannah countered. "Those endless shopping trips with Noelle. The two of you gloried in all that."

Megan shrugged. "I couldn't have enjoyed it nearly as much if you weren't there too. I couldn't dream of going to San Francisco with Ben, knowing you'd go back to Chicago and from there, to a small town hundreds of miles from me." Her gray eyes blazed with unfamiliar fire. "Our children *will* play together, Suzannah Hennessy. That's a promise I intend to keep."

Suzannah bit her lip. That promise, along with the one she'd made to Luke, was beginning to haunt her. Just as she was promising herself to never promise anyone anything again, Ben Steele walked through the arbor, a hopeful smile on his face, and said, "Megan, darling? Can I have a word with you?"

"Perhaps later. Suzannah and I are speaking."

Ben glared pointedly at Suzannah. "Go away."

Megan seemed about to chastise him, but Suzannah held up a hand to interrupt her. "Go on now, Meg, and visit with Luke and Johnny. I'll deal with Mr. Steele."

After Megan had smiled gratefully and slipped

through the back door of the Winston residence, Suzannah sandwiched Ben's sour face between her hands and demanded, "How much do you love her?"

"With all my heart."

Relaxing, she caressed his cheeks. "If you ever did anything to harm her, I don't know what I'd do."

"You'd strangle me," he reminded her fondly. "It won't be necessary, Suzannah. I'd rather die than hurt her."

"Go on."

His eyes were soft with hope. "I love her smile. Her blush. Her intelligence. Her compassion. Her loyalty to you . . ."

"Go on."

"I can't," he whispered, his voice choked with emotion. "These words—I've used them all before. I need new ones to describe this . . . this ache. This yearning. This hopeless, miserable, wonderful feeling . . ."

Tears spilled down Suzannah's cheeks. "How I envy her."

Ben cradled her gently against his chest. "You are everything Megan says you are. Will you do me the honor of being my ally in this love match?"

Suzannah sobbed against his shirt front, unable to deal with this bizarre combination of happiness and loss. "You must think I'm insane," she apologized. "But Meg and I have been through so much. When I lost Aengus, she was there. When she lost her parents, I was there for her. We've shared every loss. We wanted to share this too." Wiping her eyes, she explained haltingly, "That's why she resists you, Ben."

"I've seen it from the start," he admitted. "She can't allow herself to be happy unless she knows you're happy too. And," he smiled, the old confidence returning, "I can arrange that, I'm sure. Come to San Francisco with us. It would be an honor to make you a part of our lives—"

"As what?" Suzannah teased tearfully. "The spinster aunt?"

"The belle of the town," he promised. "Men will throw themselves at your feet. One look at that dazzling smile and provocative body, and you'll have dozens of marriage proposals."

"From city men," Suzannah reminded him. "Thank you, but no. I need open space. It feeds my soul." She reached up to pat his cheek. "Don't worry, handsome. I know what needs to be done."

"And what exactly is that?"

"You said it yourself. She needs to know that *I'm* happy before she'll allow herself the same." *Even better*, Suzannah reasoned, *if I were in love first, she'd be free to fall in love herself!*

"I'm confused."

"Of course you are," Suzannah grinned. "Love has that effect. Relax and enjoy it. But do it elsewhere. I have to confide in my best friend. Will you go inside and send her to me?"

Ben bowed, bewildered but hopeful. "I leave my future in your capable hands."

"Suzannah?"

Taking one last deep breath, and knowing what she needed to do, Suzannah turned to bestow a radiant smile on her best friend. "I spoke with Mr. Steele, and discouraged him, on your behalf. Now if only we can find you someone like Aengus, all our prayers will be answered."

"Someone like Aengus?"

Suzannah nodded. "I discovered something when he kissed me this morning. I realized—"

"Aengus *kissed* you? And you allowed it?"

"Of course. Haven't I loved him since childhood? And it was glorious, Meg. Just like I always dreamed it would be."

"Suzannah! Why didn't you tell me sooner?"

"I don't know. I suppose I was afraid you were in love with Ben. I didn't think I could convince you to settle here with us, but since you don't want to go to San Francisco, and Ben couldn't possibly stay here, everything's perfect."

"You want me to settle here? With you?"

"On the ranch. Luke and Johnny will be deliriously happy to have two stepmothers! And Aengus has agreed to add a room just for you, with a window out onto a garden—"

"Suzannah!"

"Is something wrong?"

Megan seemed to be struggling in vain for words of protest.

"I thought it would be difficult to convince you," Suzannah continued mercilessly. "But with Ben leaving today—"

"*Leaving*? Today?"

"I'm afraid so. He considered staying, for just a while longer, to try to win your heart. But I assured him you would much prefer to live with me and Aengus and the boys. It's true, isn't it?"

"Aengus broke your heart twice," Megan reminded her weakly. "I thought you despised him."

"I thought so too. But when his lips touched mine . . ." She studied her friend's reaction carefully. "Someday the right man will kiss *you*, Meg, and you'll know how exquisite it can be."

Megan sank onto the garden bench again. "I'm so confused."

"Tell me why," Suzannah insisted gently. "Is it because you love Ben?"

"I think so."

"Then you must convince him to live here, so we can all be together, just as we promised. He can sell the hotel and buy land for a ranch. He's darling in those fancy clothes, but he'll need to buy something a little more sturdy and practical. Dungarees, I suppose. And you can sew some shirts for him."

"Dungarees?"

"After a few weeks in the fresh air, shoveling hay and milking cows, he'll wonder what he ever saw in city life."

"Ben? Shoveling hay?" Megan stared for a moment, then giggled with relief. "Suzannah Hennessy, you don't mean a word of this, do you?"

"It *would* ruin his manicure," Suzannah mused. "Perhaps he'd best wear gloves."

Megan grinned knowingly. "Is there a point to this madness?"

"A lesson," Suzannah corrected. "A lesson for us both."

"And what is that?"

"If a person is fortunate enough to find the love of her life, she mustn't let anything ruin it. I love Aengus. You love Ben. We mustn't question where that leads us, even if it leads me to this place and you to San Francisco."

"You truly love Aengus?" Megan murmured hopefully.

"Truly and madly," Suzannah bluffed.

"And I love Ben?"

"Yes, silly. Don't you suppose it's time you told him?"

Megan licked her lips, as though savoring the suggestion; then she stood slowly and grasped Suzannah in a grateful embrace. "How will I bear life without you?"

"We will write to one another every day, and visit five times a year." Suzannah was struggling to keep her tone positive and reassuring. "It's not so very far away, you know. No farther than your uncle was from us all those years, and we managed to see him often, didn't we?"

Megan was nodding happily. "Ben said you secretly approved of our match, and it's true. And I thank you, Suzannah. I could never have made this decision on my own."

"Go and tell him, then," Suzannah scolded. "He could leave at any moment, and what would we do then?"

"Oh, dear." Megan wiped her eyes, then smoothed her skirt carefully. "Do I look a mess?"

"You're the most beautiful girl Aengus Yates has ever seen," Suzannah reminded her wryly.

Megan started to giggle, then frowned slightly instead. "You haven't told me how *he* feels. Does he love you? Can we trust him to treat you well? He left Katherine alone with two babies. I know he must have had his reasons, but—"

"He wants a second chance, Meg. With a warm, loving bride this time. He regrets what happened with Katherine, but he only left the boys with her because they were still little and needed a mother. He always intended to go back for them when they were old enough."

"He said that?"

Suzannah nodded. "He wants to build a future with me and the boys, and I want that more than anything in life."

"But, Suzannah—"

"He's fond of me, Meg. And I trust him completely. You couldn't drag me back out of his life if you tried, so please don't."

"I won't. You and Aengus—it's a miracle, really. It's what you always wanted. And," she added shyly, "I always wanted Ben Steele, although I never knew it. Wish me luck!"

Before Suzannah could answer, or change her mind, Megan had turned and was sprinting toward the Winstons' back porch.

Collapsing onto the bench her friend had vacated, Suzannah assured herself that the plan made sense. Megan would never marry Ben unless she knew Suzannah was happy first. She might turn her back on the love she'd found, or worse, make Suzannah come to San Francisco to live! And in the meantime, Luke and Johnny would be waiting, in misery, for the day when Suzannah would come and rescue them from Aengus.

The only way everyone could be happy was for Suzannah to set Megan free, then embrace Luke and Johnny as the sons she already loved. Aengus didn't trust the idea of a stranger as his bride, and definitely didn't trust himself to pick one out from among the local females. But surely he trusted Suzannah. They were friends, in a way, and over the years that friendship would grow stronger.

One thing was certain—a celibate marriage wouldn't bother him too much. He had made it clear—to Suzannah, Russell Braddock, and the Winstons—that he didn't intend to seek romantic love from the boys' new stepmother. In fact, the prospect of sharing his bed with a mail-order bride had made him sick to his stomach!

And since he saw Suzannah as a child, he would know that no demands of a husbandly nature would come along with the marriage. He could continue to do whatever he'd done since he left Katherine. As distasteful as it was to imagine Aengus cavorting with loose women, Suzannah would not judge him for it, since it would keep him from regretting their marriage of convenience.

Suzannah herself might have wished for something more from a marriage. Not romantic love, of course, since such dreams had died years earlier, when Aengus first broke her heart. But she had looked forward to the prospect of giving birth and mothering infants. Could she be content with just Luke and Johnny?

Of course you can, she reassured herself. *They're everything a mother could want. And as for babies, we'll leave that to Meg. You'll travel to San Francisco to help her when they're born, and they'll adore being cuddled by their Aunt Suzy, and spoiled by their cousins Luke and Johnny. Maybe even their gruff Uncle Aengus will occasionally grace them with a nod!*

Luke and Johnny, Ben and Megan—they would all be happy now. And Suzannah would be content. Aengus might never be truly happy *or* content, but if he'd meant what he said one drunken night in a letter to Russell Braddock, he wanted to provide a warm and caring stepmother for his children. It all made a sort of strange, unsettling sense—

"Suzannah?"

"Ben?" She forced herself to smile brightly as she

jumped to her feet and embraced him. "Isn't it wonderful? You and Megan—"

"And you and Aengus?" He studied her anxiously. "I thought you disapproved of him."

"My opinion changed."

"When he kissed you last night?"

"Exactly."

"I don't believe you," Ben responded flatly. "Aengus didn't give even a hint last night that he saw you as anything but a pint-sized pest. And he said you intended to travel with me and Megan to San Francisco."

Suzannah scowled. "A gentleman doesn't brag about his conquests. And it happened this morning, not last night, for your information."

Ben's eyes narrowed. "I appreciate what you're trying to do, but I won't let you sacrifice your own happiness to advance ours. I'll find another way to convince Megan to marry me."

"Do what you want," Suzannah shrugged. "I'm marrying Aengus Yates, and that's final. I've wanted him since I was three feet tall, and now he wants me too. He may have complained to you last night, but I can assure you, his opinion changed completely this morning."

"You're telling me he gave you something other than a good-bye kiss?"

"Something quite a bit more shocking. You mustn't tell Megan. She'd be appalled if she knew how I'd behaved."

"Go on," he suggested, his eyes still narrow with suspicion. "Tell me exactly what happened."

"Well . . ." Suzannah took a deep breath. "I didn't expect to spend the night at the ranch, and so I had no nightclothes. But Aengus wasn't home, and the boys were asleep, and so there didn't seem to be any harm in wearing one of Aengus's shirts to bed.''

Ben was grinning reluctantly. "I'm beginning to like this story."

"I thought you might." Suzannah stifled a smile and decided to liven up the tale a bit. "It was a rough wool shirt, and it scratched my poor skin. And sometime during the night, without realizing it, I must have . . . well . . ."

"You took it off?" Ben was now completely mesmerized. "Is that what you're saying?"

Suzannah pouted sweetly. "I didn't see any harm. After all, I intended to be up and dressed before Aengus returned."

"He left here at dawn. Were you still asleep when he came home?"

Suzannah nodded demurely. "Imagine my confusion when I awoke to see him sitting on the bed, staring at my naked shoulders and such. It was as though he couldn't resist touching me."

Ben stared in complete fascination. "Were you angry?"

"I was half asleep. I thought it was a dream. He was so gentle and loving. The Aengus I fell in love with years ago. The Aengus I never really stopped loving."

Ben cleared his throat, but still his voice was thick and husky. "That's wonderful, Suzannah. He's a lucky man."

"And I'm a lucky woman. And so is Meg."

He took her hand and squeezed it gently. "After all you've done for us, I have no right to ask another favor, but . . ."

"Ask anything, Ben."

"Could you share that story with Megan? I know

she's apprehensive about . . . well, this sort of thing. If she hears you enjoyed your first time—"

"My *what?*"

Ben backed away, but she grabbed his shirt front and snarled, "Are you insane? Do you honestly think I allowed *that?*"

Ben was chuckling nervously. "Didn't you just say—?"

"He kissed me, you reprobate. And he touched my bare shoulder. Nothing more."

Ben was struggling not to laugh harder. "Forgive me, Suzannah. You made it sound so—"

"Oh, be quiet." Releasing him, she added sharply, "No wonder Megan is apprehensive about such things, if that's the kind of behavior you find acceptable."

Ben tilted her chin so that she was looking straight into his warm brown eyes. "You say he was gentle?"

"Yes, Ben."

"And you honestly love him?"

"More than anything," Suzannah bluffed softly. Then she added, more truthfully, "My place is here, Ben. With Aengus and the boys. I can't imagine spending my life without them now."

"Well, then . . ." He hugged her heartily. "Aengus is a lucky man. When do you plan on having the ceremony?"

"I don't know—"

"Today?" he interrupted hopefully. "The judge is ready and willing—"

"Today? That's fine for you and Meg, but—"

"She has her heart set on a double wedding, sweetheart. Do you want me to speak to Aengus?"

"No!" Suzannah tried to smile reassuringly. "I'll speak to him myself. He'll be delighted, I'm sure—"

"So am I," Ben grinned mischievously. "After the bride he expected through the mail, I'm sure he felt quite fortunate to find a pretty girl like *you* in his bed this morning."

"That's enough," she scolded. "Go and make plans with the judge and Megan, while I find Aengus and tell him what we've decided." Before Ben could engage her in any more conversation, she pulled free of his hands and bolted through the archway to the front of the house.

Neither the boys nor the wagon were anywhere in sight, but the little town of Bent Creek was just down the road, so she continued halfheartedly toward the row of buildings, considering each one in turn. A general store, a livery stable, an inn with a small saloon—but still no sign of the wagon. On the other hand, a horse in front of the store looked enough like the one Ben had sold to Aengus to give her hope that her unsuspecting fiancé had finished his chores and joined them here in town.

Taking one last deep breath, and reminding herself that this course of action was the best for all concerned, she squared her slender shoulders and went looking for Aengus Yates.

Chapter Five

She paused in the doorway to study him. Her childhood hero, tall and strong, with a mane of wild brown hair around his noble face, and eyes so blue they rivaled the waters through which she had so recently sailed in the Caribbean. He was speaking to the shopkeeper, and Suzannah focused wistfully on the rhythm of his brogue. It was subtler now than it had been when he'd first arrived in Adamsville, but Suzannah had been raised by a woman with the same rich lilt to her voice, and she never tired of the lullaby-like cadence.

The shopkeeper was the first to notice Suzannah. "Well, now. Who have we here?"

Aengus turned, and a smile spread slowly over his features. "Come here, Suzy, and meet my friend Tom Whalen. He's from Boston, like myself. Tom, this pretty girl is the very brat I was just describing to you. Tom Whalen, Suzannah Hennessy."

Suzannah grimaced sweetly. "It's a pleasure to meet you, Mr. Whalen. Don't mind Aengus. He never had any manners to speak of, and it appears he's gotten worse over the years."

"He was just telling me what a wonderful cook you are," Whalen smiled. "Just like your mother, he says."

"Really?" She beamed toward Aengus. "What a sweet thing to say."

"He also told me he once turned down a marriage proposal from you," the shopkeeper continued playfully. "I'd say that reflects poorly on his judgment, to reject so lovely a bride."

Suzannah felt her cheeks warm to a dark crimson. "I was just commenting to someone that Aengus isn't one to brag about his conquests. Apparently I was wrong. If you two will excuse me?"

"Wait!" Aengus grabbed her arm before she could retreat. "We were only teasing, and it was a compliment to boot. Don't run off angry. I apologize, and so does Tom."

"It's true, Miss Suzannah," Whalen insisted. "You're like a little sister to Aengus here, but still we shouldn't have teased you."

A little sister? Suzannah almost groaned aloud in defeat. Aengus Yates hadn't taken her marriage proposal seriously seven years ago, and he wasn't going to take it seriously now! She must have been insane to believe he'd see it as the answer to his prayers.

"We don't get many visitors in Bent Creek," Whalen was informing her. "My wife will want a chance to visit with you. She's tending to her mother right now but should be back this afternoon. Will you still be in town? She's much better behaved than myself," he added sheepishly.

"I don't know if I'll be here or not," Suzannah

admitted. "And I don't want to be rude, but I need to speak with Aengus about a very urgent matter. Do you mind awfully?"

"An urgent matter?" Aengus demanded. "It's not the boys, is it? I didn't see the wagon—"

"They're fine," she assured him quickly. "It's something else entirely." She smiled at him then, just a little, to let him know she was pleased to see his concern for the children. Perhaps he wasn't as hard-hearted as he pretended.

"Well, then . . ." Aengus shrugged toward Whalen. "I'll be back to pick up my order when the wagon gets here. Tell Luke to begin loading up."

"Sure," Whalen nodded. "Go and discuss your urgent matter. And if it turns out to be another marriage proposal, don't be a fool this time."

As the two men laughed, Suzannah felt her cheeks burn again. She wanted desperately to proclaim that marriage to Aengus Yates was the furthest thing from her mind, but of course she could not, and so she tried to glare at Whalen, then took Aengus by the hand and yanked him through the doorway.

"What's your hurry?" Aengus chuckled. "And what's happened to your sense of humor? Not to mention your manners."

"*My* manners?" she seethed. "My manners are the only thing keeping me from strangling you at this moment. How could you tell a perfect stranger private details from our past?"

Aengus grinned. "What's gotten into you, Suzy? You were comfortable telling that story to Ben Steele when he was just a stranger, weren't you? Why is it such an offense when it's myself doing the telling?"

"Be quiet and let me think."

Aengus frowned slightly. "Does this urgent matter

concern Ben and Megan? Has something happened between them? He hasn't compromised her, has he? Because if he has—"

"Ben Steele is a gentleman, thank goodness. But yes, the urgent matter does concern them. They're engaged to be married, Aengus, and I've never seen Meg so happy. If you dare spoil it for her, I honestly *will* strangle you, manners or not."

"Why would I spoil it?" Aengus murmured. "It's sudden, but it was clear to me last night that he's devoted to her. If she feels the same, why would I interfere?" He smiled uneasily. "This isn't more nonsense about the mail-order bride, is it? You can't still believe I might hold her to the contract. The truth is, the more I think about it, the more relieved I am to be free of thoughts of marrying again," he added cheerfully. "It was a foolish notion from the start."

"It was not! It was the first noble thought you've had in years. Maybe even in your whole lifetime," Suzannah scolded. "You wanted a stepmother for your sons. Someone to give them the love you're too heartless to give them yourself. And you're going to do just that, Aengus Yates."

"Suzannah—"

"Be quiet," she repeated firmly. "There's something you don't know. Something about Megan and myself. We made a pledge to one another, years ago, that one wouldn't marry before the other. We wanted to raise our families together, only now it's not possible, because Meg's going to live in San Francisco. The only way I could convince her to marry Ben was to tell her I was going to stay here and marry *you*. So that's what I did."

She raised her chin defiantly. "It's best for everyone, so don't you dare be selfish about it. Ben and

Megan will be happy, and your sons will have a loving stepmother. I know you see me as a child . . ." Her voice faltered slightly. "I'm eighteen years old, Aengus Yates, and I love your sons dearly. Isn't that enough for you?"

He was staring at her as though through a haze. "Enough for me? To marry *you*? Is that what you're asking?"

"Yes. Go ahead and tease me if you must, but yes— I'm asking you again. Only for different reasons this time. You can joke with your friends about it all you like, and you can treat me like a child for the rest of my days, as long as you behave until Megan and Ben leave for San Francisco."

She could see he was about to protest, and so she added quickly, "I won't criticize or scold or nag. Not one bit. You can ignore me and the boys completely if you want and I won't say a word. Just feed us and shelter us. I'll never ask for more." A hint of impatience crept into her tone. "You'll never remarry otherwise, will you? So why not just go along with this for the sake of the boys?"

"You're asking me to marry you?"

"Stop saying that," she pleaded. "Just answer me, yes or no. But before you do, think of your sons. And think of Megan. And think of how you dreaded marrying a stranger. I'm not a stranger, am I? And I'm not a child," she added sharply. "If you'd open your eyes just for once, you'd see that. I can cook, and I can sew, and I can raise those boys for you, without asking you for anything in return other than a roof over my head, and a harmless little lie for Megan's sake. Is that asking too much?"

"Too much?" he countered softly. "Or too little?"

"Pardon?"

Aengus shrugged. "Why waste yourself on a disappointing specimen like myself? You could have any man you want."

"I don't want a man at all," Suzannah explained sadly. "Not after all the heartache I've seen them cause in my life. My father broke my mother's heart by dying. And you broke mine by leaving your family. I don't mean to be harsh, but in a way, you owe it to me to do this. To share your family with me, so that I don't have to find some stranger to father children with me, and who might then break my heart to bits."

"Suzannah . . ."

"I can't bear the thought of leaving the boys behind, Aengus. And I'd be miserable in San Francisco with Meg and Ben. This life you've built for yourself here is a glorious one. You were willing once to let a stranger share it with you. Why not me?"

"I'm more than willing to share it with you. I only want you to think it through—"

"I have!" Suzannah's heart pounded with relief and anticipation. "Our marrying will be the perfect solution for everyone. And the best part," she added, brushing his jawbone lightly with her fingertips, "is that you and I are comfortable with each other. Given the fact that you don't trust women, and I don't trust men, that's rather amazing, don't you think?"

He stared at her for a moment, a slow, appreciative smile working its way up from his strong mouth and into his cobalt eyes. "I'm not a man to make the same mistake twice, Miss Hennessy."

"Does that mean you'll marry me?"

"I'd be a fool not to."

"Oh, Aengus . . ." A shiver of relief ran through her. "We're doing the right thing. I'm sure of it.

You'll understand completely when you see Megan and Ben together this afternoon, at the ceremony.''

"Their wedding is this afternoon?"

"And so is ours." She smiled sheepishly. "Megan won't have it any other way. You'll have to pretend to be in love with me—and I with you—or she'll never go through with it. Now that she's discovered romantic love, she'll want me to have it too. I hate lying to her, but I don't think we have a choice. She'd never understand our marriage otherwise."

"I'm not sure I do either," Aengus teased.

"There's one other thing. One other lie," Suzannah added apologetically. "I hope you don't mind. It's about you. And the reason you left Katherine."

Almost instantly, she knew she'd made a terrible mistake. The smile that had lit his eyes disappeared, replaced by stone-cold resentment and hostility. "Excuse me?"

"Don't be angry," she pleaded. "I needed to convince Meg I had forgiven you—"

"That again?" he growled. "I don't recall asking for your forgiveness—"

"Shhh, Aengus. Don't lose your temper. I didn't say anything that reflected poorly on you. In fact, I made you out to be a saint."

"Did you now?" he mocked. "Let's hear it."

"I implied Katherine refused to share a bed with you. That she forced you to turn away from her. And since the boys were so young, you felt they needed their mother more than their father. But you always intended . . . *Please* stop looking at me that way!"

"You had no right to tell such tales." He shook his head in disgust. "How do you suppose Luke would feel if he heard his mother maligned in this way? Do you want to ruin the few precious memories he has left?"

"Of course not! I'd never do anything to hurt Luke or Johnny. You know that," she insisted unhappily. "Megan will never repeat the story, except perhaps to Ben. And I needed to convince her you were blameless. Otherwise, she would always have worried that you might . . . Well, that you might one day . . ."

"Leave again?" He seemed to almost choke on the words. "Is that what *you* think I'll do?"

"No. I know in my heart you must have had a good reason for leaving." She waited in vain for him to offer an explanation, then shrugged her shoulders impatiently. "You can take it to your grave for all I care, Aengus Yates. I'm done with begging you to do the noble thing. I'll just tell Megan you're not a saint after all, and the marriages are canceled."

Aengus exhaled slowly, and as he did, all the anger seemed to leave his body. "I understand why you did what you did. We can leave it as it is, and trust Megan not to repeat the story. And unless it's you that's decided against the marriage, we can go ahead with that as well."

"I still think it's best for everyone," she sniffed.

"Well, then. We should talk to Luke and Johnny."

Suzannah nodded, then touched his arm in wistful apology. "I'd never say a word against Katherine to either of them. You believe that, don't you?"

Aengus nodded in return. "In their eyes, she was perfect. Let them keep their illusions for as long as they can."

Suzannah wanted to remind him that the children had other "illusions" as well. Memories of a father who loved and appreciated them. Weren't those memories important too? Why was he so quick to sacrifice those for Katherine's sake?

Or maybe it's your own illusions you're protecting, she chided herself sadly. *You still want him to be the old Aengus. The perfect one. The one that never really existed. Leave it be, Suzannah, and be glad you've found a way to make new, true memories to replace the old, illusory ones.*

Taking Aengus's huge hand in her own, she suggested softly, "Let's go tell our boys the good news."

By the time they tracked down the children and herded them into Judge Winston's parlor, it was almost noon, and Suzannah was beginning to feel a bit giddy, despite the fact that the marriage was to be in name only. It was still the only wedding she intended to have in her life, and she wanted to look pretty. She also wanted to spend a little time with Megan before the big event. And a little less time with Aengus Yates, for fear she'd say or do something else wrong, or he'd say or do something else unforgivable, and the wedding would be over before it began.

"Did we do something wrong, Pa?" Luke asked as soon as the four were alone.

"No. Sit down over there on the sofa, next to your brother. Suzannah and I have something to tell you."

"Did somebody else die?" Johnny murmured.

"Oh, dear . . ." Suzannah knelt before him and hugged him reassuringly. "It's good news, not bad news. At least, I hope that's how you'll feel about it." With a smile toward Luke, she released Johnny and made her way to the stately blue velvet wing chair she'd chosen as the perfect place to begin her role as stepmother. When she was seated, Aengus moved to stand behind the chair, as though to emphasize, right from the start, Suzannah's role as a buffer between a grouchy father and love-starved sons.

"Are we getting a dog?" Johnny asked hopefully.

"A dog?" Aengus chuckled. "Something better than a dog. Prettier too. And just as soft—"

"Aengus!" She turned to eye him reproachfully, then swiveled back to beam toward the boys. "Do you remember how your father promised to find a woman to live at the ranch, as his wife, and take care of you?"

The two children nodded solemnly.

"He was hoping that the new wife would be someone you could love and trust. He wanted—"

"That's enough," Aengus interrupted impatiently. "Suzannah and I are getting married. She's going to be your stepmother from now on. How does that sound?"

"Does that mean she's staying?" Johnny asked cautiously.

Aengus chuckled again. "Does that meet with your approval?"

"Yippee! Suzannah's staying!" The younger boy flew into Suzannah's lap and began to hug her wildly. "I knew you wouldn't leave us! Not again!"

"Never again," Suzannah promised. "I'm so glad you're pleased, sweetie."

"Are you going to make biscuits every night? And tell us stories?"

"Of course. And I'll help you with your lessons, and teach you to dance—"

"*Dance?* We're not *girls*, Suzannah."

"But you'll be wanting to dance with girls some day," Aengus reminded him. "Be glad you'll have such a pretty teacher."

"Do you know how to dance, Pa?" Johnny marveled. "With girls?"

"It's been a few years, but I'm sure I remember a bit of it."

"Did you dance with Mama?"

Suzannah winced and hugged the child closer. "Of course he did. But do you know who was the best dancer in Adamsville? Megan Braddock. And guess what? Megan's going to be married too. To a man named Ben Steele."

"The man who gave us money?" Johnny marveled. "I like him."

"He gave you money?" Suzannah frowned. "Why?"

"So we'd go away. So he could talk to Megan alone."

Suzannah exchanged grins with Aengus, then checked for Luke's expression, certain that the older boy would have half suspected Ben's motive. To her surprise, Luke was still seated on the sofa, his face frozen in an expression that was something less than joyous.

"Luke?" she murmured. "Is something wrong?"

The boy looked past her to Aengus. "Should I go load the wagon now, Pa?"

Aengus nodded. "Then hurry back. You and Johnny will need to wash up for the festivities. If there was more time, I'd send you home to change into your church clothes—"

"They don't fit us anymore," Luke interrupted coolly. "Come on, Johnny. Let's go load the wagon."

The little boy slid off Suzannah's lap and joined his brother in the doorway. "We'll be fast, Pa. Don't change your mind while we're gone."

When they left, Aengus patted Suzannah's shoulder. "That went well."

"No thanks to you," she smiled. "But Luke's reaction was odd, don't you think? I hope he doesn't resent my trying to take Katherine's place so soon."

"That boy's moody," Aengus said. "Don't take it to heart."

"He's moody like his father," Suzannah teased. "Just the same, I should go and talk to him. Unless you want to?"

"I can't talk to him," Aengus shrugged. "Isn't that why you're marrying me in the first place? Because I don't talk to those boys?"

"It's one of your many charms," she smiled, pecking his cheek playfully as she passed by him on her way toward the front door.

The wagon was about to pull away, but when Luke caught sight of her, he reined in the team, then jumped down from the driver's bench to confront her directly. "Don't marry him."

"For heaven's sake, Luke! I thought you'd be happy."

"To see you with *him?*"

"Oh, dear, is that it?" She lowered her voice and pulled him out of earshot of Johnny. "I know you and your father haven't been getting along, but—"

"He's mean, Suzannah. Don't do it. I like the other plan better anyway."

"The other plan? You'd rather he married some stranger—"

"A year's not so long, just like we said," Luke insisted. "We'll miss you, but once you come back and take us away with you, we'll be with you forever."

Suzannah stroked his cheek lovingly. "Aren't you forgetting something?"

"That I might get 'the old Pa' back?" His tone was every bit as harsh as Aengus's could be. "I believed that last night. Even this morning, I believed it a little. But . . ." His hazel eyes were dark with concern. "What if he hurts you?"

"Hurts me?" She was honestly confused by the question; then her heart sank. "Has he raised a hand to you or Johnny?"

"No."

"Are you saying he raised a hand to your mother?" Luke shook his head.

"Then I don't want to hear that kind of talk."

The boy lowered his gaze to the ground and repeated stubbornly, "He's mean."

"I've seen him be grouchy, and I've seen him be wonderful," Suzannah said gently. "I'm hoping that this marriage will bring out the best in him. Give it a chance, won't you, Luke?"

"What if he's not the old Pa in a year? Will you still keep your promise?"

She flushed but nodded. "Yes, sweetie. If you're not happy here in a year, I'll keep my promise."

"Suzannah?"

"Yes?"

The child blushed but finally met her gaze. "I know what men do to ladies in bed. Are you going to let him do that to you?"

Panicking at the unexpected question, she considered telling him the truth. It would reassure him to know that she and Aengus had no intention of engaging in lovemaking of any kind. But Aengus's words rang in her ears: *Let them keep their illusions for as long as they can.*

Shouldn't a little boy be able to believe that marriage was a sacred bond, both physical and spiritual? Shouldn't he be allowed to believe that love could triumph over all? Wouldn't it be best for him to believe that his father was the kind of man a girl could trust with her most precious and irreplaceable gift?

"Your father and I have a fondness for each other, Luke," she insisted finally. "We want to share that feeling with each other. When you grow up, you'll understand and respect that. For now, you need to trust us to make the right decisions for all of us." Cradling his face in her hands, she added shyly, "You mustn't believe everything you hear about lovemaking. When the time comes, your father will tell you the truth about it, and you'll be glad you didn't worry about me too much."

"I heard it's how babies get made. Are you and Pa going to make babies?"

Suzannah bit her lip before hedging, "In a few hours, I'm going to have two new stepsons to love. That's enough children for me for a start, don't you think?"

"I guess." Without warning, the boy threw his arms around her neck, hugged her fervently, then turned and sprinted back to the wagon.

"I think I'm going to cry," Dorothy Winston gushed as she stood back and admired her handiwork—a soft pink satin ball gown, hastily altered at the waist and in length to accommodate Suzannah's proportions. Never in her life had the girl worn a dress with a "neckline," much less one with so fancy and provocative a bodice. The thought of Aengus or Ben seeing so much of her bosom made her want to wrap herself in a blanket from head to toe, but her hostess insisted it was fashionable, and Megan, of all people, agreed that they must be "visions of loveliness" by any means at their disposal.

"Why not just parade around naked?" Suzannah grumbled, pulling stubbornly at the fabric, willing it to cover more. She wished now she hadn't insisted on wearing her hair in a soft French braid with golden tendrils framing her face. If her thick locks were hanging loosely, she could use them to hide all this skin!

"That raises another interesting question," Dorothy was teasing. "Do you want to borrow one of my lace nighties, or will you sleep au natural tonight?"

"I'd like to borrow something pretty," Megan admitted. "Ben's used to city women—"

"I don't want to hear this," Suzannah protested, covering her ears in mock dismay. "Honestly, Meg, isn't it bad enough you've chosen that provocative gown?"

"It doesn't provoke," Dorothy corrected. "It simply defines. That long, slim body of hers was made for flowing satin."

Suzannah had to admit it was true. Megan Braddock was positively radiant in the ice blue gown. And to Suzannah's delight, the dark-haired beauty hadn't once worried about her mother's legacy, even when Dorothy had innocently observed that Megan had the legs and poise of a prima ballerina.

"Everything's perfect," Dorothy pronounced finally. "I'm going to give you a few minutes to collect yourselves while I make sure Ben and Aengus are situated properly. Thank goodness they're handsome men," she added, half to herself. "It makes the decorating so much easier."

"That's why we chose them," Suzannah teased.

"Hush now," Dorothy scolded fondly. "You want this to go perfectly, don't you? Now, where was I?"

"You're going to situate our handsome grooms," Megan prompted.

"Right. Then you'll hear me start to play the piano. Walk in slowly, carrying these bouquets. And try to smile, but don't make eye contact with anyone." Embracing each bride in turn, she sniffed back a sob. "You're so beautiful, both of you. I only wish we'd had time to invite more guests—"

"You've done so much for us as it is," Megan smiled. "The food, the flowers, the gowns—this wedding would have been a disaster without your help. How can we ever thank you?"

"You can send me letters from San Francisco, so I'm not so woefully out of touch. And you . . ." She turned to Suzannah, her eyes shining. "You've already done so much. Rescuing our darling Aengus from loneliness and despair! And taking those darling boys into your heart . . ." She pulled a handkerchief from her sleeve and dabbed gently at her eyes, then turned reluctantly toward the doorway leading to the parlor. "Five minutes, and not a second more. Listen for my cue."

When she'd left, Suzannah picked up a bouquet of gardenias and pine branches, inhaled it deeply, then passed it to Megan. She wanted to remind her friend of the times they'd pretended to be brides, walking through a grove of trees with wildflower bouquets in their hands, using bedsheets as veils. But Megan was clearly remembering those days without any prompting, and if they started reminiscing aloud, they might cry and ruin the dabs of face makeup their hostess had applied to their cheeks and eyes.

Then strains of piano music reached them, and Megan murmured nervously, "I barely know Ben Steele."

"And I know Aengus too well."

The observation made Megan giggled. "Between

the two of them, they're perfect.'' Then she admitted, ''I'm terrified about tonight. Aren't you?''

Suzannah winced, knowing that while Megan's night would be one of both discovery and anxiety, her own would be predictable and reassuring. Megan would be touched and prodded and challenged. Suzannah would bake some biscuits for Aengus, crochet a bit, and retire early. ''Ben will be gentle. Try not to worry.''

''Aengus will be gentle too. You always said Aengus was gentle. We *know* Aengus. But we don't know Ben at all.''

Suzannah smiled sympathetically. ''He's a bit of a rascal, isn't he? Wait until he sees you in that dress.''

''Suzannah!'' Megan giggled again. ''We'd better hurry. Dorothy said she only knows how to play two songs.''

They embraced, directing each other to ''take care, and don't worry, it will be wonderful,'' then exchanged nervous smiles as they carefully positioned their bouquets to hide their exposed cleavages before hurrying toward the parlor.

Suzannah had known Aengus Yates for almost ten years, and in her imagination she knew every inch of his body by heart. Tall and lanky, strong and quiet, slow smile and blue eyes—she could picture him in every detail whenever she closed her eyes. Still, when she walked into the Winston parlor and saw him standing by the fireplace in the clothes he'd borrowed from his friend Tom, she almost gasped to realize that he was as much a stranger to her as Ben Steele was to Megan.

Had she ever seen him in a dress shirt and trousers?

She was certain she hadn't. She'd rarely even seen him indoors! To her, Aengus had been a wrangler, moving masterfully among a string of horses, with the dusty clothes and confident attitude of a man at home on a ranch.

Now, with music playing, a fire burning, and a small audience of strangers watching every move, Aengus looked like a prince. His hair was pulled back, his posture regal yet relaxed, and his eyes, as blue as ever, were the truest and most mesmerizing point of reference in the room. She had never, *ever*, seen this man before in her life!

Then he caught his first glimpse of her, and his reaction caused what was left of her composure to desert her. Try as he might to look at her face, she could see that her daring neckline had captured his attention. *At least now he knows you're not a little girl anymore,* she consoled herself shakily. Still, it was awkward, and she prayed desperately for a quick end to the ridiculous ceremony.

Look at Ben instead, she counseled herself, and the tactic seemed successful. In contrast to Aengus, Ben looked to be a nervous wreck, and Suzannah understood exactly why. Aengus's responsibilities as a husband would end as soon as he and Suzannah left this parlor and headed for the ranch. Ben, on the other hand, had to play that role for life! He had to usher Megan into womanhood that very evening, and then make her happy, father her children, and remain faithful to her forever. No wonder Aengus was so calm! All he had to do was stand there and look devastatingly handsome.

Still, Ben seemed to draw strength from the sight of Megan, and Suzannah's smile grew less stiff and more genuine as she noted the true adoration in his eyes. He would take care of his bride. There was simply no doubt about that. And the wedding night would be a blissfully exciting one, because Ben was a ladies' man, and knew what a girl wanted to hear, and feel, and believe.

Through the haze of uncertainty and sentiment, Suzannah noticed the Yates boys, seated to the right of the fireplace, staring at the brides as though they were strangers, and she almost giggled with delight. They were *so* adorable! Miniature versions of Aengus—Johnny with his smile, and Luke with his sincerity.

And the moment you and Aengus speak your vows, those boys become your sons, she reminded herself firmly. It was all she needed, and when she reached Aengus's side, she took his arm as casually and confidently as if they'd been married for years. In her heart, they almost had been.

Judge Winston married Ben to Megan first, and while Suzannah felt a tear slide down her cheek, she felt only joy at the genuine happiness that shone in both the bride's and the groom's face as they spoke their vows. Then the judge directed Ben to kiss his new wife, and Suzannah smiled, suspecting another of the passionate, heart-searing exchanges she'd witnessed between the two. Instead, Ben's lips barely brushed those of his bride; then he held her at arms' length and studied her with pride and amazement, as though he'd never really believed she'd go through with it.

And Megan, who had seemed so nervous, now radiated confidence and contentment as she teased softly, "Do you remember when you told me you always win, Mr. Steele?"

"I was bluffing, Mrs. Steele," Ben replied hoarsely.

Judge Winston chuckled. "I believe that's the first time I've allowed gambling in my chambers." He turned then to Suzannah. "Shall we proceed?"

She looked to Aengus, who nodded solemnly.

The words were a blur, even when Aengus responded, his brogue richer and more pronounced than usual. He even used the charming and unexpected "Aye" when asked if he took Suzannah as his wife. She hadn't heard him use that since the early days of his arrival in Adamsville, when he'd spent homesick afternoons in her mother's comforting kitchen.

He must be nervous, she sympathized silently. Her own voice sounded stilted and unfamiliar, despite her efforts to appear calm and self-assured for Luke's sake. Then the judge pronounced them man and wife, and directed Aengus to kiss the bride, and she turned to him in relief, knowing that with one simple brush of his lips against hers, the worst of it would be over. She only hoped he remembered to make the kiss appear romantic and loving, for Megan's sake.

Her new husband rested his hands on her waist and gave her an inquiring glance, as though asking for permission, or at the very least confirmation, of her instructions. Relieved that he was putting on so romantic a show for Megan, she slipped her hands behind his neck and smiled her most encouraging smile.

Lowering his mouth to hers, he tasted her, gently but insistently, and as she pretended to respond, she found herself actually enjoying herself. After all these years of wondering, it was nice to know that she'd been right. Aengus Yates would have made a wonderful lover. His lips were soft, and she could feel just a hint of his tongue against her mouth.

Interesting, she thought ruefully. *Katherine was such a fool not to appreciate this.*

Then he pulled her hard against himself, and the kiss became infused with a hungry, insistent heat that made her gasp with dismay. That gasp was a mistake, allowing his alert tongue access to her mouth, where it probed with bold and irreverent thoroughness. Fearful of losing her balance, she had no choice but to wrap her arms around his neck and pray that he would come to his senses. But Aengus only deepened his attack, devouring her with such maddening enjoyment that she wondered why no one in the audience had the presence of mind to intercede on her behalf.

She was determined to protest as soon as she regained her strength, but when would that be? Time had been suspended for the onslaught, and her body was so weak with confusion that it actually molded itself to Aengus's for support, despite the ungodly bulge of his manhood that was beginning to greet her. Her knees began to buckle, and when they did, Aengus broke off the kiss in time to scoop her up into his arms.

"Apparently," Ben Steele observed cheerfully, "Aengus *wasn't* bluffing."

The audience burst into laughter, and to Suzannah's mortification, Aengus announced, "I'll be taking my bride home now. Megan? Best of luck to you. Ben? Treat her well or you'll have me to deal with."

"Worry about yourself, my friend," Ben chuckled. "You've got yourself a wildcat there."

"Aengus, put me down!" Suzannah wailed. "I want to say good-bye to everyone." Wriggling free as soon as he'd begun to lower her, she scanned the faces of strangers until she spied her new stepsons. With a hopeful smile, she knelt and opened her arms to them, and was pleased when they ran to embrace her.

"We're going to be a wonderful family," she predicted in a whisper. "Be good tonight for the judge and Mrs. Winston, and tomorrow, when you come home, everything will be different."

"We'll be good," Johnny promised.

"Luke?" She studied the boy's clouded expression. "Aren't you just a little bit happy about this?"

Luke said nothing. Instead, he glanced pointedly over toward Aengus, who was shaking hands with Judge Winston.

She realized that the kiss must have annoyed him, and the thought made her smile. "You're as stubborn as your father, do you know that, Luke Yates?"

The boy scowled. "Are you *still* going to keep your promise?"

Rumpling his dark brown hair, she assured him, "My promise is now a guarantee. One year from now, and hopefully much sooner than that, you'll be happy."

"Me too?" Johnny interrupted.

"Absolutely."

"And Pa too?"

"All of us. We're a family now, Johnny. What do you think of that?"

"I think it's good." Noting Luke's scowl, he added firmly, "It's good as long as Pa isn't mean to you. Did he kiss you too hard, Suzannah? It almost made you fall down."

The bride laughed lightly. "It was a fine kiss, believe me."

Johnny smiled with relief. "At least Pa did it better than Mr. Steele. *He* almost missed Megan's face!"

Even Luke had to laugh at that, and the sound was

music to Suzannah's heart. Then Megan was there, tapping her on her shoulder and whispering, "You mustn't keep Aengus waiting any longer."

Standing to gaze into her friend's laughing gray eyes, Suzannah sighed. "You look so happy, Meg. Radiant, just like a bride should look. It's a beautiful sight."

"I love Ben," the girl explained simply. "It's a miracle, but it pales in comparison with the miracle of you and Aengus. All these years, all the misunderstandings and disappointments, and now this!" Lowering her voice, she admitted, "I didn't believe you. I thought you were just marrying him for the sake of the boys. But that kiss . . ." Tears welled in her loving eyes. "You're his bride, just like you always wanted to be."

But it wasn't the way she'd always wanted it to be, and for a moment Suzannah questioned the course she'd chosen. She'd wanted so much more for herself. To be Aengus's bride, in more than name only. To walk hand in hand with him. To sleep by his side. To share his secrets, both joyous and sad. To bear his children. To lavish upon him the love that once blazed in her heart every time he stepped into view.

Stooping to embrace her stepsons one last time, she murmured, "Be good," then turned back to Megan. "Be happy, Meg. Be happier than any woman has ever been."

"I already am," Megan assured her through her tears.

"You won't leave Bent Creek without saying goodbye?"

"Of course not, silly. Ben's taken a room at the hotel, and he promised we could stay for at least a week. He knows how sad I'll be to leave you here."

Suzannah smiled. "Why don't you and he bring the boys back to the ranch tomorrow? That way you can see where I'm going to live, and we can . . . well, you know."

"I can't wait to hear every detail," Megan agreed slyly. Pulling Suzannah safely out of the children's earshot, she asked for the tenth time that day, "Do you suppose it will hurt?"

"You'll survive," Suzannah teased. "Our mothers did, didn't they?"

Megan giggled nervously. "You're so much calmer about it than I am. But then, you've always been braver than me."

Suzannah resisted an urge to assure her that, if she were facing a true wedding night, she might be just as nervous as her friend. It was the only real advantage to a loveless marriage, she decided with a wistful smile. No wedding night apprehension.

"I suppose I should go and visit with some of my new neighbors."

"They all seem so nice, Suzannah. Especially the Whalens. And the Winstons, of course."

"The Whalens?" Suzannah winced. She'd almost forgotten about Aengus's friend Tom, and it annoyed her to realize that someone here in town knew the truth: that Suzannah was nothing more than a pesky "little sister" to Aengus Yates.

From the corner of her eye, she now saw that Aengus and Tom were talking and laughing as they enjoyed a cup of Dorothy Winston's apple cider. Were they chuckling over the marriage proposal? Or worse, the scandalous kiss Aengus had inflicted on her?

If Tom shares the truth with his wife, then everyone in town will soon know, she worried. *How could Aengus be so foolish? Especially after scolding me for telling tales to Megan!*

Marching across the room, she eyed the two men haughtily. "Good afternoon, Tom. Aengus, could I speak with you for just a moment?"

"I'd like a chance to congratulate you first," Tom smiled. "And to kiss the bride."

"Perhaps later," Suzannah sniffed, and to her dismay, the two men began to chuckle again. "That's enough, both of you. I know you see this wedding as a source of great amusement, but to Luke and Johnny, it's a very solemn occasion. I wish you'd treat it with more respect."

"I didn't mean any disrespect, Suzannah," Tom murmured. "It's customary where I come from—"

"She's just nervous," Aengus interrupted, fixing Suzannah with a disapproving stare.

"She's entitled to be nervous, marrying an ornery cuss like yourself." Tom hesitated, then took both of Suzannah's hands in his own. "I don't know what you see in him, darlin', but as his friend, I'm more pleased than you can guess to know he has a wonderful woman like you to take care of him. To save him from himself."

There was no mistaking the sincerity in the man's words, and Suzannah flushed with embarrassment. "What a lovely thing to say. Forgive me for being so rude, Tom. I suppose it's just as Aengus said. I'm nervous." Rising up onto her tiptoes, she pecked her new neighbor on his cheek. "Thank you for coming today."

"It's been my pleasure, Mrs. Yates."

Mrs. Yates? Suzannah's gaze shifted to Aengus, to see if he found the sound of her new title disconcerting, but he still looked annoyed over her treatment of his friend, and so she smiled apologetically. "Aengus?"

Tom gestured toward the other side of the parlor. "I should go and spend a little time with my own bride. We'd like you both to come to supper soon. With the children, of course."

"We'll be looking forward to it, Tom."

The shopkeeper nodded, then slapped Aengus on the shoulder. "Congratulations again. Try to remember that you don't deserve a wonderful girl like her. It'll make the whole marriage go more smoothly."

"I'll bear it in mind," the bridegroom growled.

Aengus took Suzannah by the elbow as soon as his friend moved out of earshot. "I've had enough of this."

"I'm sorry, Aengus! It was a misunderstanding—"

"Wave good-bye to Megan so she doesn't think we're arguing. Then go and get into the wagon."

"But, Aengus—"

"Now!"

Suzannah took a deep breath and reminded herself that he had cheerfully cooperated with her somewhat unreasonable demand that they pretend to be marrying for love. Now he was tired of the pretense, anxious to get back to his predictable existence, and justifiably angry with her for her rude treatment of his friend.

Still, she wasn't about to take orders from him, and so she observed quietly, "I shouldn't have insulted Tom the way I did. And I'm grateful to you for putting on such a lovely show for Meg and the boys. So I'll go and get into the wagon. But not because you told me to. I'll do it because I agree, it's time to leave."

When his only response was a cool nod, she turned away and called out, as brightly as she could, "Meg! Ben!" Then she threw the couple a kiss, gave the boys one last, reassuring smile, and allowed her stone-faced bridegroom to lead her silently away.

Chapter Six

Although Aengus Yates was annoyed with his new bride, he was infinitely more annoyed with himself. Sure, she had been rude to his friend, but as Tom had said, it had only been because she was nervous. After all, she was a virgin, and her wedding night was only hours away. She had a right to be wary of her first time with a man, assuming she still intended to allow it tonight, given the unfortunate timing of this quarrel.

Why hadn't he been more patient with her? Or better still, why hadn't he followed his instincts and carried her out of that parlor directly after their incredible kiss? She had been ready then—on fire, in fact. Now she was cool to him, and he was going to have to begin the seduction anew. It was a frustrating turn of events, and he had only himself to blame.

He'd spent the last six weeks dreading the prospect of remarriage, but ever since Suzannah's unexpected proposal this afternoon, he had begun remembering some of the advantages wedded life had to offer, most notably the convenience of having a woman in his bed. No more quick trips to Virginia City. Instead, he would have the opportunity to linger over lovemaking. To savor it. Not with a stranger, but with an attractive young woman he admired and trusted. They were an odd match in many ways, but he had learned, during their first amazing kiss, that they were well suited to one another in one very important regard.

"There's a blanket in the back," he offered, if only to break the silence. "Are you cold?"

"I'm fine," she murmured; then she turned to him and blurted, "I saw you laughing with Tom, and I thought you and he were making a mockery of our marriage. Not that it isn't one, of course, but it's the only marriage I'll ever have, and I didn't want it to be a joke."

"I don't see our marriage as a mockery."

"I thought you were telling him that the wedding was just for convenience's sake, and that you weren't my husband in the way . . . well, in the way our kiss might have led him to believe. I don't want our neighbors thinking that, Aengus. It's your right, I suppose, to say whatever you like to your friend—"

"Why would I tell him I wasn't your husband?" Aengus interrupted. "He was right there watching when the judge married us."

"But he knows the rest," she countered stubbornly.

"The rest?"

"That you see me as a child. A bratty little sister, as you called me this morning. He knows you don't find me appealing in the way a bridegroom usually finds his bride."

Aengus grinned, relieved that they were resolving

their first spat so easily. "We were laughing at myself, not at you. At the fact that I could have mistaken you for a child, especially given the way you look in that dress."

Her gaze darted downward, to her provocatively showcased breasts, and she wailed, "Are you saying you were laughing about my—my chest?"

"No, Suzy," he assured her fondly. "We were marveling at it, and at my good fortune in having married so comely a female."

She eyed him warily. "I don't want the whole town knowing our business, Aengus. I want our marriage to appear normal in every way to them. I'm not asking you to lie to your friends," she repeated quickly. "Just don't share details with them that might make them think we only married for the sake of your sons."

"Tom Whalen knows I married you as much for myself as for the boys," Aengus assured her gently. "No one who watched us together today could doubt that."

"Because of the kiss?" Suzannah smiled sheepishly. "At the time, I thought you went too far, but you were right. It convinced Meg, and everyone else, that we were marrying for the right reasons."

He studied her hopefully. "You liked it more than I thought you would, given your inexperience and all."

"That's absurd. I hated it!"

"Is that so?" He chuckled at the indignant tone. "You had us *all* fooled, then."

"You're teasing me again?" A warm smile lit her face. "Does that mean you've forgiven me for behaving so rudely?"

He hesitated, then dared to pat her knee. "I know you're nervous, Suzy. It's only natural."

"I was nervous at the Winstons', but not now." She beamed again. "It's like I said this morning, Aengus. I'm so comfortable with you. In some ways, it's almost a perfect arrangement."

"You're not anxious? About being alone with me?"

"Not at all. But you should hear poor Megan. She's terrified. Not that I blame her, of course." Suzannah blushed but added frankly, "I'd be nervous too if I were facing what she's facing tonight."

"I'm glad you're so comfortable with me," Aengus smiled, grateful to know that their long years of acquaintanceship made so great a difference in her ability to give herself to him freely. It made sense, of course, but females weren't always sensible about such things.

"I trust you," his bride was explaining. "Even though you've made mistakes, I know you have a good heart." Before he could respond, she added softly, "We'll both make mistakes in the days and months to come, but if we really and truly trust each other, we can make this alliance a good one for everyone. You believe that, don't you?"

He nodded again, impressed by her wisdom and her commitment. And she was right. If they were to share a bed and a life, they had to trust one another. *He* had to trust *her*. Not with each and every secret, of course. But with enough of the truth to allow her trust in him to grow, without hurting Luke or Johnny in the process.

"You asked me this morning about the reason I left Katherine—"

"I did not! Honestly, Aengus, are you still angry about that? Meg promised me she wouldn't say anything, not even to Ben, and—"

"Suzannah?"

"Yes?"

"I'm going to tell you why I left Adamsville."

Her vibrant green eyes widened dramatically. "You are?"

"You're my wife, and so I'm going to trust you with the truth. I've never told this to anyone else."

"I'm honored, Aengus."

He smiled at the sincerity in her tone. "Considering the honor you're paying me tonight, it seems the least I can do. And it seems important that you of all persons should know the truth about one thing. I was never in love with Katherine."

"What?" Suzannah gasped. "I know you stopped loving her—"

"I was *never* in love with her," he repeated firmly. "There was a time when I sincerely appreciated her, for giving me sons, but there was never any love. Not in the sense you mean it."

"Then why . . . ?"

"Why did I marry her? Because she was carrying Luke."

"What!"

He nodded grimly. "I'm not proud to say it, Suzannah, but I'm not ashamed either. Do you remember when Katherine first came to town? To visit the Monroes?"

She nodded, clearly still speechless.

"The first night of her visit, she came out to the bunkhouse and presented herself to me in my bed. It took me by surprise, to say the least, and I didn't have the presence of mind to consider the consequences. Such opportunities were rare in Adamsville, especially for an eighteen-year-old ranch hand with no money."

"Katherine came to you that way? She must have

been as taken with you as . . ." Suzannah's blush deepened to a dark crimson. "I'm not judging her, of course. I loved you madly myself in those days. But it seems odd to imagine Katherine behaving that way. She was so dignified and ladylike."

He bit back an unkind observation, reminding himself that Katherine was dead, and it would be unseemly to malign her any more than was necessary. "She ignored me for the rest of the visit, until the day she was scheduled to go back to Chicago. At the last minute, she came to me in tears and said she was carrying my child. I was flabbergasted, to say the least. I did what I thought was the only honorable thing—"

"Oh, Aengus, how awful. I mean, it's not awful that Luke was conceived, but . . . well, you know what I mean. I always just assumed that you fell in love at first sight. But it was Luke that brought you together. That's sweet too, in its own way."

Aengus watched as his bride innocently traveled down the same road that had led him to his present dilemma. It didn't occur to decent people like the Hennessys and the Yateses that a person might scheme so malevolently to ruin another person's chance for happiness. Suzannah now believed that the marriage of Katherine and Aengus, while perhaps not romantic, had been a blessing in disguise, because it had led to the births of Luke and Johnny. Little did she know the boys would have been born even if Aengus and Katherine had never met.

"Could I have the blanket now?" she asked suddenly.

For the first time, he noticed she was shivering. "I'm sorry, Suzy." Pulling the team to a halt, he hastily fetched the coarse woolen blanket and draped it around her shoulders. "It's a bit of a shock, I suppose."

Wrapping herself more completely, she murmured, "You did a noble thing, marrying Katherine that way. Can you forgive me for all the times I've dared to judge you?" Before he could answer, she continued. "I know the rest. It was a loveless marriage, and you yearned for more. She spurned your manly attentions—"

"She had an affair with another man."

"*What?*"

He patted her shoulder, then picked up the reins and urged the team to resume the journey back home. "That's what you needed to know, Suzannah. I didn't leave because I was bored or restless or neglected. I left because I could no longer bear the sight of her."

"An affair? Are you sure?"

"I found them together."

"You saw them?" Suzannah buried her face in her hands. "In all my imaginings, I never imagined this. I knew she didn't appreciate what she had. But to think she turned from you—*you!*—to another, lesser man. I can't bear it, Aengus. I simply can't bear it."

He watched in amazement as her simple, childlike loyalty colored the tale in his behalf. She was so certain he was a prize. So certain the other man was the "lesser" of the two. It did his heart, and his pride, good to know there was someone on this earth that had held him in such esteem, even if it had tarnished a bit over the years.

Suzannah peeked between her fingers and asked warily, "Was he someone I knew? Someone from Adamsville?"

He hadn't meant to tell her, and was surprised

when he heard himself revealing, in an unfamiliar monotone voice, "It was Alex Monroe."

The instant he said it, he regretted it. The revelation was clearly too much for his naive young wife, and as he watched, helpless to take it back, her every illusion of love and honor and trust began to crumble before his very eyes.

"He was your friend," she whispered unhappily. "You *saw* them together? Kissing?" She read the truth in his eyes and wailed, "Oh, Aengus! How I hate them!" Throwing herself into his lap, she hugged him fiercely. "My poor Aengus. Why didn't you come to us? Mama and Megan and I—we would have taken care of you. Didn't you know that?" Before he could answer, she added mournfully, "It was Katherine who should have left town. You should have stayed with the boys—"

"That was what I wanted at first," he agreed, cuddling her gratefully against himself. "But Katherine wouldn't hear of it. She wanted the boys for herself, and she had Monroe's money to back up her cause. If it had gone before a judge, she would have prevailed, and there would have been the shame of it for the boys. I didn't want to put them through that."

Suzannah stroked her fingertips along his cheekbone. "I see why you don't want them to know the truth. Perhaps someday, if they insist, you'll tell them. But for now, it's best that they believe she was blameless. All of your choices have been noble ones, Aengus."

"Thank you."

She smiled weakly. "Remember yesterday, when we said we were glad she was dead? Now I see the true justice in it. You have the boys back, just as it should be. Megan said this was all a miracle, and now I'm beginning to see it that way myself.''

He knew he could kiss her then, and she would melt in his arms, but he didn't want it to be that way. Not their first time. He wanted it to be a joyous, playful joining, not a mournful sharing of loss, and so he contented himself with cupping her pretty face in his hand. ''Now that you know, we need never speak of it again. Do you understand?''

''But, Aengus—''

''It's in the past, Suzannah, and it makes no sense to dwell on it.''

''I suppose not.'' She gathered the blanket tightly around herself and slipped off his lap and back onto her seat. ''Thank you for sharing the truth with me. You'll never know how much it means.''

''I thought it might help for you to know. You said you're comfortable with me, but—''

''But now I'm even more comfortable.''

''That's important,'' he smiled. ''Anything I can do to put you at your ease tonight, you should tell me. I want it to be perfect for you.''

''I want it to be perfect for you too,'' Suzannah assured him. ''That's why I'm going to cook you anything you want. And biscuits too, of course.''

Aengus grinned at the innocent suggestion. ''Do you see the picnic basket wedged between your trunk and the corner of the wagon bed? Dorothy sent along some chicken and dumplings, and a bottle of wine imported from France. All you need to do tonight is relax. I'll take care of the rest.''

''It sounds lovely,'' Suzannah sighed. ''If only the boys could have come home with us tonight, it really would be perfect. But I suppose that would have seemed a little odd.''

Aengus chuckled at the extent of his bride's maternal instinct. "It would be awkward for them as well as for us."

"True. Luke has ideas, even at his young age. And as you said, we should preserve their illusions, so it's best they stayed in town. But you'll miss them just a bit, won't you, Aengus?"

"I like having you to myself, Mrs. Yates," he murmured seductively. "For this first night, at least."

"I like it too. It gave you a chance to confide in me about Katherine and Alex." She winced anew. "Do you suppose it was just the one time between them?"

"You don't need the details, Suzy."

"Alex Monroe," she mused. "He pretended to be your friend." Her eyes widened suddenly. "Did Elaine know about it?"

"I doubt it. And I don't want to discuss it any further."

"Did you hit him when you found them together?"

"That's enough, Suzannah. Don't make me regret telling you."

"Elaine couldn't have known," the bride continued as though she hadn't heard her husband's objection. "She would have divorced Alex the minute she found out he had a wandering eye, and he would have lost all that wealth and power. Do you suppose that's the only reason he married her? Someone should tell her what kind of man—"

"Suzannah, that's enough!"

She grimaced at the harsh tone. "I won't say anything to anyone else. Not even to Meg. But you can't blame me for being shocked. He was your friend—"

"Apparently not."

A long, wistful sigh signaled her agreement. "To

INTRODUCING BALLAD,
A BRAND NEW LINE OF HISTORICAL ROMANCES

As a lover of historical romance, you'll adore Ballad Romances. Written by today's most popular romance authors, every book in the Ballad line is not only an individual story, but part of a two to six book series as well. You can look forward to four new titles a month – each taking place at a different time and place in history.

But don't take our word for how wonderful these stories are! Accept our introductory shipment of 4 Ballad Romance novels – a $22.00 value – ABSOLUTELY FREE – and see for yourself!

Once you've experienced your first four Ballad Romances, we're sure you'll want to continue receiving these wonderful historical romance novels each month – without ever having to leave your home – using our convenient and inexpensive home subscription service. Here's what you get for joining:

- 4 BRAND NEW Ballad Romances delivered to your door each month
- 25% off the cover price (a total of $5.50) with your home subscription
- a FREE monthly newsletter filled with author interviews, book previews, special offers, and more!
- No risks or obligations…you're free to cancel whenever you wish… no questions asked.

To start your membership, simply complete and return the card provided. You'll receive your Introductory Shipment of 4 FREE Ballad Romances. Then, each month, as long as your account is in good standing, you will receive the 4 newest Ballad Romances. Each shipment will be yours to examine for 10 days. If you decide to keep the books, you'll pay the preferred home subscriber's price of $16.50 – a savings of 25% off the cover price! (Plus $1.50 shipping and handling.) If you want us to stop sending books, just say the word… it's that simple.

think I praised him for having looked out for Katherine and the boys during her illness. But it was the least he could do under the circumstances. Was it difficult for you, going back to Adamsville to fetch them? Seeing them there at Alex's house? Johnny told me you argued with Alex that day, and now I understand why. It must have been awful for you. And I won't nag you any more about the way you treat the boys, now that I know the source of it."

"And what exactly is that?"

Her voice grew hushed and mournful. "You can't look at them without seeing her face, and her betrayal. Isn't that so?"

Aengus gritted his teeth. He didn't see Katherine when he looked at them. He saw Monroe—in their eyes, their expressions, and their futures. And he *didn't* want to discuss it anymore. He didn't want to discuss anything, in fact. He just wanted to keep Suzannah reassured and receptive, so that the consummation would not be jeopardized.

He wondered what had possessed him to tell her a portion of the truth. She clearly wouldn't rest now until she'd made sense of all of it, which meant there was a real danger she'd realize one day that the boys were Monroe's.

And what then? Would she be so anxious to be their "stepmother" when she knew the truth about them?

He cleared his throat. "If the only subject worth discussing on our wedding day is my first wife's infidelity, this is a sorry marriage for sure."

Suzannah flushed. "Forgive me, Aengus. I won't mention it again."

He tried to think of a less volatile subject, but Suzannah succeeded first.

"I can't wait to change out of this silly dress," she announced cheerfully. "The sooner it's back in Dorothy Winston's closet, the better."

"Are you sure she wants it back? They may have intended it as a gift. And if not, I'd be willing to buy it from them."

"Why on earth would you do that?"

"Because it's your wedding dress. And," he added huskily, "because you look lovely in it."

"Don't you mean my bosom looks lovely in it?"

"Your bosom is hardly *in* it at all, Mrs. Yates," he teased.

Suzannah drew the blanket closer and pretended to be offended. "At least you can see I'm not a child any longer."

"Not a child, but still a brat," he grinned, adding silently that he was more than willing to share a bed with so shapely a brat. "You've no need for that blanket anymore, Mrs. Yates, now that you have a husband to keep you warm. Why don't you slide over closer to me?"

"Are you going to tease me for the rest of our marriage?" she laughed. Then her face softened into an affectionate smile. "You seem happier already, Aengus."

"I can't remember when I've felt this good," he admitted.

They were turning onto the dirt trail to Aengus's property, and Suzannah's green eyes began to dance. "I can hear the river! We must be almost home. Can you imagine a more beautiful night to begin our life together? It's barely dusk, and already there must be a thousand stars in the sky."

Aengus gave silent thanks for the romantic setting and for the bride who seemed so at ease in it. The fact that she still wasn't showing any signs of nervousness or doubt amazed him, but he wasn't going to question it. He would concentrate on continuing to make her feel at home, and with any luck, she'd be out of her borrowed dress and into her husband's bed before she recognized the raw lust that was beginning to strain the limits of his best behavior.

"Put it over there by the fireplace for now." Suzannah watched admiringly as her husband hefted her giant trunk off his back and onto the floor with a thud.

"I don't see why you needed it right away. Not that I'm complaining," he added hastily.

"Complain as much as you'd like," she smiled. "I know it's dreadfully heavy, but I honestly need everything that's in it."

She couldn't wait to dive into its contents and find a more comfortable, less revealing, dress, but she knew if she mentioned that again to Aengus, he'd take it as an opportunity for more teasing. Better to settle him down at the dinner table first. "Come and have some of this chicken. I tasted it, and it's not too awfully bad."

"We're going to eat first?"

"Aren't you hungry?"

"Ravenous," he murmured. "Shall I open the wine?"

"I won't be having any, but you should if you'd like."

"You don't drink wine?"

"I'm not allowed . . ." She caught herself and smiled sheepishly. "I suppose that's not true anymore."

His blue eyes twinkled. "As your husband, I give you permission."

"I'll give *myself* permission tomorrow night, when Meg and Ben come to dinner. Unless you want some now."

He was studying her intently. "It might make tonight go easier, Suzannah."

"Are you uncomfortable?" She was truly amazed at the thought. "I'm sorry, Aengus. I thought it was all going so well." Before he could respond, she added sincerely, "It's more difficult for you, because of all you went through in your first marriage. Would you like to be alone for a while?"

"That's the last thing I want," he chuckled, tucking the wine bottle back into the picnic basket. "We'll just save this for tomorrow, then. The last time I drank alone, I called myself Dennis Riordain and ordered a bride through the mail."

Suzannah laughed lightly. "It was such a lovely letter. Do you remember it?"

"No."

She knelt before the trunk, opened it, and freed the letter from between the pages of her worn leather-bound prayer book. "Meg gave it to me. Come and read it. It's a tribute to your love for your sons, and . . ." Catching herself, she smiled apologetically. "Listen to me. Married less than a day, and already I'm breaking my promise not to interfere." She replaced the letter carefully. "If you ever want to see it, it will be here in this book."

Before she stood, she rummaged until she'd located a soft white nightgown, embroidered with red roses along its high neck and cuffs. "Where shall I put my things, Aengus?"

"That can wait until morning, can't it?" Crossing

to join her, he took the folded nightgown from her and spread it open across the trunk. "All you need is this, or less. Or you can borrow my shirt again. It suited you—"

"It was too big for me and you know it, so stop your endless teasing." She smiled to soften the criticism. "It'll be time for bed before we know it, so I suppose we should talk about all that."

"I agree." Aengus put his hands on her waist and stared down at her with such an uncertain expression that she realized the issue of their sleeping arrangements had been weighing on him more heavily than she ever could have guessed.

Had he been concerned with how their celibate match would appear to the boys? Did he want them to see their stepmother and father in the same bed for the sake of their "illusions"? Suzannah found the thought both charming and reassuring. As much as he pretended otherwise, he truly wanted his sons to feel that their lives were normal. The Dennis Riordain letter had proven that, although the sobering conversation concerning Katherine's betrayal had shaken Suzannah's confidence just a bit.

"We'll do this however you want," he was informing her gently. "Just tell me what would make you feel most comfortable, and that's what I'll do."

Resisting the temptation to throw her arms around his neck and thank him for being such a wonderful father and husband, she decided instead to adopt the same serious, respectful tone he'd been using, and to echo the concerns she supposed he was having. "Tonight you and I can do whatever we want, but once the boys come home, it's important that we behave in an appropriate way. They may be children, but Luke seems to understand a little about what goes on between a man and his wife. They have their illusions, as you once said, and we should respect that.''

"But tonight," Aengus confirmed carefully, "we should enjoy being alone? That's what you're saying?'' When Suzannah nodded, he exhaled sharply. "Tell me, Mrs. Yates. How can I make it most enjoyable for you?''

"It's you who's making the larger sacrifice, Mr. Yates," she smiled. "Why don't you tell me how *I* can make it enjoyable for *you?*''

A slow, disbelieving grin spread across his features, and he seemed about to speak. Then he tipped her chin up, cupped her face in his hand, and brushed his lips across hers, much as Ben had done with Megan during the wedding ceremony. Overwhelmed by the feelings of gratitude and respect he was showering on her, she found herself responding in kind, despite the absurdity and futility of it all.

They shouldn't be kissing. Friends didn't kiss. It was blissful and innocent and fun, just for this one night—their one evening alone together before the boys came home and they had to behave forever—but it also seemed naughty. And confusing. And pointless.

But she had always wanted to kiss Aengus Yates this way. She had dreamed of it, and when he'd broken her heart, she had wept for the loss of it. Gentle, respectful, perfect kisses. If this was how he wanted to spend their one evening alone together, could it honestly be wrong?

Then the hand that still rested on her waist tightened, pulling her closer against him, and the hand on her chin moved to the bodice of her dress, fumbling at the laces while also caressing the soft, exposed, forbidden skin of her breasts, and suddenly she knew exactly why their "innocent" kissing was wrong. Pulling free without surrendering to the panic his touch had created, she gently explained, "Aengus, we mustn't. It was lovely, but we mustn't. Not ever again."

"It's fine, Suzy," he corrected, pulling her back with a firm but tender hand. "Don't be frightened—"

"I'm not frightened." She pulled free more sharply and backed away with a disapproving frown. "I'm being sensible. Can't you see where this is leading?"

He exhaled again, this time like a man in pain. "I was hoping it was leading to the bedroom."

"Aengus Yates!" She looked around wildly for her blanket, but it was nowhere to be found, and so she grabbed her nightgown instead and clasped it against her chest. "What a thing to say!"

"You'll be more comfortable in the dark—"

"Be quiet!" she wailed. "What are you thinking? You can't possibly think I'd go into a bedroom with you when you're in this state! What kind of girl do you think I am?"

"A married one," he growled. "I'm trying to be patient, Suzannah, but the time has come—"

"The time will never come!" She shrank from the flash of angry confusion in his eyes. "Honestly, Aengus, this is all a horrible misunderstanding. I never intended for us to be married this way. I thought you *knew* that. I thought you agreed to it. I thought you *preferred* it."

She tried desperately to smile despite the knot that was forming in her stomach. "Look at me, Aengus. Little Suzy Hennessy. If you'd wanted a child bride, you'd have married me years ago. Remember?"

When he simply stared, she continued frantically.

"It's a misunderstanding, Aengus. It's something we should have discussed—"

"Apparently."

She backed another step away. "We'll work it out somehow."

"And how will we do *that?*"

She winced but decided to stand her ground. "By remembering what's important. We married for the sake of the boys, did we not?"

"I thought we married for Megan's sake," he drawled.

"Well, that's true. For the boys and for Meg."

"Those were *your* reasons."

"And what were yours?" she demanded, then blanched at the dark, disrespectful look in his eyes. "Aengus Yates!"

He laughed then, an unfamiliar laugh, and shook his head in disgust before turning toward the front door.

"Where are you going?"

"To sleep in the stable. Be ready to leave at dawn."

"To leave? Back to town? Oh, no, Aengus. You can't mean to divorce me! Not until we've talked this through—"

"Divorce is for married people," he informed her icily. "Fortunately, we aren't that yet. Without a legal consummation, you're not a wife, you're just a pest. Same as you always were." With that, he strode toward the door, slamming it behind himself with such force she actually felt the floor reverberate.

Suzannah stared after him, whispering unhappily, "It's just a misunderstanding," despite the fact that it was clearly more than that. Somehow, in some unfathomable way, she had given this man the impression that she would surrender her virginity to him despite the fact that *she* didn't love *him*, and *he* didn't love *her*.

Men are different from women, she reminded herself numbly as she sank into the rocking chair in front of the fireplace. *You've heard it a thousand times, Suzannah Hennessy—I mean Yates!—but now you finally understand. They're blinded by wanting to do things with women—any women! Even women they consider pests, or children, or who knows what else? This is exactly why Mama warned you about them, and it's the reason you warned Meg about Ben! You should have listened to your own advice.*

She thought of the way Aengus had pawed at her breasts. Then she remembered the kiss at the wedding, and the way he'd drawn her against himself. And the way he'd looked at her that morning when she'd been lying, half naked, in his bed.

Drink the wine, Suzannah . . . Relax, Suzannah . . . Wear the nightie, Suzannah. . . . . What a beast he was! Why hadn't she seen the telltale signs? They'd been so obvious!

Then she remembered the most telling sign of all, and as she did, the tears that had been so absent now flooded from her eyes. He'd told her about Katherine. The secret he'd never shared with anyone else. He had trusted her with his most private and personal secret because he'd believed she was about to share with him her own most private and personal gift. She had told him he could trust her, and he had believed her.

And now he planned to divorce her. How could it all have gone so wrong so quickly? The boys would be miserable, living with a father who could barely stand the sight of them; and Suzannah would be miserable too, growing into a bitter old maid in San

Francisco with Meg and Ben; and Aengus would feel like a fool for the rest of his life for having trusted a woman again.

She simply couldn't let it happen. She had to salvage it all somehow, for everyone's sake. There had to be a compromise that would repay Aengus for his trust, preserve Suzannah's dignity and self-respect, and seal the marriage legally.

"Suzannah?"

"Oh, Aengus!" She jumped up and spun toward his voice, wiping her tears with the nightdress she still clutched in her hands. "I didn't hear you come back in."

"I shouldn't have raised my voice to you," he murmured contritely. "I've no excuse, except that I'm a weak and lonely man. And when a man such as myself believes a woman has agreed to . . . well, to be with him, it can be a terrible frustration when she changes her mind. I don't tell you this to excuse my behavior," he added hastily. "Just to explain it."

"You mustn't apologize," she sighed. "I didn't mean to mislead you, but I did, and I'm sorrier than I can say."

"Don't cry anymore," he pleaded. "Go and sleep in Luke's bed tonight, and try not to worry. Judge Winston will know how to correct all this in the morning."

She hesitated, then took his hand and held it tightly. "Can I ask you something, Aengus?"

"You're not going to propose again, are you?" he complained, only half in jest.

"In a way, I suppose I am."

"Suzannah—"

"No, listen. Please? I need to know what you would have said if I'd made myself clearer this morning. If

I'd told you I had no intention of sharing your bed. That you could go elsewhere for female companionship, and I'd never complain. That I was here to see to your other needs, but not that one. And that I'd take good care of your sons. Would you have agreed?''

She could see that he was about to explain the concept of "marriage" to her again and so she added hastily, "I'm proposing a legal marriage this time, Aengus. I understand now that I can't be the boys' true stepmother unless I'm legally married to their father, and I can't be legally married to you unless we c-c-consummate this union one time. I understand that clearly now, and I accept it. As long as *you* accept the fact that it will only be this one night between us.''

Aengus was studying her suspiciously. "What are you saying?''

"I'm saying, one time. Can it be clearer than that?''

He took a deep breath. "I'd like it a bit clearer, given our earlier misunderstanding. You're saying you'll be my bride tonight the way Megan will be with Ben?''

"Once. Is that enough for you?''

His expression softened. "Why are you doing this, Suzy? For two boys who aren't even yours? For a friend who would die before she'd see you make this kind of sacrifice? What are you thinking?''

"I'm thinking it's as much for us—for you and me—as it is for them," she confessed. "Do you remember when I told you you didn't need to tell me what happened with Katherine? I said you could take it to your grave, for all I cared.''

"And?''

"And that's what I intended for myself as well. To take my virginity to my grave with me. But you shared your secret with me, Aengus. And now I'll share what I have with you. It will be the way we seal our pact. One secret, one night, and a lifetime of trust. Can you accept it on those terms?''

She locked her eyes with his, certain he'd be overwhelmed by the solemnity of her latest proposal, but instead he was staring again, as though she'd lost her mind. Then to her mortification he threw back his head and began to roar with laughter.

"Aengus!"

"Taking your virginity to your grave, were you?'' He was barely able to speak through his chuckling. "I can guarantee you wouldn't have succeeded."

"Why not?''

"Come here and I'll show you."

"That's silly." She tried to glare, but failed. "Stop laughing at me!''

"I'm trying. But you make such ridiculous claims." Stepping close to her, he put his hands on her shoulders and held her steadily. "Haven't you wondered how it would be with us? Did you think you could sleep in the same bed with me, night after night, and not grow curious?''

"It's not enough to be curious. A girl like me has to be in love before she wonders about such things. It's different for a man—''

"Is it?''

"Isn't it?''

Aengus shrugged. "There was a time I was sure I'd love a girl before I married her, but twice I've proven myself wrong. This time, at least, I know what I'm getting.'' One hand moved behind her neck, caressing her gently. "I don't deserve you, Suzy. I know that for a fact. And I don't deserve this night with you, but I want it more than I've ever wanted anything. If you're still willing."

"One night," she reminded him weakly. "To make it legal. After that, you'll have to find your pleasure elsewhere, with my blessing."

"One night to make it legal," he echoed. "After that, I won't touch you again unless you ask me to."

"I won't ask you to," she assured him. "Not ever again."

"We'll see."

Her heart was beginning to pound in her chest. "You mustn't tease me about it. And you must never, never refer to it in the years to come. I'm trusting you, Aengus."

"You can trust me," he murmured huskily.

She could see it was happening again, only this time she fully recognized the signs. He wanted to have her—to pleasure himself in outlandish ways with her—and she wanted it too, although for different reasons. This night would make her a part of this family, in the eyes of the law, and in the eyes of Aengus Yates. And for all his teasing, it would bind them together—his secret in exchange for her maidenhood.

"Do you want to kiss me now, Aengus?"

"Aye. Are you ready this time?"

She smiled shyly, remembering how foolishly she'd offered to dedicate the evening to his enjoyment, not knowing what he had in mind for her. Now she knew, and she was ready. "Do whatever you'd like, Aengus. This is my wedding gift to you."

"Whatever I'd like?" He arched an eyebrow playfully. "Do you mean it this time?"

She nodded, and to prove it, took his hand and

moved it to the bodice of her dress. "Do what you want. I trust you."

His lighthearted mood vanished again, consumed by the passion that flamed in the dark blue depths of his eyes as his fingers played across her bare skin. "We should go into the bedroom."

"Whatever you want. Shall I change into my nightie first?"

"Not on my account." Bending down, he hoisted her into his arms, and while she felt a wave of panic, she didn't even consider protesting. Instead, she slipped her arms around his neck and tried to smile through her apprehension. It helped that his face— so familiar and so handsome—was a face she had once loved with all her heart. *Remember those days,* she counseled herself silently. *And remember why you're doing this tonight.*

Chapter Seven

In what seemed like one giant stride, Suzannah's bridegroom carried her to the bedroom and deposited her on top of the coverlet. Then before she could decide whether to sit or lie down, he was stripping off his shirt, revealing a bronzed, muscled chest, and arms that rippled with every move. It was a glorious sight, and she might have taken a few moments to enjoy it, but when his fingers moved to the waistband of his trousers, she had no choice but to avert her eyes and scurry under the covers, pink gown and all.

"You're overdressed, Mrs. Yates," he teased when he climbed into bed and snuggled up beside her. "Shall I do the honors?"

"I'll do it," she assured him, but her nervous fingers couldn't work the laces, and soon his warm hand covered her own, urging it aside.

As he unfastened the bodice, he began to nuzzle her neck, and the warmth of his breath and lips caused ripples of delight to flood through her from head to toe. Then he whispered, "Shall we kiss for a while first?" and she nodded gratefully, knowing that this, at least, was something familiar she could do that would please him.

As he'd done at the wedding, he began with a gentle tasting of her lips that deepened quickly, until his tongue was thrusting hungrily into her gasping, appreciative mouth. This time, however, his hands were making demands as well, and when he had freed her breasts completely, his fingers went to work on them, teasing and playing until the peaks had hardened with desire. His mouth abandoned hers then, traveling quickly down to tug and taste at her nipples until she thought she might go mad with embarrassed delight.

Then he was kissing her mouth again, and this time her own greedy tongue joined in, while her fingers laced themselves into his hair, pulling his mouth more completely against her own. Never had she imagined herself so alive with need, and she wanted to kiss him forever, but knew his thoughts were concentrating elsewhere now. His hands were feverishly pushing her gown lower and lower on her torso, and she wanted to plead with him to stop—to be content with the kissing and the feel of her nipples against his bare chest—but it was already too late. One hand had forced its way under the fabric and between her legs, and as she wriggled in frantic protest, his fingertips grazed the tender, wet folds she had insanely granted him permission to invade.

"Aengus, no," she begged. "Not yet."

He stopped immediately, withdrawing his hand while lifting his head to gaze down at her. She expected to see annoyance, or at least frustration, but there was only desire mingled with apology in his deep blue eyes. "It was going well until then?"

She blushed frantically. "Very well. I just didn't expect you to touch me there. I mean," she corrected sheepishly, "with your hand. I knew about the other. But," she eyed him desperately, "I'm not ready for that yet either."

His smile was the one that had lingered so stubbornly in her memory. Slow and steady and warm, as though they had all the time in the world, and she began to relax a bit. "I like the kissing, Aengus."

"So do I. It's the gown I don't like. It's forcing us to struggle, do you see?"

She nodded and, without unlocking her gaze from his, she inched free of him, brought the coverlet back up to her neck, then reached under it to tug and wriggle until she had completely shed the bulky gown and undergarments. Then she moistened her lips and smiled. "I'm naked, Aengus."

"Come here, and we'll kiss a while more."

"I want to, but . . ." She wondered if he'd laugh if she told him how she feared the feel of their bodies together now—now that there was no fabric to shield her from the hard, male member that had been straining against her during their kissing.

"Give me your hand, Suzy."

She smiled uncertainly and shook her head. "Not yet."

"Do you know what I think?" He edged closer, a reassuring smile on his lips. "I think you're making too much of it."

"I don't think so."

He was clearly trying not to chuckle. "You've seen it before, when you watched me swimming years ago—"

"It wasn't like this," she scolded.

"Because you weren't like this," he grinned. "Now you're a woman, and nature's just trying to take its course. Give me your hand, and I'll make the introduction, and then we can kiss some more. How does that sound?"

It sounded wonderful, to have their mouths locked together, and their chests rubbing against each other, and their legs tangling beneath the coverlet, and so she reached forward shyly to stroke his cheek, then lightly down his chest and down toward his stomach. Aengus was watching her, as though fascinated by the progress; then the first hint of impatience showed in his expression and he covered her hand with his own and dragged it gently downward to his rock-hard erection.

Startled, she tried to pull her hand free, but Aengus held it firmly in place and as he did so, he lowered his mouth over hers again, and suddenly it all made sense. Even the size of it, huge as it seemed, made sense to her, as though her body knew instinctively how much pleasure he could give her with it. As her hand began to explore, Aengus groaned and again slid his fingers between her legs. And now she understood that too, and while she still resisted his attempts to urge her thighs apart, she also craved the moment when he would succeed.

"It's time, Suzannah." His voice was low and gravelly. "You have to trust me now more than ever."

"I do," she gasped. "More than I ever dreamed I could."

"You feel so good," he moaned. "So soft. So ready for me."

"I'm ready," she echoed. "More than ready."

The words seemed to empower him, and with one final kiss, he pressed her thighs apart and began to

pleasure himself between them while his fingers
probed gently, scouting the wet folds for the intrusion
to come.

And all Suzannah could think was that if for some
tragic reason the huge erection didn't fit where it
was supposed to go, she would die of frustration and
shame. Or perhaps she'd die anyway! Her heart was
pounding so hard, and Aengus's breath had grown
so ragged, she thought they *both* might succumb to
heart failure there in the bed if they didn't just try
to make it happen soon.

"Suzannah," he groaned.

"I know." She took his member in her hand again
and urged it toward its target. "I understand, Aengus.
Don't wait any longer."

"I don't want to hurt you . . ." Even as he spoke,
he began, with maddening gentleness, to enter her.
One tentative thrust, then another, more forceful one
that made her gasp.

"I'm fine," she assured him quickly. "Don't stop."

He nodded and began to pump, still slowly and
gently, but with a rhythm that told her it was too late
to turn back, even when a raw moment of resistance
signaled that she had truly become the man's bride.
"I'm fine," she whispered again, and to prove it,
she grasped his face between her hands and pulled
his mouth down to her own for a searing, love-starved
kiss.

His thrusts, still rhythmic, grew more and more
demanding, and he began to groan with hedonistic
abandon, as though the sensations he had discovered
at her core were driving him insane with pleasure.
Then, as Suzannah clung to his neck, frightened and
fascinated, he completely exploded within her, and

a single, final groan confirmed that his madness was drawing to an end.

Aengus continued to move, savoring her for a few seconds more, before raising his head to smile sheepishly down at her. "Thank you, Suzannah."

She nodded shyly.

"I intended to be gentle with you—"

"You were. It was fine."

Brushing his lips across hers, he pulled his satiated member free, then began to gently massage the damp, raw folds that had given him such enjoyment. "Let me take care of you now."

His concern for her discomfort pleased her, and while she didn't feel at all sore, she closed her eyes and allowed him to soothe her, knowing that somehow it made him feel less beastly for what he had done. Although it seemed unlikely that she could relax while a man was touching her in so intimate a spot, she found that her trust for him was indeed complete, and she actually sighed aloud as his fingertips stroked and petted.

"That's right, Suzy," he murmured into her ear. "Does that feel good?"

"It feels wonderful. You didn't hurt me, Aengus," she explained softly. "But it's sweet of you to take care of me this way."

When his fingers soothed deeper, she smiled self-consciously. "It almost feels naughtier than the other, Aengus."

"Does it?"

"Yes, isn't that silly? Oh . . ." A sharp, delicious surge had come from nowhere, and she had to force herself to take a more even breath before admitting wistfully, "I'm fine now, Aengus. You don't need to . . . Mmmm . . ."

He nuzzled her neck for a moment, then moved his mouth to her nipple and pulled, playfully but gently, with his teeth. It caused another shock wave, radiating all the way down her torso, and without thinking she arched against his fingers in a successful attempt to prolong the stab of pleasure.

As embarrassed as she was to realize Aengus had probably noticed her behavior, she was even more ashamed of the single, incredible thought that was racing through her mind. *If only he was still hard and inside me now . . .*

"Suzannah?"

"Kiss me," she pleaded, and when he rolled on top of her, she gasped with relief at the erect, huge feel of him against her stomach. Reaching her hand to stroke him, she said softly, "I'm ready now for sure, Aengus."

"Ready to be kissed?"

"Aengus . . ."

"I know, Suzy. I know." Confidently separating her thighs with his hand, he began to thrust himself into her without waiting for further permission, and while the movements were still gentle, there was more insistence. More authority.

And Suzannah was a part of the motion this time, moving her hips to welcome and encourage him, giddy with the waves of pleasure his every thrust evoked. She was conscious of every sensation now— the feel of his hands on her buttocks, the warmth of his breath on her neck, the roughness of his tongue and the softness of his lips. The delicious frustration of wanting him deeper than deep, harder than hard, hotter than hot.

And then there was nothing but wave after wave of cataclysmic ecstasy, and a grateful, greedy Suzannah clung wildly to her husband's neck, knowing from the mindlessness of his pumping that he too was in the throes of an incredibly perfect release.

Arms and legs entwined, they stayed together, still and satiated, for what seemed like hours before Aengus murmured, "You are an amazing female, Mrs. Yates."

She pulled back, just enough to stroke his cheek with her fingertips. "Is that how it always is?"

"That's the best of it."

Still a bit dazed, she drew her hand down along his shoulder, then began to lazily trace the muscles of his arm. "I'll always remember this, Aengus. I'll always be glad it was you who did it."

"You must be exhausted. And starved, for good measure. Tell me what I can do for you now."

What could he do for her? For an instant, she actually considered giving him an honest answer to his painfully innocent question. *You can act like the old Aengus again, out of bed as well as in. Hoist Johnny on your shoulders, and praise Luke to his face. Tell them you love them despite what Katherine did. Then fall madly in love with me, and court me as though your very life depended on it. Don't give me any choice but to fall in love with you again. Then bring me flowers every day and make love to me every night, and I'll never ask you for another thing for the rest of our lives.*

"Suzannah?"

"I'm not hungry. But I am a little tired."

"Sleep, then." He pulled the coverlet over her, then brushed his fingertips across her cheek. "You're the prettiest sight I've ever seen."

"And you're the handsomest," she admitted wistfully. "Could you find my nightdress for me before you go?"

He hesitated, but only for a moment, before nodding. "Where shall I sleep, Suzannah?"

"In the boys' room, for tonight at least. If you don't mind."

"I don't mind at all." He studied her intently before adding, "Get some rest. We'll talk in the morning."

"I'll be in a dreadful mood," she warned.

Aengus chuckled ruefully. "I'm sure that's true enough."

She watched as he ambled into the outer room, returning in less than a minute with her nightdress in one hand and a plate of food in the other. "I'll just leave this chicken on the bedstand in case you get hungry later."

"Thank you." She clutched the coverlet up to her chin with one hand while reluctantly extending the other into the open air to accept the gown from him.

His blue eyes twinkled at the show of modesty. "So? That's how it's to be?"

"Yes. That's how it's to be."

"But you'll always remember how you liked it, and you'll always be glad it was me who did it to you?"

"Go away," she suggested with an exaggerated yawn. Then she closed her eyes and snuggled into the bed, hoping he'd take the hint and leave without making any further jests at her expense. After a moment, she peeked out to discover that her husband had indeed left her alone in their wedding bed, just as she'd asked. With a confused sigh, she slipped into the soft nightgown and cuddled back under the covers, knowing she'd sleep easily. Knowing she'd dream, as she did every night, of being Mrs. Aengus Yates. Only this time it would be true.

When Suzannah awoke, daylight was streaming through the window of her husband's bedroom, and she smiled despite all the confusion of the night before. What a glorious place to live out the rest of her days! The air smelled of rainwater and pine. And coffee. Which meant that Aengus Yates was already prowling the house, waiting for her to come and talk to him about the night before. Fortunately, she was more than ready for that particular discussion.

Of course, it would help if she was properly dressed, and so she peeked cautiously into the outer room and was relieved when he was nowhere in sight. Scampering to her trunk, she gathered up what she needed, grabbed a pitcher of fresh water from the sinkboard, and hurried back into his room.

When she emerged again, she was wearing her favorite high-necked green gingham, along with the buttery soft ankle-high boots Russell Braddock had had specially made for her in Chicago. She smiled as she thought of the marriage broker. What would he say if he knew she was married already? And to Aengus Yates, of all people!

There'd been so many times she'd wondered what her future would hold. Now, overnight, she had become a wife and a mother. There was strength in that, and she would draw from it when she faced her husband for their first full day of married life.

Still, when he burst through the front door, a cheerful, satisfied grin on his face, it was all she could do to keep from running back to his room and slamming the door behind her.

"Good morning, Mrs. Yates. You're as pretty today as you were when I left you last night."

"Good morning, Aengus. Any sign of the boys or Megan yet?"

"I imagine Megan and Ben will stay in bed late this morning." He arched an eyebrow mischievously. "Speaking of which, how are you feeling? I'm hoping you're not too sore."

"What if I am?" she sniffed. "I have the rest of my life to heal. Do I need to remind you we agreed not to refer to all that, ever again?"

"All what?"

She couldn't bear the smug look on his face, as though he believed her cooperation in the success of their wedding night would propel her into a lifetime of naughty misbehavior with a man she didn't love! Men!

"It's obvious you have something on your mind," she informed him haughtily. "Feel free to say it. We have no secrets between us."

"The truth?"

"Of course."

Aengus folded his arms across his chest and studied her openly. "I'm thinking you've had a taste of it now, and you'll be wanting more."

"You're mistaken. And you're a hypocrite. You agreed to one time—"

"And you helped yourself to a second time," he grinned. "I suppose that's when I decided there was hope for a third."

"A second—?" She bit her lip to keep from uttering an impolite word. "It was all one night, Aengus Yates, and you know it. That was our agreement."

"Our agreement was to consummate the marriage.

The rest was your doing. Not that I'm complaining. It was the finest night of my life."

"Well, I hope you enjoyed it, because it's the last time you'll have a fine night under this roof." She flushed and added lamely, "I knew you'd find a way to tease me about this, Aengus. Must you always be disrespectful? I honored our bargain. All I'm asking in return is that you allow me my dignity."

He stepped closer and smiled encouragingly. "When we made that bargain, you didn't know what you were bargaining away. Now that you know, there's no dishonor in changing your mind. In admitting that you have needs, same as a man. You're my wife—"

The sound of horses' hooves beating against the road distracted him and he frowned pointedly. "Who could that be?"

"Megan and Ben!" Suzannah crowed. "Do you see, Aengus? We aren't all barbarians. They've come for a visit—"

He had moved to the doorway and now announced sourly, "It's Luke and Johnny. I thought the Winstons would have more sense than to send them back so early in the day. Me being such a barbarian and all," he added darkly.

"Promise you won't be gruff," Suzannah pleaded. "They're probably so happy to have this stepmother business resolved. They were fearing she'd be an ugly, unpleasant stranger too, I'm sure, just as you were."

"Ugly and unpleasant by day, but in the dark—"

"Aengus Yates!" Disgusted with his innuendo and attitude, she literally shoved him out of her way in her haste to reach the porch, where she waved cheerfully to her stepsons. This was the arrangement, after all, was it not? Suzannah would shower the boys with love, and Aengus would be ornery and unpleasant. It was time she abandoned any secret hopes of changing all that. She would concentrate instead on being the best stepmother the world had ever known.

"Suzannah!" Johnny didn't stop running until he'd knocked her right off her feet. "Are you our new mama now?"

"It's all legal," Aengus drawled from the doorway. "I saw to that detail personally."

She turned to glare at him, then hugged the child close. "Isn't it wonderful? We'll never be apart again."

"It's good," the child sighed. "Does it mean we never have to sleep at the judge's house again?"

"I can't guarantee that," Suzannah smiled. "But I'll do my best to protect you from lumpy beds and salty food."

Johnny giggled happily. "Even Ben Steele wouldn't sleep there anymore. He moved to the hotel, and he took Megan with him."

"She's his wife," Aengus explained coolly. "Wives always sleep where their husbands sleep, John. That's how it works."

"I know. Luke told me." Johnny sent his father a vaguely accusatory glance, then turned back to Suzannah and whispered, "You're not hurt or nothing, are you?"

"Of course not, silly."

"What exactly did your brother tell you?" Aengus demanded. Then he stomped past the two, muttering, "Never mind. I'll ask him myself."

"Aengus, don't scold him," Suzannah protested, jumping to her feet and half dragging Johnny by the hand as she trailed her grim-faced husband. "If you'd spoken to them about it yourself, the way any other father would, they wouldn't have to rely on silly gossip from other boys."

Aengus whirled, his blue eyes blazing with annoyance. "Are you criticizing me again? I thought that was part of our danged bargain."

"We agreed you'd let me raise the boys my own way," she countered unhappily. "I can't bear it when you're harsh with them."

"Then you shouldn't have come."

She stared, unable to reconcile this hurtful man with the gentle, patient lover from the night before. In her heart, she knew he was being torn apart by the anger he felt toward Katherine, but how could he allow that anger—righteous as it was—to ruin his relationships with his own flesh and blood?

"Pa's right."

She turned her gaze to Luke, and winced at what she saw. The same anger. The same stubborn refusal to salvage something—anything—from the unfair hand that life had dealt him. He was Aengus, through and through, and the thought sent a shiver of foreboding through her spine.

"You should go to San Francisco with Megan and Ben," the boy continued woodenly. "We'll be fine for a while without you."

She could see that Luke was beyond her grasp for the moment, as was Aengus. But Johnny's bottom lip was quivering, and so she drew herself up and announced haughtily, "It's a little late for that, don't you think? I'm Suzannah Yates now, for better or for worse. I have two sons I intend to love forever, and a husband I'm willing to respect if he gives me half a reason to. I'm not going anywhere, so you'd better get used to having me here."

"I'm used to it already," Johnny murmured. "Don't send her away, Pa. *Please?*"

She saw a flicker of something in Aengus's eyes. Remorse? Pain? Despair? Whatever it was, it was enough for now, and so she knelt to hug Johnny close. "Don't worry, sweetie. No one's going anywhere."

Aengus took a step closer to Luke and spoke his name in a firm but quiet voice. The boy returned his gaze for a long moment, then nodded for the man to continue.

"I don't want you filling your brother's head with nonsense about my marriage to Suzannah. Do you understand?"

Luke shrugged his slender shoulders. "It wasn't nonsense, Pa. It was the truth."

"I see. And what is the truth?"

"That I'll kill you if you ever hurt Suzannah."

As Suzannah's heart crumbled in her breast, she waited for Aengus's reply, knowing that it would make things even worse, but powerless to intervene.

But to her surprise, her husband's response was even and respectful. "I won't hurt Suzannah, Luke. You have my word on that."

When the boy nodded and turned away to finish unsaddling the horses, Suzannah felt the world spin, just a bit. What had just happened? A twenty-seven-year-old man and a little boy, one-fourth his age and size, had just come to an understanding, the way two grown strangers might. Under other circumstances, it might have seemed comical, but between father and son it was cold and disturbing. She almost wished

Aengus had punished the boy for his insolent words, even though they'd been said in Suzannah's defense. A boy shouldn't speak that way to his father, and a father shouldn't allow it. But nothing was as it should be with these two, and she was at a loss to know how to fix it.

"I'll be in the stable if you want me, Suzannah."

She didn't bother responding to him, or even checking his expression to see if he'd meant the remark as a reproach. She was too busy wondering what to say to Johnny about the scene they had just witnessed. Her first true challenge as a stepmother.

And Johnny seemed to know what was coming, so he prompted her. "Luke sassed Pa."

"Yes, he did."

"That was bad."

"Yes, it was," Suzannah nodded. "It was very disrespectful."

"Pa didn't get mad, though."

"No. He didn't get mad."

The boy waited, patient but clearly expecting further explanation, and so she decided to give it a try. "Your father and Luke are too much alike. That makes it hard for them to argue with each other. And it makes it hard for them to apologize to each other, even when they know full well they've done something wrong. I think that's why your father won't make Luke apologize."

Johnny nodded slowly. "That's what I think too."

"Really?"

"Luke's not mean, but he's mean to Pa. And Pa's not mean, but he's mean to us." He paused for a moment, then asked softly, "Why is he mean to *me*, Suzannah?"

"Oh, Johnny." She kissed his cheek, then cuddled his tiny body closer. "Do you know who Aengus Yates is meanest to? Himself. He doesn't allow himself to enjoy being a father, even though being a father is the most joyous thing a man can do. I don't understand it, and I don't approve of it. And I don't intend to allow it to continue. I'll find some way to make it all right, I promise."

"Are you going to cry, Suzannah?"

"No, sweetie. Even if I wanted to, there isn't time. We're having guests for dinner tonight."

"Megan and Ben?"

"That's right."

"Will he give us money to go away again?"

"If we're fortunate, he'll give your father money to go away," she guessed. When the boy gasped, she amended her statement contritely. "I meant that as a jest, Johnny, but it wasn't a very nice one. Your father's not going anywhere. Not ever again. I'd never wish for that."

"But we might leave, in a year. That's what Luke says."

"That's what Luke says now. But a year's a long time. Anything can change. And I promise, we won't want to leave at all by then."

"Good."

"Do you want to come help me in the kitchen?"

Johnny winced and wriggled free of her embrace. "I will if you want. Or I'll go help Luke with the raft if you want me to do that."

Suzannah grinned. "You should absolutely go and help your brother. When you get hungry, come home and I'll fix you something yummy."

She watched until he'd disappeared into the woods, then forced her thoughts to turn to the dinner she should be preparing for her visitors and for her new family.

"You're finally here! I feel like I haven't seen you in years!" Suzannah threw her arms around her friend and squeezed her tightly, then turned to Ben Steele and eyed him with pretend disapproval. "You look much too pleased with yourself, sir."

Ben grinned and kissed her cheek. "There's something different about you, Mrs. Yates. Aengus has been busy, I see."

Suzannah flushed and pointed to the stable. "He's out there. Go find him and ask him yourself."

"In other words, you and Megan want to compare our performances. Be kind, darling. I did my best."

Megan giggled sweetly and raised herself onto tiptoes to brush her lips across his. "Fetch Aengus, but hurry back. I'll miss you dreadfully." When he'd sauntered away, she added to Suzannah, "We haven't been apart more than five minutes at a time since the wedding. He's been so attentive." Her gray eyes twinkled impishly. "Tell me about Aengus. Has it been a dream come true?"

"More or less. Was Ben a gentleman?"

"I don't know what a gentleman is anymore," Megan confessed with a rueful laugh. "I only know Ben's perfect in every way. I'm so grateful to you, Suzannah, for helping me see that."

"Come inside and stop gushing," Suzannah teased, ushering her onto the porch.

"Where are Luke and Johnny?"

"They were too hungry to wait, so they've already

eaten. I'm sure they're working on that raft of theirs—they'll do that right up to sundown, I suppose—and then they'll be eager to visit with you before bed. You're late," she added more solemnly than she'd intended.

Megan caught her friend by the elbow. "Let's not go in just yet, Suzannah. I'm dying to hear what you thought of . . . of last night."

The hostess took a deep breath, remembering how tricky these moments could be with Megan, because of the girl's insistence on looking for signs that she was a "fallen woman" like her mother. With that in mind, she admitted honestly, "I liked it more than I thought I would."

Megan exhaled in relief. "Wasn't it wonderful? Ben was so gentle and tender and patient."

"Aengus was gentle too."

Megan's eyes twinkled. "Last night, at *the* most inappropriate moment, I remembered how we used to peek at Aengus while he was swimming. How we used to marvel at his body. Especially—"

"I remember," Suzannah interrupted sharply. "I hope you didn't share that memory with your husband."

Megan collapsed against a post in a fit of laughter. "We're ruined, Suzannah. Who could have thought it could be so wonderful?"

Suzannah grinned in defeat. "Look at yourself. You're positively giddy. Didn't you get any sleep at all?"

"We napped in between, but never for long. I don't think we really fell asleep until dawn, and even then—"

"Megan Braddock!"

"It's Megan Steele now." She studied her friend cautiously. "Tell me what's wrong. Did it not go well with you and Aengus?"

"It was fine," Suzannah hedged.

"Fine?" Megan seemed aghast at the concept. "Shall I ask Ben to speak with Aengus about it?"

"Pardon?"

"Well . . ." She blushed prettily. "As we suspected, Ben has been with many women. I wish it had been otherwise, but I believe it may have benefited me last night, because Ben knew just what to do."

"Aengus knew what to do too," Suzannah assured her. "He has two sons, Meg. Where do you suppose *they* came from?"

"I didn't mean it as an insult." Megan took Suzannah's hand in her own and squeezed it contritely. "I was just thinking that Katherine was so cold. She couldn't have been very receptive. And so Aengus might—"

"Might need instruction from Ben? Honestly, Megan, I can see you're going to be insufferable now. Wait until I tell Aengus you have doubts about his manhood."

"Suzannah, don't!"

"Here they come now. Shall we ask them to drop their pants so we can—"

"Suzannah Hennessy!"

Suzannah grinned. "Do you promise to stop bragging about Ben? And it's Suzannah Yates now, remember."

"Suzannah Yates," Megan marveled. "You always said you'd marry him, and now you have. Are you happy, Suzannah?"

"Yes," she lied. "Happier than I've ever been. But not as happy as you, of course, given that I'm married to a eunuch by comparison."

Megan shrieked with laughter again, and Ben, who was just stepping onto the porch, was more than happy to allow her to lean against him. "Has Suzannah been telling you all about her wedding night?"

"That's right, Ben Steele," Suzannah sniffed. "But she didn't believe a word of it. She's convinced it's all about playing cards."

He grinned malevolently. "I should have known you'd take the romance out of it, Mrs. Yates. Aengus, I feel sorrier for you by the minute."

"You've no idea," Aengus grumbled. "Suzannah, did you still want me to open that wine?"

"Yes, please." She winced when Aengus proceeded into the house without a backward glance. Hadn't he noticed how Megan and Ben were behaving? Cooing and cuddling, as though they couldn't bear to be without one another's touch for even a minute. If Aengus wasn't careful, Megan would suspect the truth about Suzannah's marriage of convenience, and the whole bargain would be off!

Hurrying her visitors into the dining area, she demanded brightly, "Are you hungry? I've been cooking all day."

"I'm starved," Ben assured her, nibbling at his bride's neck as though to illustrate the point. Then he commandeered a chair at the dining table and pulled Megan into his lap. "It smells delicious, Suzannah."

"Ben, behave," Megan giggled. "I need to help Suzannah."

"Aengus will help me. Just settle your husband down somehow while we serve you."

Moving to the sideboard, where Aengus was wielding a corkscrew, she whispered, "Can you believe how silly they are?"

When he scowled without answering, she insisted, "For heaven's sake, don't sulk. I want her to believe we're in love the way they are—"

"That isn't love, Suzannah," he grumbled. "It's a wife taking care of her husband."

A peal of laughter from Megan illustrated the point, and Suzannah smiled apologetically. "They're obnoxious, but they'll be gone soon. Won't you please just pretend we're as happy as they are? If you do," she added warily, "I'll do something for you in return."

"Something?"

"Whatever you want," she offered. Her cheeks heated quickly, and she checked to see if Megan was watching, but Ben was keeping his bride occupied and so Suzannah added carefully, "That's fair, isn't it?"

He cocked his head to the side and studied her. "Is this to be the way of it? I'm not complaining. Just asking."

"The way of it?" She frowned when his meaning hit her. "This will be the last time, I assure you. To thank you for your cooperation."

"Well, then . . ." He grinned mischievously. "If you want to convince them, you should make a fuss over me, the way Megan does over Ben."

Suzannah grimaced but nodded. "As long as you know it doesn't mean anything."

"It never does."

She stared for a moment, wondering if he truly believed that; then she decided she couldn't afford to care, and so she wrapped her arms around his neck and gave him a quick but intimate kiss.

"Very nice." He nuzzled her neck appreciatively. "I don't think they noticed, though. Try again."

"Bring the wine," she directed haughtily. "And try not to embarrass me."

As Aengus distributed the glasses, Suzannah served stew and biscuits, then tried to take a seat. But her husband had other ideas, and to her embarrassed delight, he pulled her into his lap, just as Ben had done with Megan. Then he raised his glass to their company. "A toast. To Suzannah Yates. The prettiest cook in all the Sierras."

"To Suzannah," Ben echoed, tasting the wine with an expert flair.

Megan smiled and moved her glass to tap against Suzannah's. "To my best and closest friend. If only I could cook as well as she."

"You have other talents," Ben assured her fondly.

"That's true," Aengus smiled. "She has the voice of an angel. Have you heard it, Ben?"

Before Suzannah could warn the men against this course, Megan's proud husband turned to beam at his bride. "Is that true, darling? Perhaps you'll sing something for us later this evening."

"And would you like me to dance as well?" she snipped.

"Huh?"

"For heaven's sake, Meg," Suzannah intervened. "Why do you always assume—?"

"Could we change the subject?" Megan scowled. "Ben? Didn't you want to discuss our travel plans with Suzannah? So she wouldn't be shocked when we left?''

''Your travel plans?'' Suzannah shrank from the thought. ''It's so pretty here, don't you think? And Bent Creek needs a bigger hotel. Ben. Couldn't you find a way to stay?''

''There's no money here, Suzy,'' Aengus explained quickly. ''Don't make him feel worse than he does. He knows how close the two of you are.''

''San Francisco isn't so far away,'' Ben added.

Megan's soft eyes were filling with tears, and so Suzannah interceded quickly. ''We're being silly, Meg. It's clear that Ben will do whatever you ask, so you'll simply ask him to bring you here every year. At springtime. On the anniversary of our weddings. And again at Christmastime Won't that be lovely?''

''I suppose.''

''And this beast''—she paused to elbow Aengus— ''will bring me and the boys to San Francisco. And so it's settled. Don't you agree?''

Ben smiled at her gratefully. ''What will we do without you, Suzannah?''

''You'll behave, or I'll be on your doorstep.''

The gambler grinned toward Aengus. ''How did you ever turn her down the first time?''

''Pardon? Oh, that?'' He chuckled, then nuzzled Suzannah playfully. ''She was pretty then too, only in a different way. And so I didn't realize the mistake I was making.''

''Tell us about it. The pint-sized marriage proposal,'' Ben insisted. ''I've heard the females' version, but I'd like to hear how it really went.''

Suzannah turned to Aengus, eyeing him with a combination of threat and plea that made him grin more mischievously than ever. ''Imagine a pretty little child not taller than this table. I doubt she even came up to my waist. In fact, I had to look around for a moment just to see where the bratty little voice was coming from—"

"Aengus!"

The husband continued unabashed. "Have you ever seen my bride when she puts one hand on her hip and points the other one at your face like you're a common criminal?"

Ben nodded vigorously. "Unfortunately, yes. You left out the part where she stomps her foot."

Megan had been dissolving into laughter against her bridegroom's chest. "They don't mean it, Suzannah."

"I remember her exact words," Aengus grinned. "She said, 'I can see you're getting restless, Aengus Yates, but you'd better wait for me. I'm not much to look at now, but shapely women run in my family, and I intend to do a lot of growing in the next few years.'"

"He remembers every word," Megan marveled. "Isn't that sweet, Suzannah?"

She nodded, hoping Aengus couldn't see how impressed and confused she was.

Ben chuckled fondly. "She was right about that. She's just about the most shapely female I've ever seen, and I've seen quite a few."

"I'm sure Meg appreciates hearing *that*," Suzannah chided. "Honestly, Ben Steele, I'm beginning to regret matching you to my friend."

"So now it's you who matched us?" Ben laughed. "The truth is, it was a gentleman in Chicago I have to thank for meeting my darling Megan."

"Oh?"

"It's true, Suzannah." Megan smiled. "Ben won

full passage from New York to San Francisco in a card game. And the man he won it from said to him . . . What was it, Ben?''

''He said, 'May this ticket change your life for the better.' And it did.''

''Do you see, Suzannah? We both have romantic stories of how we met. You loving Aengus since childhood, and Ben winning me in a poker game.''

Suzannah smiled at her friend. ''And to think you almost let your uncle match you with a stranger.''

''And so did you. What were we thinking?''

''See here,'' Aengus grinned. ''I'll not have Dennis Riordain maligned in my presence.''

''Nor will I,'' Ben echoed, lifting his wineglass high before their eyes. ''To Dennis Riordain.''

''To Dennis Riordain,'' they repeated heartily. Then Suzannah and Megan exchanged sheepish glances and gingerly downed their first, tentative mouthfuls of forbidden alcohol.

The rest of the meal went by like a dream. Aengus cuddled Suzannah against himself as though she were precious cargo to be guarded with his life, and Megan beamed like a girl whose every wish had come true. Suzannah was careful not to lock eyes too frequently with Ben, knowing, as Megan had so aptly put it, that he was ''the brother she'd never had,'' and might sense the uncertainty in her cheerful facade.

Still, all in all, the performances were flawless, and when Megan and her husband left for Bent Creek, Suzannah knew they believed both couples would live happily ever after. That had to be enough, for as Suzannah had learned that afternoon during Luke's confrontation with Aengus, the situation at the Yates ranch was hopeless, unless she could somehow convince Aengus to change. She would give anything for that, including a lifetime of lovemaking. Perhaps even especially that.

And so she would try to get up the nerve to suggest just that before the night was through.

Chapter Eight

While Aengus conducted his final check of the stock for the night, Suzannah tucked her sleepy stepsons into bed, changed into her lightweight nightgown, and nervously took down her hair so that it hung like a golden veil around her shoulders. Then she turned down the lamp, but not so much that she wouldn't make an impression on him when he entered the bedroom. Then she waited for him, her pulse racing all the while.

"Suzannah?"

She moved to peek through the bedroom doorway. "I'm in here. Keep your voice down or you'll wake the boys."

When a slow, deadly smile spread across his features, she couldn't help smiling in return. It was so silly, really. Just the natural way married couples everywhere behaved, but somehow Aengus made it seem like more. Or perhaps it was she who made it seem so momentous, by claiming that each time was the last. If so, that would change shortly. The prospect made her shiver with excitement.

"So?" He closed the door before surveying her admiringly. "Look at yourself. Prettier than ever, and not wrapped in a confounded blanket either."

"We're married. And I'm very fond of you. Why would I need a blanket?"

"We'll have to invite Ben and Megan to dinner every night," he teased as he began to strip off his clothing.

Suzannah forced herself to watch, although she kept her eyes high on his chest. She even considered following his lead and taking off everything herself. He'd never really seen her naked—at least, not naked standing—and she knew it would amuse him greatly. On the other hand, she could clearly save that particular amusement for another time. From the expression on his face, she had done more than enough for now.

Stepping to within inches of her, Aengus pulled her close and began to trail his lips along her neck, murmuring, "We're husband and wife, Suzannah. There's no reason we shouldn't enjoy each other this way every night. If it's romance you want, I could try—"

"No!" She touched his cheek in apology. "It's not romance I want, Aengus. At least, that's not what I'm asking for tonight."

"I know exactly what you're asking for tonight," he grinned, lifting her off her feet and setting her on the bed. Stretching over her, he slid his hand up between her thighs. "I thought for sure you'd be skittish again, but here you are. More than ready—"

"Shhh . . ." Covering his mouth with her hand, she insisted, "This is nice, Aengus, but there's something else I want, too. Something infinitely more wonderful than romance. If you would offer me that, I would give you anything you wanted in return, for the rest of our lives.''

"What is it?'' he demanded eagerly. "If it's within my power, it's yours.''

"If you could find it in your heart to be gentle and loving to your sons—''

His angry curse shocked her into silence, and she watched in helpless misery as he rolled to his feet and pulled his pants over his long, lean legs. "You'll never let it go, will you? I should have known that from the start.''

"But, Aengus—''

"I won't bother you again, Suzannah. Keep your precious body to yourself, along with your opinions and your infernal nagging, or we'll be getting ourselves that divorce we talked about last night.''

"They're your sons—''

"Enough!''

"Wait!'' She ran to block the door as tears began to stream down her cheeks. "I know it's too complicated for you and Luke right now. But what about Johnny?''

"What about him?''

"I saw something today. I know it wasn't just my imagination. There's some feeling there, isn't there? Feelings that aren't tainted by Katherine's betrayal.'' When he didn't scowl or protest, she continued desperately. "Perhaps it's because he's so young. So innocent. So sweet and blameless in every way. Or perhaps it's just because he doesn't resemble Katherine as much as Luke does. Johnny looks so much like you—''

"Does he?''

"Yes. He has your smile.''

"You see that?" Aengus demanded. "A resemblance to me?"

"Of course. Haven't you ever noticed it?"

He seemed almost pleased for just a second; then his blue eyes clouded. "You said you saw something today. Something in the way I acted toward Johnny. What was that?"

"There was something in your eyes when he spoke to you. It seemed as though he touched your heart, just for the briefest of moments."

"Do you think Luke noticed it?"

"Luke?" She tried without success to understand the question. "I don't know what you mean, Aengus."

"Never mind." He sank onto the bed and cradled his head in his hands. "Why are you doing this to me, Suzannah?"

In an instant she was kneeling before him, stroking his hair contritely. "What am I doing?"

"You're opening wounds that can't be healed. Don't ask me to explain. Just believe me when I tell you I can't go through it again. I have to let it go."

"I'll let it go too, then," she promised, guilt-stricken over the intensity of his distress. "For a while at least. I promise."

"No, you'll never be able to do that," he countered softly. "I should have realized that from the start. Bringing you here was a mistake—"

"Bringing me here was the best thing you ever did," she corrected him firmly. "I made a mistake just now, but that doesn't mean we can't go back to our original agreement. You won't have to think about the boys again, because I'll take care of them completely. I won't nag, not ever again. And tonight, to thank you for cooperating with me in front of Meg and Ben—"

"That's not necessary, Suzannah. We're both tired." Kissing her forehead, he shrugged to his feet and walked out the door without another word.

"So that's that," she announced to the empty room. "You didn't make it better, you made it worse. It's torture for him to talk about the boys, because of what Katherine did, but you keep asking him to talk. No more, Suzannah Yates. It's time you started keeping your end of the bargain."

Plumping handfuls of hay into a makeshift pillow, Aengus settled back for the night, trying *not* to wonder about little Johnny. It never did any good—he'd never know for sure if the boy was his son or not—and it only caused him pain. And it caused Luke pain too. Aengus was sure of it.

Luke was amazingly perceptive. Surely he had noticed how Aengus responded differently toward his younger brother. While Aengus hoped Luke saw that as nothing more than a tribute to Johnny's age, he suspected the child saw right through such facile arguments. Luke Monroe hungered for a father, just as Aengus hungered for a son. While Luke wondered why Aengus couldn't be that man, Aengus wondered why fate had cruelly taken from him the joy and wonder that being Luke's father had given him for four blessed years.

And so he came to the same conclusion as always, that it was best to believe Johnny was Alex's son. That way, at the very least, Aengus could treat the boys equally. It wouldn't be fair to Luke to do otherwise, and it wouldn't be fair to himself to fall in love with fatherhood again, the way he'd done with Luke, only to learn one day that Alex Monroe had stolen that honor from him all over again.

"Aengus?"

"I'm here, Suzy."

She wandered toward him through the dark and sat down beside him, gathering her shawl around her shoulders and positioning the skirt of her nightgown as modestly as possible. "Are you feeling better?"

"I'm fine."

"Is there something I can do to make you feel good again?"

"Aye." He pulled her into his lap and ran his hand along the soft, bare skin of her legs, amazed—and grateful—that she'd come to him after all the confused emotions with which he'd so unfairly burdened her. "If you're still willing, I'd like to take you up on your offer."

"Enjoy yourself," she advised with a weak but loving smile. "This will be the very, *very* last time I ever allow this."

"Taking it to the grave after this, are you?"

She giggled and wrapped her arms around his neck. "If only you weren't such a handsome beast, we wouldn't keep having this argument."

"And if only you weren't such a pretty little tease, I'd be able to stay angry with you, instead of craving you every waking minute." He plunged his finger into her and enjoyed her appreciative gasp. "I see I'm not the only one who's been having naughty thoughts."

"I haven't," she protested lightly. "But if you kiss me, I might have one or two before the night is through."

He covered her mouth with his own, grateful for the invitation, and even more grateful for the distraction. He knew this was the reason she had come to him tonight—not to keep her promise, but to soothe the wounds she'd opened with her well-intentioned meddling. She was a softhearted, unselfish girl, and he intended to cherish and protect her as best he was able.

She was also a curvaceous, responsive female, and he intended to cherish that too, in every way she'd allow. And so, as he kissed her, he caressed her breasts through the flimsy fabric of her bodice until her nipples hardened with arousal. Then he coaxed her hand downward to stroke his manhood, while his fingers played under her gown, readying her for the slow, sweet night of ecstasy to come.

She vaguely remembered Aengus carrying her back to his bed after their night of lovemaking, and smiled to herself when she found pieces of straw under the covers and in her hair. He hadn't stayed with her after that, but somehow had managed to continue his ritual of making coffee before she awoke. One day, she'd have to surprise him by getting there first, but in the meantime, it was a wonderful way to start her day.

She was already settling into a routine, as easily as if she'd been a member of the family for years. It helped that the Yates men weren't very demanding. In fact, they were almost embarrassingly appreciative of her every contribution, marveling over a simple pie or a darned sock until she wanted to scold them for spoiling her.

Her stepsons had a routine themselves, and as she observed it, she realized she had probably misjudged Aengus. The boys had their chores but seemed able to finish them quickly, then were off into the woods, exploring and working on the raft they refused to let her see until it was finished. Aengus was hardly the tough taskmaster she had expected. He also used an even voice with them most times when he addressed them. Unfortunately, he rarely did so, but at least he didn't berate them the way she'd suspected he might.

He just ignores them, she decided finally. Somehow, she was beginning to understand what Johnny had meant when he said his father was mean to him. He hadn't been referring to cruel words or harsh demands or physical punishment. Just the absence of love and attention at a time when the child had a bottomless craving for both.

And so Suzannah supplied copious amounts to the boys, rumpling their hair, spoiling them with pie and cake, praising their muscles, and insisting that they endure her endless embraces. It embarrassed Luke, but he didn't complain, and she in turn was careful not to hug him in front of Aengus, knowing that the boy liked to be treated like a grown man when his father was around.

That night, when the table had been cleared and the boys had been settled into bed, Aengus went out to the stable without any discussion, and while Suzannah was tempted to invent some pretense to join him, she decided against it. Just as they needed a routine by day, they needed certainty by night, and since she wasn't ready to agree to permanently surrendering to him, it was best that she stayed within the old, dependable rules.

She wasn't sure what to expect the next day, but it proved to be as delightful as its predecessor, although Aengus had gone to town and thus wasn't around for her to watch and admire from behind the kitchen curtains. Concentrating again on her stepsons, she was a bit concerned when she spied Luke in the corral with the huge and "skittish" stallion that Aengus had acquired so recently from Ben.

Johnny was on the porch watching his brother, and so she sat on the step next to him, wrapped her arm around his shoulder, and asked as casually as she could, "Didn't your father tell Luke not to ride that stallion?"

"He's not riding it. He's gentling it. See? Just like Pa does."

It was true! As Suzannah watched in pure amazement, Luke stroked the stallion's neck firmly, then pulled an apple from his pocket and moved a few steps away, offering it casually. When the horse snorted and shook his mane, disdainful of the gift, Luke simply shrugged and took a bite. Then he proffered it again.

"I've seen your father do this dozens of times. Do you think the horse will eat it?"

"If Luke does it right, he will."

She bit back a smile. "*Is* he doing it right?"

Johnny considered the question soberly. "He's standing too close. Pa knows just where to stand."

Almost as though he'd heard, Luke took a full step backward, then nibbled again on the apple. Instead of offering it a third time, however, he put it back into his pocket.

"Why's he doing that?" Suzannah demanded.

"I don't know."

Picking up a pitchfork, Luke began tossing hay around the corral until the stallion whinnied in protest.

"He's asking for the apple," Johnny explained exuberantly.

"I think you're right."

As they watched, now completely mesmerized, Luke

offered the half-eaten apple a third time, and the huge black horse approached cautiously.

"I wish Aengus could see this," Suzannah whispered, more to herself than to her stepson.

"He watches Luke sometimes," Johnny informed her. "Luke doesn't know it."

"Really?"

"He watches me too. But I *know* it." After a short pause, he asked wistfully, "Why does he watch us, Suzannah?"

"I'm not sure." She gave his little shoulder a squeeze. "I used to watch your father when I was a little girl and he was a full-grown boy. I used to watch him work horses at the Monroe place. I'd hide in the bushes, so he wouldn't know. Because I didn't want him to see how much I loved him."

"Do you think that's why Pa watches us?"

"I hope so."

"Me too. *Look!* Midnight's going to take it."

"Goodness! Look how calm Luke is about it."

"Just like Pa."

"Yes," she sighed. "Just like him."

Luke's face broke into a proud grin that made her want to rush over and congratulate him, but she could see he wasn't quite finished. And so she waited while he reached up and began to vigorously rub the horse's neck. Thanking him. Taming him. The master, but with the utmost respect and appreciation. *Just like Aengus . . .*

She prepared a ham for dinner that night and quickly learned that it was the way to the Yates men's hearts. If it had just been Aengus who had praised her cooking skills, she might have suspected an ulterior

motive, assuming of course that he was craving
another night together as much as she. But the boys
showered her with compliments too, the most effec-
tive one being the way they alternately savored and
devoured their triple servings.

We're almost an ordinary family at this moment, she
marveled happily as she presented them with an aro-
matic apple pie. They groaned that they wished they'd
saved room, then panicked when she offered to take
it away and serve it the next day. They'd each have
a little slice, they assured her. Not too little. And not
necessarily just one.

As Johnny was cleaning his dessert plate he looked
at Aengus and ventured carefully, "Pa?"

Aengus nodded slightly, indicating that he should
continue.

"Do you know what happened today?"

"What?"

"Luke made Midnight ask for an apple."

Aengus turned his full attention to Luke. "Is that
so?"

"Yes, sir. But I didn't ride him."

"You put the apple in your pocket, and he asked
for it?"

Luke nodded self-consciously. "It wasn't so hard.
That horse is mostly tame. Just skittish is all."

Aengus seemed to consider this soberly before
replying. "Sometimes the skittish ones are worse than
the wild ones. Too many bad habits."

The boy flushed with pride.

"Do you think you can handle riding him?"

"Yes, sir."

"You'll stay inside the paddock until you're sure
who's boss?"

"Yes, sir. I promise."

"Fine, then." He turned to Suzannah. "I'll be gone early tomorrow. Before dawn, most likely. It could be two days, or even three, before I'm back. Tom and I are going to catch some new stock."

"Catch it?" Suzannah smiled. "Not buy it?"

Aengus smiled in return. "There's no need to buy it out here. There are wild mustangs for the taking, and Tom says he knows of a canyon some real beauties use as a refuge. He needs the money," he added soberly. "So they can take his mother-in-law to a doctor in San Francisco. So we're going to give his canyon a try."

"He'll help you catch them?"

Aengus nodded.

"Will he help you tame them too?"

"Him?" Aengus snorted. "He's useless with all that." Turning to Johnny, he announced, "I want you to pay attention this week while I work the mustangs, so you can learn like your brother did."

"I already learned it all, Pa," Johnny bragged. "I'm just not tall enough yet."

Aengus chuckled at the "pint-sized" bravado. "Time'll take care of that. Did you do all your chores today?"

"Yes, sir."

"Fine, then. Thank Suzannah for the dinner, then go and get ready for bed."

"Thanks, Suzannah," the boy enthused. "I never ate so much."

"You're welcome, sweetie."

"Can I go too?" Luke asked, rising half out of his chair as he spoke.

Aengus nodded.

The older boy paused to grin at his stepmother. "Thanks, Suzannah."

"It was my pleasure, Luke," she assured him fondly.

When the boys had raced away, she gave her husband a curious glance. He'd been so sweet about Luke's success. And so darling to Johnny! Was it this way sometimes between him and his sons? If so, perhaps there was less to worry about than she'd suspected.

"What now?" he growled.

"Nothing."

"You have a complaint about *that*? They need to learn to work horses, Suzannah. How do you expect them to run a ranch one day if they don't?"

She smiled as she assured him, "They're fortunate to have you to teach them."

Aengus shook his head. "Still sounds like a criticism somehow. But since I need my sleep tonight, no harm done. Unless you have other ideas?"

She pretended to sniff indignantly, knowing he was suggesting another moonlit rendezvous despite their clear understanding to the contrary. Still, she wasn't actually annoyed. Not when he'd been so good to his sons. In the three days since she'd married him, she'd seen no hint of cruelty or mean-spiritedness. He was strict, perhaps, and unloving and blunt, but also genuinely concerned about their character and their training and their future. Surely in time the boys would see that for what it was—Aengus's awkward attempt at expressing his dormant love for them.

And in the meantime, it was thrilling to feel his eyes on her as she went about the business of clearing the table. The air was charged with him wanting her, and she was half tempted to offer herself to him, just one final time. How much sleep could he need, even for mustang wrangling? Surely he could spare an hour or so for his grateful bride. She wouldn't see him for days, or nights . . .

Then Johnny raced back into the room, his face freshly scrubbed and his flannel nightshirt neatly pressed, courtesy of Suzannah. "Did I get ready for bed fast?"

When Aengus didn't respond, Suzannah assured the boy, "Faster than lightning."

The little one beamed. "Are you going to tell us another story tonight, Suzannah?"

"Of course. After you hop into bed." She smiled toward Luke, who had just entered the room at a more judicious pace. "I'll be in soon. But first, come over here."

The two boys approached her with knowing grins, and she didn't disappoint them, hugging and kissing each in return. "I love you both."

"I love you too," the boys chorused; then Luke added, "Don't forget the story."

She watched fondly as they ambled toward their room; then suddenly Johnny turned toward his father, who was standing before the fireplace. "Pa? Should we tell you we love *you* too?"

Suzannah's heart swelled, and she could feel tears of joy sting her eyes. Fortunately, her stepsons didn't notice. Their eyes were on Aengus, and Suzannah held her breath, waiting for the reply that might unite them as a family on the spot.

Then Aengus answered calmly, and without appearing to consider it, "That's not necessary. Good night, boys."

The plates she'd been carrying crashed to the floor, and Johnny and Aengus both shot startled glances her way. "Are you hurt?" Aengus demanded as he began to cross the room to her.

"Stay there!" she gasped. "Please, just stay there." To Johnny she added in an eerie and unfamiliar voice, "Run along now. I'll be in when I've cleaned up this mess."

"Do as Suzannah says," Aengus added carefully. "And take good care of her tomorrow while I'm away."

"We will, Pa," Johnny assured him.

If the child's heart was broken, he didn't show it. But it didn't really matter. Suzannah's was broken enough for all of them.

And through her despair, she realized that Luke hadn't moved or spoken, and she turned to see his hazel eyes, still narrowed; his nostrils, still flared; his little hands, still clenched into fists at his sides. The father's thoughtless answer hadn't broken *his* heart. It had simply confirmed his suspicions, and so, rather than saddening him, it had hardened him more completely. Perhaps irrevocably.

"Go on to bed now, Luke," Suzannah instructed him in a hoarse but insistent tone. "I love you."

Without a word, the boy spun and stalked to his room, slamming the door behind him.

"Suzannah? Don't you want some help with that?"

An angry tear slid down her cheek and she brushed it away with the back of her hand. "I don't want anything from you, Aengus Yates. The one thing you could have given ..." She stopped herself and crouched to the floor to gather bits of broken pottery. "Never mind."

He crossed the room to her and leaned down to take her by her shoulders, urging her to stand and face him. "Suzannah—"

"Don't." Still fighting a true flood of tears, she accused softly, "Couldn't you see how much it meant to him? Are you as heartless as all that? You don't deserve those boys. You truly don't.''

"I never said I did. I don't deserve you either, but—''

"Go away, Aengus. Get your sleep, and catch your mustangs, and stay away from me from now on.'' She stood and locked pain-filled eyes with his. "Is that clear?''

"Aye, it's clear. Just try not to cry for too long tonight. I'm not worth it.''

"I'm not crying for you. I'm crying for them.''

"You're crying for us all,'' he corrected, cupping her face in his rough hand and kissing her mouth gently. "I'd say I never should have brought you here, but those boys need you, and that's a fact.''

"Aengus, don't. Please don't kiss me. I can't bear it.''

He smiled wryly and kissed her forehead. "I haven't seen either of the boys this happy since I went to fetch them at their—at their Uncle Alex's place, so don't cry for them either.''

She wanted to throw herself into his arms and let him comfort her, but the solution was simply too absurd, given that he was the cause of all the grief. And so she pulled free, wiped her eyes one last time, and murmured, "Go to the stable and get a good night's sleep. I'll go and take care of my stepsons.''

True to his promise, Aengus was gone long before sunrise. He didn't even make coffee this time, and she suspected he hadn't come back into the house at all. The last thing she wanted was to create an even greater chasm between the father and his sons, but there was nothing she could do about it for the time being, not with him gone and her head pounding from lack of sleep.

Luke took one look at her face at the breakfast table and nodded coolly. "Didn't I warn you? He's mean."

"Did Pa hurt you, Suzannah?" Johnny murmured. "Is that why you cried?"

"No, sweetie. Your father was very gentle and understanding with me last night."

"Him?" Luke snorted.

"You didn't come and tell us a story." Johnny studied her intently. "Were you sad because the plates busted?"

Suzannah shrugged, grateful for the excuse but not quite comfortable with lying. "Let's forget about last night, shall we? Let's make some special plans for today. Why don't we pack a picnic, and you can take me to see the raft?"

Luke's head snapped up, as though the idea had galvanized his attention. "We could pack a lot of food and use the raft to go down the river to Sacramento. And when we run out of stuff to eat, there are trout in the river, and I can catch 'em easy."

"Sacramento?" Suzannah smiled. "That's days away, isn't it?"

"And Pa said we can't take the raft in the river," Johnny reminded his brother sternly. "Only in the creek."

"Who cares what he says?" Luke's hazel eyes flashed with contempt. "The creek doesn't go anywhere. We need to take the river if we want to get away from here."

"Oh, dear—"

"I heard there are jobs in Sacramento for most anybody. I'm real strong, Suzannah. I can find some way to take care of us. Just don't say we have to wait a year," he pleaded quickly. "You've seen how he is now. You see he won't change. Not ever. 'The old Aengus,' " the child added harshly. "Maybe he never was good at all. Maybe it was just our wanting him to be good, like you're doing now. Did you ever think of that?"

She'd thought of it more often than she'd like to admit, but to hear it from a seven-year-old unnerved her to the core. "I've seen proof that the old Aengus still exists." When the boy began to scoff, she added quickly, "I'm not saying he's going to be that way again. Not even in a year. But in his own way . . . Luke! Where are you going?"

The boy turned to fix her with an icy glare. "You're just like Ma. Not seeing what he is because you like kissing him."

"Luke Yates!"

"I have to do my chores."

"Luke!" She winced as the door slammed against her words; then she turned to Johnny and smiled weakly. "He's in a bad mood, isn't he?"

The little one nodded. "He used to yell at Ma too."

She studied the boy intently. "He said your mother didn't see how your father was, just because she liked kissing him?"

"Not Pa," Johnny explained. "He's talking about Uncle Alex. Ma liked kissing *him*, and it used to make Luke mad. It made me mad too, only I didn't yell about it."

"I see." She patted the child's arm. "They used to kiss right in front of you?"

"No. More like you and Pa. Like when you think we don't know."

Suzannah coughed nervously. "Your father and I are married, Johnny."

"Uncle Alex was married too. To Miz Monroe."

Suzannah bit her lip, then dared to ask, "Did Mrs. Monroe know how much your ma liked your uncle?"

"Maybe. 'Cause she didn't like Ma, and she didn't like us. Exspecially not Luke."

"I can imagine," Suzannah said. "Do you feel the way Luke feels, sweetie? Would you like for the three of us to get on that raft and float away and never see your pa again?"

"I don't know. I like it here sometimes."

She nodded pensively. "So do I. And I think it's going to get better and better. Slowly, though. And it will never be perfect. But it doesn't sound like Adamsville was all that perfect either, toward the end."

"After you left, it was bad. And then Ma got sick, and it was really, really bad. Then Pa came . . ." The boy shrugged his little shoulders. "I like it best when you're around."

"Well, then . . ." She reached and pulled him into a quick hug. "That settles it, don't you think? You and I like it here, and we like it that we're all together. So we'll stay for a while at least and see what happens."

He nodded, clearly relieved. "I better go help Luke before he yells at *me* too."

"I'm still going to pack a picnic for us."

Johnny grinned. "Luke'll be grouchy till he tastes it, then he'll be good." Racing toward the door, he turned only to give her a cheery, " 'Bye, Suzannah!" before racing out of sight.

* * *

She might not have been successful in affecting her husband's moods, but she wasn't about to let a seven-year-old boy set the tone for her household, and so she plotted to subvert her older stepson's grouchiness. Apple pie, compliments, stories, and teasing, then more apple pie—slowly, over the three days she was alone with the children, she watched Luke's cool demeanor melt until he was as close to sunny as she could hope, given his reserved nature. He'd gotten that from Aengus. But he also had Aengus's appreciative manner, not to mention the direct, honest quality that made a person instinctively put his trust in a man.

As much as she missed Aengus Yates—and she missed him in ways she'd only dreamed of before—she found herself dreading his return. What if he was harsh or cold? It would hurt her, and worse, it would destroy the tentative happiness she was establishing with the boys. Still, when she heard the pounding of hooves on the afternoon of the fourth day, she burst through the door and onto the porch without hesitating for a moment, desperate to be seen by those amazing blue eyes at any or every cost.

He cantered into view, dusty but relaxed, trailing a string of wild mustangs behind himself. The sight almost took his young bride's breath away. So tall in the saddle. So commanding. Just as he was in their bed. She wanted to lure him into a bubble bath and to have her way with him right there in the foam.

But he didn't even glance in her direction. Instead, he corralled the new stock, then rode over to Johnny, who had been watching in open-mouthed admiration. Reining his horse to a stop, Aengus leaned down to the little boy and, in one smooth move, deposited something into the child's arms. A squirmy, golden-haired puppy that had been concealed under the wrangler's long, dusty coat until just that moment!

After Johnny had squealed with predictable delight, Aengus turned his chestnut toward the upper pad-dock—toward Luke—and proceeded onward toward the elder of the two children.

And Suzannah found herself whispering aloud, to Aengus, or perhaps to someone even more powerful, *"Please, please, please . . ."*

Chapter Nine

Aengus rode toward Monroe's older son, wondering what to say to begin to make peace with the boy. He'd had time to think these three days and nights, and he knew Suzannah was right. There had to be a way to settle this, once and for all.

And for all his conflicted feelings, he couldn't help feeling proud over the way the boy was now handling Midnight. There was no way that bastard Monroe could ever take credit for this! It was pure Aengus Yates. Pure Dennis Riordain. Pure generations of Riordains and Yateses—wranglers and horse tamers all.

Still, when Luke looked him straight in the eye, as though they were equals, Aengus grimaced. The kid was a pain in the behind. But Aengus had promised himself he would try and so he announced diplomatically, "I'm home."

"This stallion isn't skittish anymore," Luke countered evenly.

"So I see." Aengus was careful not to smile at the youthful bravado. "I brought a puppy for you and your brother. And if you'd like, you can have Midnight too, since you gentled him. Or," he added casually, "we can sell Midnight and split the profit, and you can tame one of the mustangs for yourself." He smiled to himself even as he made the offer, remembering the first horse he'd tamed as a boy in Ireland. No amount of money could have convinced him to part with *her*.

Luke hesitated, then nodded stiffly. "Let's sell Midnight and split the profit."

Aengus struggled not to allow his disappointment to show. To see greed in his own son . . . Then he reminded himself harshly that this was Alex Monroe's son, and Alex Monroe was the greediest son of a gun he'd ever had the misfortune to meet. If the boy had inherited his father's avarice, who was Aengus to judge?

And so he quietly assured the boy, "You'll have your profit, although I don't know what you need it for."

"I need it for Suzannah."

A moment of relief swept over the bone-weary wrangler. Was that all the boy had meant? He wanted to buy a present for his stepmother? Mustering his resolve, he told the boy, "Dollars can't buy what Suzannah wants. She wants *us* to get along. I want that too."

"You want that so she'll kiss you," the boy accused coolly.

Without even realizing it, Aengus pulled back on the reins, causing his horse to back a few feet away from the child. *Fitting*, he realized soberly. Mending fences with this one was going to be more difficult than he'd thought. "I know I haven't been the father you wanted—"

"You haven't been a father at all."

Aengus winced but persisted. "It'll take time for me to learn—"

"You *used* to know how."

"I used to believe I knew how," Aengus explained wearily. "There's a difference, Luke. But I'm going to try."

"Because you love Suzannah?"

Before Aengus could answer, the boy shrugged his narrow shoulders in dismissal. "She loves you too. She'll do whatever you want. That's how it is with ladies. So"—his hazel eyes grew cold—"you don't need to give us gifts."

"Just the same," Aengus growled, "the puppy is for you and your brother. And if you can tame one of the mustangs, she'll be yours too."

"And half the profit for taming Midnight?" Luke countered. "I earned that."

"You'll have it by noon tomorrow."

The boy nodded, turned the black stallion away from Aengus, and galloped unceremoniously away.

So much for that, Aengus thought with a self-mocking smile; then he turned his own steed toward the ranch house to see if Suzannah's reception of him would be equally cold.

She wanted to throw her arms around him, to thank him for making Johnny's face light up with such a glow, but she contented herself with brushing a smudge from his cheekbone with her thumb. "You should get cleaned up while I warm some soup. After that, I'm headed into town.''

"Oh?"

She savored the disappointment in his tone before answering. "Dorothy Winston is serving afternoon tea for Megan and myself and a group of women from town. To say farewell to Meg, you know. There'll be Tom's wife—Jenny, isn't it?—and someone named Marilyn.''

"Marilyn Potter," Aengus nodded. "She's a mean one.''

Suzannah laughed. "I appreciate the warning." Her tone grew perceptibly warmer as she added, "It was darling of you to bring the puppy.''

"It was nothing.''

"It was darling," she corrected. "Johnny already named him Nugget. Because of his gold coat.''

"I brought something for you too.''

"Oh?"

"Another kind of nugget. Found it in a stream bed." He proffered an inch-thick hunk of ore sheepishly. "It would make a fine wedding ring, don't you think?"

"Aye," she sighed; then a flush of apology graced her face. Did he think she was mocking his way of speaking? Or did he see it as it was, a sign of how deeply the offer had affected her? "There's soup and pie," she offered lamely. "I'll set it out for you, but then I'll need to leave for Dorothy's house.''

"I'll take you into town.''

"Don't be silly. You must be exhausted. Luke can—"

"I'll take you, Mrs. Yates. And when you've had your fill of foolish female chatter, I'll bring you home.''

The bride blushed with delight. "I understand you

can get a bath and shave at the hotel for less than a dollar."

"A bath and a cigar," he agreed cheerfully.

"Well, then . . ." She tried to lock gazes with him, but failed, and so she stared instead at the floorboards. "Shall we go?"

Jenny Whalen, Tom's wife, was six months pregnant, overburdened with responsibilities thanks to her mother's illness, but still such a delight that Suzannah and Megan responded to her instantly. And Dorothy Winston was, as usual, the consummate hostess and entertainer. She had gotten it into her head to convince Ben and Megan to delay their departure to San Francisco long enough to meet some close friends who lived in Sacramento during the winter months, but moved up into the mountains every April to savor the springtime beauty and to escape the intense heat of the valley in summer.

"Their housekeeper is also a marvelous seamstress. She made the gowns you two wore on your wedding day, in fact. Every year she designs an entirely new wardrobe for me while I visit them in their home near Donner Lake."

"Donner Lake?" Megan sighed. "I'm not sure I'd like to go there, knowing all the suffering that poor wagon train endured there."

"That was ages ago! These days, there's a good-sized town that's sprung up nearby, what with all the flurry from the railroad and the lumberjacks and all. You girls could come with me—"

"I'm not going anywhere," Suzannah interrupted firmly. "I have three hungry men to fuss over."

"And I'd miss Ben," Megan smiled. "Even if we were apart for just a day."

"Bring him along! He can play cards with the judge and his cronies while we visit."

Suzannah sent her friend a sympathetic smile. "Ben's anxious to begin your new life in San Francisco?"

The bride nodded. "I have to admit, I'm looking forward to it a bit myself."

"I wouldn't be in such a hurry to live in San Francisco if I were you," Dorothy's friend Marilyn warned. "It's filled with criminals and prostitutes and foreigners. And dreadful foreign diseases too."

Suzannah rolled her eyes. "We were only there for a few hours before we moved on to Sacramento, but it was clearly the most beautiful city on earth."

"I agree," Dorothy said heartily. "Really, Marilyn, must you be so discouraging?"

Aengus's description of the Potter woman as a "mean" one proved more and more accurate as the afternoon wore on. But Suzannah was unwilling to allow anyone or anything to taint her last social event with her best friend, and so she laughed off Marilyn's cynical observations about men, San Francisco, and gambling, knowing that the only way such remarks could hurt Megan would be if she sensed Suzannah took them to heart.

Jenny Whalen also tried valiantly to keep the conversation on a positive note, mostly by lavishing compliments on Aengus, and gratitude on Suzannah for having allowed him to go off with Tom so soon after the wedding.

"Aengus loves wild horses," Suzannah assured her. "I wouldn't dream of interfering with that. He inherited a gift from his ancestors—the gift of gentling

hem without hurting them. He's grateful to Tom
or having shown him where to find so many new
prospects for his talent."

"You're a smart wife," Marilyn Potter informed her
heartily. "Let them have their wild, immoral fun away
from home, so they're decent when they're with us.
That's really all we can ask."

"Marilyn," Dorothy scolded. "Suzannah and
Megan are new brides. They don't need to hear such
talk."

"You're saying I'm wrong?" Marilyn challenged.
"You're saying the judge doesn't have a taste for
immoral women? Why else would he go into Virginia
City so regularly? Like Aengus," she added, arching
an eyebrow toward Suzannah.

"Like Aengus did *before* he was married," Dorothy
corrected loyally. "Don't listen to her, Suzannah. Her
complaint is against her own husband—"

"At least my husband is honest. He doesn't pretend
to want only one woman." Marilyn eyed Megan with
cruel amusement. "I suppose yours claims he doesn't
need any woman but you? What would you say if I
told you men have needs that a woman like you, or
me, or any of us in this room, could never fulfill?"

"That's enough, Marilyn," Dorothy scolded.

"What kind of needs?" Megan asked, a little too
curiously, and Suzannah felt her heart sink. Was this
never going to end? Was Megan going to wonder
about "naughty women" and her mother to her dying
day, responding to every hint that she hadn't sprung
from decent stock? Where was it to end?

"If Marilyn can't meet her husband's needs, that's
her own sad problem," Suzannah announced
sharply. "You needn't concern yourself with it, Meg.
One has only to see Ben's eyes when he looks at you

to know that you are the only woman he sees or needs. And as for *my* husband . . ." She stared into Marilyn Potter's small dark eyes and informed her haughtily, "I've had no complaints about my meeting his needs. My condolences if you've had some from yours."

Dorothy Winston and Megan giggled behind their hands, but Marilyn seemed unashamed. "My husband respects me enough not to deceive me. I asked him once, straight out, why married men are drawn to women of loose virtue. And when he told me the reason, I gave him my permission to do so whenever the urge struck him. Better that he turn to those women than ask me to fulfill his unnatural needs. That's all I have to say."

"Well, that's a relief," Dorothy said firmly. "Shall we just change the subject and have some cake?"

"What kind of unnatural needs?" Megan persisted. "He actually told you what he does with them? With loose women?"

"Meg," Suzannah warned nervously. "This woman doesn't know what she's talking about—"

"My husband told me!" Marilyn countered angrily. "I admire Mrs. Steele for being willing to listen and learn. You, Mrs. Yates, are just like Dorothy. Hiding in your fantasy that you satisfy your husband, when the truth is, only a whore can satisfy a man completely."

"Gracious sakes alive!" Dorothy wailed. "What if the judge walked in here right now and heard this? I'd never be allowed to entertain friends again. I agree with Suzannah—"

"I want to hear what Marilyn's husband told her," Megan interrupted. "Suzannah, if you and Dorothy don't want to hear, Marilyn can whisper it to me."

"Good grief," Suzannah sighed. But when Megan leaned her ear toward the Potter woman, Suzannah followed suit, as did Dorothy Winston. Within seconds, the three women had been treated to a true earful, and it was clear that Marilyn had only just begun to list the various exotic pleasures and practices in which certain people indulged.

"I won't have this kind of talk in my parlor," Dorothy announced sharply, her cheeks bright red with embarrassment. "And, Megan, I know we only met last week, but since I'm the closest thing to a mother you have in these parts, I forbid you to pursue this subject any further. Is that understood?"

Grinning from ear to ear, Suzannah turned to her friend, ready to tease her for having received such a sound scolding, but her smile evaporated in the face of Megan's clear distress. The girl's face was as white as fine paper, and if Suzannah hadn't known better, she would have guessed her friend was about to faint dead away.

"Look how you've upset my guest," Dorothy fumed. "Really, Marilyn, my husband warned me not to invite you this afternoon, and he was right. Megan, darling, you mustn't believe a word this shrew says. Her own marriage is such a disaster, she can't stand to see anyone else happy. But I assure you—"

"Excuse me, won't you?" Megan blurted unhappily. Jumping to her feet, she brushed against the tea cart and almost toppled it in her haste to escape toward the garden.

"Poor darling, she's in shock," Dorothy murmured. "She must be terrified that one night soon, Ben will do what Marilyn just described! Suzannah, go and tell her it's all an exaggeration, won't you?"

Suzannah nodded, knowing that the situation was even worse than Dorothy suspected. Knowing that Megan was at this moment imagining that her own mother had performed such bizarre rituals with strange men in strange places. Poor Meg!

She found her friend in a heap on the red brick bench and embraced her staunchly. "You're being such a goose, Megan Elizabeth Steele! Your mother never did any such thing. Not with any man, for any reason! The whole idea is preposterous, and if you don't forget all about it this instant, I'm going to go to Ben and tell him every bit of it."

"*No!*" Megan clutched wildly at Suzannah's arm. "You mustn't say a word about this to him. Not ever. Promise me this instant."

"I won't make any such promise," Suzannah countered. "Not until you give me your word you'll forget all about that awful Marilyn and her lurid tales. I knew your mother, Meg. I loved your mother with all my heart. She was a good and decent—"

"This isn't about her!" Megan wailed. "It's about Ben! About what *he* did. What he told me! After I trusted him."

"Ben?" Suzannah murmured. "Don't tell me you think he wants harlots to do things with him—"

"He doesn't need harlots for that! He has me," Megan interrupted bitterly. "He told me that it would hurt less, and be more comfortable. And he was so gentle and handsome and convincing, and I trusted him. I *trusted* him, don't you see?"

"Good grief, Meg. Are you saying . . . ? Oh, no . . ." Suzannah fought a wave of disbelief, followed closely by an even stronger wave of laughter. "Oh, dear . . ."

"It was the very first thing he did on our wedding night," Megan was confiding, her voice choked with humiliation. "Any other girl would have said no. Any other girl—any *decent* girl!—would have known instinctively. But not me. He made such a fool of me . . ." Covering her face with her long, graceful fingers, she burst into a torrent of sobs.

Pulling her friend tightly against her chest, Suzannah patted her shoulder while searching for something to say that didn't sound either frivolous or cruel. Was it possible Ben Steele had actually done such things, and on their wedding night, no less? And if so, had Megan enjoyed it?

But of course she had. Wasn't that the point? Wasn't that the real reason she was so upset? "Listen, Meg. We both know what a rascal Ben is—"

"A rascal?" Megan cried. "What does that make *me*?"

"Well, I think it makes you a goose," she teased carefully. "You love him so much you'd do anything for him. And he's mischievous enough to take advantage of that. But not out of mean-spiritedness or depravity."

"I should have said no. *You* would have." When Suzannah didn't respond immediately, Megan pulled free and demanded sharply, "Wouldn't you?"

"I don't know," Suzannah admitted. "On our wedding night, I told Aengus I'd do whatever he asked. So I suppose . . ."

"You wouldn't have done *that*," Megan glared. "Admit it. And Aengus never would have asked, because he's a gentleman, and he respects you as a lady. I don't want to talk about it anymore."

"You need to talk to Ben," Suzannah corrected. "You need to tell him how upset you are. And you need to tell him about your mother—"

"Stop mentioning her!"

"Fine."

"This doesn't have anything to do with her."

"I agree."

Megan wiped her gray eyes cautiously. "You don't think I inherited weak morals from her, do you? It's all Ben's doing, isn't it?"

Suzannah winced. "I loved your mother, and I love Ben, even though he's a scoundrel. But most of all, I love *you*. I don't know whose fault this is, but I know it's not yours. And"—she drew a deep breath—"if Aengus had asked this of me, on our wedding night, I believe I would have acquiesced. And you know what a Puritan *my* mother was."

When the quip didn't elicit even the hint of a smile from Megan, Suzannah frowned. "You need to talk to Ben. Hit him with a book and tell him what a weasel we think he is. But don't just feel poorly about it. That's not the way to deal with this."

"You should go home to Aengus now," Megan announced suddenly. "You're fortunate to have a husband like him. One who respects and loves you. As miserable as I am right now, I can still be happy that you found someone to cherish you. So go home and don't worry about me. I'll be fine."

Suzannah studied her friend anxiously. "Do you want me to talk to Ben? You two can't possibly leave tomorrow as you planned. Not under these circumstances."

"We won't leave tomorrow," Megan agreed darkly. "I can guarantee you that, at least."

"And you'll speak with him?"

"I'll deal with it in my own way. In my own time." Wiping her tears with a lace handkerchief, she squared her slender shoulders proudly. "Will you make my apologies to Dorothy? I can't face her right now. I can only imagine what she thinks of me—"

"She thinks you were shocked by Marilyn's words—"

"Because a new wife like myself would never have guessed men could be so depraved?" Megan smiled sadly. "How fortunate for me that I'm a stranger here. In Adamsville, they wouldn't have made so kind an assumption, would they?"

Before Suzannah could protest, she added quickly, "Don't worry, Suzannah, I'm fine. It's not as though Ben's been cruel, and heaven knows, he hasn't neglected me. I'll find a way to deal with this—"

"Let me help! I'm your friend. And I would have done the same thing if Aengus had asked," she repeated weakly. "I swear it."

"You know it isn't true," Megan sighed. "And you know he never would have asked. Marilyn said it herself. He goes to whores in Virginia City for such . . . activities. I mean," she amended hastily, "he went to them before he married you. He'd never go now. I know that in my heart, no matter what that awful woman says."

Suzannah pursed her lips thoughtfully. Until now, she'd been so preoccupied with Megan's dilemma she hadn't given any thought to her own, but wasn't Megan right? Aengus had gone to Virginia City in the past, and would go even now, wouldn't he? Or perhaps Marilyn Potter was wrong, and Aengus had never even wanted to do such things and never would!

Or perhaps he *craved* such things, but not from Suzannah! Why not? Because he had too much respect for her, or because he wasn't as passionate about her as Ben was about Meg? "This is making my head ache," she announced suddenly. "I have two hungry sons at home to worry about, and a dusty husband who hasn't had a decent meal in days. You should come out to the ranch with me, Meg. We'll send word to Ben to join us there for dinner, and the four of us—"

"No! I'm humiliated enough without letting Aengus Yates know what I've done too. Do you want him to see me as a harlot?"

"Megan Braddock! I mean—"

"Megan Steele, for better or for worse," the girl agreed wryly. "I'll speak to Ben myself, Suzannah. Promise me you'll mind your own affairs and not meddle in mine?"

"What Aengus Yates does in Virginia City is my affair, is it not?" Suzannah's tone softened quickly in response to the anguish in her friend's eyes. "Do you know what I think, Meg? I think it doesn't sound awful at all. Perhaps Aengus was just . . . well, just waiting before he suggested such a thing. You know what a temper I have. He may have been afraid of how I'd react, but the truth is, it sounds exciting."

Megan smiled through her unhappiness. "You're just saying that to make me feel better, but I love you for it anyway. We both know you'd never consider—"

"I'm considering it right now! Are you completely deaf? Right after dinner, I'm going to ask Aengus—"

"Suzannah, don't! Please?" She bit her lip and added cautiously, "You'd really talk to him about such a thing? Aren't you afraid he'd think less of you for repeating such scandalous talk?"

Suzannah knew exactly what Megan needed to hear at that moment, and so she bluffed, "I'm not going to repeat it, I'm going to request it."

"Suzannah Hennessy!"

"I'm his wife and I trust him," she shrugged. "And I suppose in a way I trust Ben Steele more than *you* do, because I've seen how much he loves you, and I know he wouldn't do anything to disgrace you. So it must be perfectly respectable. Odd," she added impishly, "but respectable."

Megan's gray eyes narrowed. "I know you too well, Suzannah. We grew up together, and we learned right from wrong together. You'd say anything right now to make me feel better, but you don't mean it. I don't even want you to mean it. I just want to go back to the hotel and rest. And think for a while."

"Talk to Ben."

"I will."

"If you don't, then you know *I* will," Suzannah warned, but Megan didn't seem to have heard her. She had a faraway look in her eyes—a look Suzannah knew well, although she hadn't seen it in years. Megan was remembering the rumors, and the murders, and the doubts, as though time had been turned back and they were vulnerable little girls again.

She won't talk to Ben, Suzannah told herself silently. Which meant it was up to Suzannah to speak to the gambler. But did she dare? Could she find the words? What would he think of her for broaching such a subject? Not that he'd had any trouble broaching it with a sweet, innocent virgin, of course. What a scoundrel he was! If Aengus knew how the gambler had treated Megan, Suzannah was certain he'd teach him a lesson.

So tell Aengus, she counseled herself in relief. *Let him handle it, man to man.*

"Don't worry too much, Suzannah," Megan instructed her friend wistfully. "In a day or two we'll talk again, and I won't be so glum. Make my excuses to Dorothy, won't you? And give Aengus and the boys my love."

Suzannah nodded, and when Megan had disappeared through the front gate, she trudged back into the house to face her hostess.

"I feel just terrible," Dorothy gushed. "Our little Megan is so sensitive and sheltered, she must have been shocked to the core by Marilyn's ridiculous story."

Suzannah studied the older woman warily. "Did it shock you?"

"Me?" Dorothy laughed self-consciously. "I don't shock easily, Suzannah. Being married to a judge, I hear all sorts of sordid details."

Suzannah nodded. "Sordid" was the perfect word for it. And Ben Steele was a menace! "Did Marilyn and Jenny leave?"

"I sent Marilyn away so Meg wouldn't have to face her again. But Jenny's in the hall visiting with Aengus."

"Aengus is here?" Suzannah gasped. "Right now?"

"He came to fetch you. I offered to feed him, but he claims you promised him biscuits, and he's going to hold you to it."

"You didn't say anything to him about—"

"Goodness, no!"

"Thank heavens," Suzannah murmured, then she pulled herself together and embraced her hostess. "It was a lovely tea party, almost until the end. You'll have to come out to the ranch soon, so that I can return the hospitality."

"I'm just pleased you're not angry with me," Dorothy smiled. "Go and find your handsome husband now. After four days on the trail, I have a feeling he's anxious to be alone with you."

*   *   *

The initial homecoming had been warm, so Aengus didn't know what to make of his bride's behavior during the long, quiet wagon ride home from the judge's house. She wasn't being unfriendly, or at least not exactly, but she was sitting so far from him she was in danger of falling off the side of the seat. And it wasn't just physical distance she was putting between them. Her mood was distant too, but in a skittish sort of way that just didn't fit so feisty a female.

What did you expect? he challenged himself ruefully. *You're still a disappointment to her. It'll take more than a puppy and a hunk of gold to change that.*

Still, he had hoped that the presents, especially the one for the boys, would soften her a bit. He'd missed her to the point of madness during the short separation, dreaming about her along the trail by day and aching for her under the stars at night. And for some reason, he'd been confident that, for all their troubles, she would be missing him too. Now he wasn't so sure she was even glad he was home!

"I had that bath we talked about." He rubbed his fresh-shaved chin self-consciously. "How do I look?"

"That's a silly question." She eyed him nervously. "You look the same as you always do."

"Then why are you looking at me differently?"

"I'm not!" A crimson blush spread over her pretty features. "I wasn't even thinking about you, Aengus Yates. I have more on my mind than how handsome you are, *or* how clean."

He found the response intriguing. It was almost as though she was embarrassed to be alone with him! After all her claims of being "comfortable" with him, what could have changed so suddenly?

Maybe she had missed him after all, in a raw sort of way, and was uncomfortable with the implications.

It was a fascinating theory, and so he decided to pursue it. "Have I told you how pretty you look in that dress? Green suits you because of those emerald eyes of yours."

"Stop talking nonsense." She squirmed visibly. "Can't you see how miserable I am over Megan's leaving?"

"I wanted a chance to see her myself, but Dorothy said she left abruptly. What was that about?"

Suzannah glared. "I just told you, she and I are upset over being separated from one another after all these years of being closer than sisters. Are you so heartless you can't even see that?"

"It's Ben who's heartless, for taking her away," Aengus chuckled. "You should turn that temper loose on him, not me."

"Don't mention Ben Steele's name to me. If you knew him better, you'd ..." She clasped her hand over her mouth and finished with a weak, "Never mind."

"Is that it?" Aengus grinned in relief. "The insufferable lovebirds have had themselves an argument? That's why Megan was upset—"

"I didn't say that," Suzannah interrupted. "But in a way, it's the truth. They've had a misunderstanding, Aengus. Or at least, Meg and I don't understand what Ben could have been thinking when he did what he did. I'm furious with him, although the truth is, I'm more worried than angry." She exhaled slowly, then gave him an encouraging smile. "It's sweet of you to be concerned. You're very fond of her, aren't you?"

"Aye."

"Almost like a brother, wouldn't you say?"

He considered the question carefully. "Are you saying she needs a brother?"

"Needs one?"

"Has Ben mistreated her?" When Suzannah didn't answer right away, Aengus felt a twinge of foreboding and reined the wagon team to a forceful stop. "Suzannah, answer me directly."

"For heaven's sake, Aengus, he hasn't hurt her like that, I promise. It's more complicated than that."

"He hasn't hurt her 'like that,' but he's hurt her some other way? Is that what you're saying?"

"Never mind. I can't talk to you about it. Not that you'd understand, even if I could. Not that I even pretend to understand it myself—"

"Suzannah? Could you make a little sense, just for a minute or two?"

She smiled sheepishly. "You know how sensitive she is on certain subjects, because of the rumors about her mother."

He nodded, immediately reassured. "She finally talked to him about that? Good. I'm sure it was hard for her, and maybe he didn't say all the right things, but it's best they not have secrets between them."

"That's true. I'm hoping they'll talk it through tonight. I don't envy them that, but as you said, it's best."

He cleared his throat, then suggested huskily, "I was hoping you and I would have a chance to do some talking tonight ourselves. After the boys are asleep."

To his surprise, she seemed immediately uncomfortable again. "You should concentrate on getting some rest tonight, Aengus. Sleeping on the trail can't be too restful, and you'll have a full day tomorrow taming the new stock."

"Those nights on the trail were lonely," he smiled,

patting the empty length of seat beside him. "Come and sit closer. I've missed having you nearby."

She edged away instead. "You said you wanted to talk. We can talk just fine like this."

"Did I say talk?" he murmured. "I meant whisper. Come over here and let me whisper how much I missed you."

She stared, as though he'd proposed something exotic but fascinating, and once again he suspected she'd been having wanton thoughts about her husband.

Then she moistened her lips and smiled shyly. "May I ask you something, Aengus?"

"Anything."

"And you promise you won't judge me? Or tease? Or be shocked?"

He arched an eyebrow playfully. "There's nothing shocking or improper about missing your wedded husband, Mrs. Yates."

"Pardon?"

"It's the most natural thing in the world. If I were to tell you some of the thoughts I've been having about *you* in the middle of the night—"

"Aengus, be quiet!" She slapped her hands over her ears. "I don't want to hear that kind of talk, *and I didn't miss you that way,* so please, just be quiet and take me home."

"Fine," he growled. "I suppose I had that bath and shave for nothing, then."

"I suppose you did," she sniffed in return. "Just because you were gone for a few days, you can't expect me to act like—well, like some sort of harlot."

"Harlot?" He stared in amazement. "I'd expect that kind of thinking from Megan, I suppose, but not from you."

"Megan doesn't think any differently than I do!" she snapped. "And neither of us is the kind of girl who'd give herself to a man just because he was clean and brought her a gift."

"From what I saw of them when they visited last week, Megan allows Ben to do *whatever* he wants *whenever* he wants, gift or not, clean or otherwise."

"Aengus Yates! How dare you say such a thing!" Her eyes flashed with emerald green fire. "If she acted that way, it's because she trusted him."

"He's a lucky man, either way."

"Well, he's not lucky anymore," she snarled. "If that's the kind of women you and Ben want, the both of you should go to Virginia City from now on. Just don't you dare think I'm interested in such things."

"I wouldn't dream of it," he drawled. "All I want from you tonight is a decent meal and some undisturbed sleep. You can take everything else to the grave with you for sure."

To Suzannah's relief, Aengus didn't seem to hold her bizarre behavior during the wagon ride against her that evening. He even stayed with the family after dinner, rather than heading right out for his sleeping quarters in the stable.

For her part, she was dying to apologize, just so that she could ask him candidly about Megan's problem. Surely he'd understand. He might even have some good advice. He'd been a man of the world himself for a few years, hadn't he? Perhaps not in the same way as Ben Steele, but undoubtedly he'd been with naughty women. He might be able to explain to Ben the necessity for begging for Megan's forgiveness, promising never to abuse her trust again, and assuring

her it wasn't any quality he sensed in her that made
him behave so presumptuously. He was just an incorrigible rascal. She'd known that from the start, hadn't
she?

In the meantime, she tried to relax and enjoy the
hilarious antics of Nugget, a bundle of boundless
energy that seemed intent on exploring every inch
of the ranch house, bounding into the lap of every
member of the Yates family, licking every inch of their
faces, and wearing Johnny to a frazzle in his efforts
to keep up.

Luke, who was sitting by the fire, poring over one
of Aengus's maps, seemed content to allow his
brother to be the dog's only owner, but Nugget clearly
knew otherwise, taking every opportunity to try to
draw the older boy into the fun. Finally, in a brilliant
maneuver, the puppy seized the map itself in his teeth
and scampered across the room, depositing it proudly
at Suzannah's feet.

"Why, thank you, Nugget," she smiled, picking up
the paper and wiping away traces of the exuberant
dog's mouth. Studying the details of the map, she
noted wistfully that it covered the area between the
Sierras and San Francisco. As sad as she'd been to
think of herself and Megan being separated by such
a distance, it felt stranger still to now wonder whether
Megan would be going with Ben at all.

Luke crossed to her and held out his hand patiently.

"I don't see Bent Creek on this map," she told
him. "Shouldn't we mark it somehow?"

"This thin line is the creek," he explained, tracing
a tributary with his finger. "And the town is here,
where the river is closest to the creek."

"That's right," Aengus interjected. "Have you seen
the creek yet, Suzy?"

"The boys took me over there to see the raft. And we had a picnic."

"But she wouldn't let us take her for a ride 'cause she was scared," Johnny added.

"I wasn't scared. I just wasn't properly attired for a dunking." She smiled sheepishly toward Aengus, and the answering twinkle in his eyes sent a stab of need through her. If only she could go to him. Ask him. Kiss him.

"Come here, Suzy."

"Pardon?" She flushed, wondering if he'd read her mind.

"I said, come here." He patted his knee invitingly. "I want to talk to you."

Acutely aware that the boys were watching her reaction, she stood and smoothed her skirts, then crossed to Aengus and sat primly on his lap. "What did you want to talk about?"

His hand settled on the small of her back, pulling her closer, and she was suddenly aware of how clean and fresh he smelled. And his face was so smooth, she wanted to brush her lips across it. Before she knew what she was doing, she looped her arms around his neck, murmuring, "Welcome home, Mr. Yates. We missed you."

A slow smile spread over his handsome features; then his hand slid up her back until it was cradling the back of her head, so that his mouth could descend firmly onto hers. Then he kissed her as he'd done at their wedding, and she abandoned herself to it easily, knowing he couldn't take it further with the boys in the room, and loving the waves of innocent pleasure his tongue was sending through her.

For all his faults—and she couldn't remember *any* of them at that moment—he was a wonderful kisser.

And he'd brought the puppy home to the boys! She wanted him to know how much she appreciated that, and so she allowed her tongue to spar playfully with his, for just a decadent moment or two.

Then a small voice, only inches from her ear, murmured, "Wow," and she pulled free to see Johnny standing right beside them, his hazel eyes wide with admiration.

"You should teach Ben to do that, Pa," the boy insisted with innocent admiration. "He almost missed Megan's mouth at the wedding. You *never* miss."

Suzannah stifled a giggle, while Aengus threw back his head and roared with laughter that vibrated right through his wife's modest green dress, stimulating her beyond all propriety. She was about to whisper a naughty compliment into his ear when he teased, "What do you think, Suzy? Should I give Ben Steele some advice on how to make love to his wife?"

Wincing at the irony of the question, Suzannah swiveled to see how Luke was reacting to all the hilarity, only to see that he had noiselessly left the room. Completely sobered now, she slipped from Aengus's lap onto her feet and murmured to Johnny, "It looks like your brother went to bed. It's time you and Nugget did the same. Go on now, and I'll be in to kiss you good night in a minute or two."

"Will you tell us a story?"

"Yes, if you hurry."

"We will! Good night, Pa. Good night, Suzannah." Scooping up the wriggling puppy, he added exuberantly, "Thanks for the dog, Pa."

"You're welcome, John."

As soon as her stepson was out of the room, she turned to Aengus and pleaded, "Could I ask a favor?"

"Of course." He stood before her, a little too close,

and smiled encouragingly. "What's bothering you, Suzannah? You haven't been yourself for hours."

"Could you sleep in the stable tonight? Alone, I mean. Not because I'm angry, because I'm not. And not because I'm not glad you're home, because I am. I just need you to sleep there tonight." When he arched an inquiring eyebrow, she added lamely, "There's something I need to ask you, but I'd prefer to ask it in the morning. In the daylight. It's a daylight sort of question."

He grinned ruefully. "You haven't made a lick of sense all day, woman. Do you know that? But I'm too tired to argue, so I'll go."

"Wait." She rose up onto her tiptoes and brushed her lips across his cheek. "I'm sorry, Aengus. I know I've been acting peculiarly. I have a reason, believe it or not."

"Don't apologize." He caressed her cheek with the back of his rough, warm hand. "It's my fault and I know it. I should have been honest with you on our wedding night."

"Pardon?"

He grinned again. "You said it was only for one night, and after that, we'd just be friends. I pretended to go along, but the truth is, I always knew I couldn't live with a pretty little half-naked female like yourself and not try to win your affections on a nightly basis."

"Half-naked?" She touched the collar of her sturdy green dress self-consciously. "What a thing to say!"

His eyes traveled over her with unmitigated longing. "When I was on the trail, I had a picture of you in my mind. Wearing your nightgown, or less. It's how I see you now, Suzy, no matter what you're wearing."

She knew it was only fair. After all, *he* was never wearing his shirt in any of *her* fantasies, so she allowed herself to smile rather than scold. "I think about you too. All the time. I wish your homecoming could have been less complicated, but something happened today—"

"At that damned tea party? I knew it!" he exploded. "I suppose it was Marilyn Potter who caused the trouble. Is that why you said Ben and I should go to Virginia City? I don't know what she told you about me—"

"She didn't say a word about you. Or at least, not a word I bothered listening to. It was something else, Aengus. Something I need to think through, before I ask your advice."

"Advice? Is that what you mean by a daylight question?" He patted her shoulder, then turned away from her and ambled to the front door. "Sounds like we've both got a sleepless night ahead of us, Mrs. Yates. If you change your mind and want some company, you know where I'll be."

"Good night, Mr. Yates." She waited until she heard his footsteps resounding on the porch boards before adding quietly, "Thanks for the puppy, Aengus Yates. And for paying attention to our sons. You'll never, ever know how much it means to me."

Chapter Ten

She woke up at least a dozen times that night, and each time she asked herself the same questions. Should she go to Aengus and seek his advice? Should she go to him, not mention Megan's problem, and just thank him in wifely ways for bringing the puppy? Should she go to him for no other reason than that she wanted to be with him? Or should she behave herself and stay in bed alone?

There was no answer, but finally, blessedly, there was morning, and to her delight, she detected the strong aroma of coffee before her eyes even opened. Hoping Aengus had lingered, waiting for her to appear, she dressed quickly in her prettiest blue-striped dress and nearly tripped in her eagerness to exit the lonely bedroom.

"Good morning!" she gushed. "The coffee smells heavenly." Kissing Johnny's cheek quickly, she hurried to stand before her husband, who was waiting patiently by the fire. "Did you sleep well, Mr. Yates?"

"It's daylight."

She felt her cheeks flush. "Let me fix some ham and eggs first. Then we'll talk. Johnny, did you find something for Nugget to eat?"

"He had pie." The boy grinned as he admitted, "So did me and Luke. It's all gone now."

"Imagine that. I suppose I'll just have to bake another one. Do you still have room in that tummy of yours for some eggs?"

"Yep."

"Where's your brother?"

"Outside."

"He went out to look over the new stock," Aengus explained. "I told him he could pick the one he wants to work."

"He must be thrilled," Suzannah beamed. "Are you sure he's ready?"

"I'm sure."

"You'll watch him carefully, to be sure he doesn't get kicked?"

Aengus and Johnny both chuckled; then the boy explained, "If he's smart, he won't be on that end."

Suzannah pretended to glare. "It's a wild horse. If it decides to rear up, neither end is safe. Isn't that so?"

"Luke knows what he's doing, but I'll keep an eye on him just the same," Aengus promised. "I'll go now, in fact. Send Johnny running when breakfast's ready and we'll all sit down together."

"I'd like that," she said, her voice huskier than she'd expected. "Thank you, Aengus."

"She wants you to kiss her again," Johnny announced mischievously.

"John Dennis Yates!" She scooped him out of the chair and tickled him until he screamed with laughter. "You stop teasing your pa about that. Do you want him to stop kissing me altogether?"

"No danger of that," Aengus assured them, turning Suzannah to face him, then brushing his lips across hers. "I'll be outside when you're ready."

She stared after him, even after the sound of his boots on the porch steps faded. Breakfast together as a family? Puppies and kisses and good-humored patience? When had life turned so suddenly perfect? If only Megan's life were half as wonderful right now, she'd be able to relax and enjoy it.

And there was always the possibility that it was—that Megan had confided her hurt feelings and unhappy secrets to Ben, who had then apologized, and reassured, and cast a new and more lasting spell over her.

There was no way of knowing without another trip into town, but neither Aengus nor Luke would have time for that today. Perhaps Suzannah could make the trip alone, or take her younger stepson for company. It would be worth it to find that Megan was happy. But if they found the opposite was still true, what good would more talking do, unless Suzannah had first spoken with Aengus?

The puppy, who had been dozing in the corner, woke up just then and scampered gleefully to Suzannah, jumping up on her legs until she relented and knelt down for a profusion of sloppy kisses. Then she bundled Nugget into Johnny's arms. "Take this wild animal out of my kitchen so I can get cleaned up and start breakfast. But don't let him startle the new horses. Understand?"

"Can he start all the chickens instead?"

"Startle, not start all." Suzannah grinned. "Is that

the thanks our poor chickens should get for providing our breakfast? Just keep your little gold friend out of mischief, and come back in a few minutes to wash up. And, Johnny?''

''Yeah?''

''Thank you for being such a wonderful boy. I don't know what I'd do without you.''

''Me neither. 'Bye!''

When Luke declined the opportunity to eat with the rest of the family, Suzannah felt a twinge of apprehension. The boy had been quiet and distant the night before, too, even when she'd told one of her most hilarious Noelle Braddock doll stories. Aengus noticed her concern and reassured her, commenting that Luke had selected his subject—a feisty dapple-gray mare—and was in the middle of introducing himself to her, a crucial moment in horse taming that shouldn't be taken lightly.

''I should be getting back out there myself,'' he said quietly as he finished the last of his meal. ''Luke's got the right idea, working them right away. So?''

Suzannah grimaced and turned to Johnny. ''Can you do your chores with Nugget, or do you want to leave him here with me?''

''He's gonna help me.''

''Good. When you're finished, you can play with him as much as you like. But I don't want you going on the creek with that raft unless someone's with you. Someone human,'' she added firmly. ''And there's a chance I might ask you and Nugget to escort me into town today, so stay close by.''

The boy swelled with pride before their eyes. ''I know the way. I can even hitch the wagon mostly without any help. Are we gonna show Nugget to Megan?"

"Perhaps. So you two run along and finish your chores." She leaned to peck him on the cheek, then scooted them away from the table.

"Into town again?" Aengus arched an eyebrow. "You're still worried about Megan? And about Luke too? I never knew you were such a worrier."

"I know," she sighed. "Isn't it awful? Let's hope most of it is my imagination, but the truth is . . ."

"The truth is, you want daylight advice about Megan's troubles." He nodded solemnly. "Let's go sit on the porch so we can keep an eye on those stepsons of yours. And then, out with it."

To her delight, he gallantly took her arm as they headed into the beautiful spring morning. Once they'd seated themselves on the steps, she admitted, "I scarcely know how to say this, so I'll just say it right out."

He nodded, studying her expression intently.

"It might help if you didn't look at me."

He shrugged and turned his gaze toward the upper paddock, where Luke and the mustang were taking one another's measure. "Go on."

"You know how Meg is. In spite of everything we know in our hearts about her mother—the gentleness, the goodness, the decency—she can't accept the fact that a woman might dance or sing for paying men without being . . . well, without being just like women who do other things for paying men. And so she thinks of her mother that way. And you know how everyone—you included—says Megan's just like her mother. In looks, and the beautiful voice, and the gracefulness—"

"Her mother had a gift. She should be proud of that, not ashamed."

"You don't have to convince me. Eliza Braddock was like a favorite aunt to me, and I adored everything about her. I would have given anything to be able to sing and dance like her.

"That's the root of the problem, I suppose," Suzannah explained. "Those were the qualities that impressed us as children. Meg saw them as signs of talent and culture, and she was proud to share in them. Then, when the rumormongers used them as signs of wantonness, she shared in that too. Felt tainted by it."

"And now Ben's said something that reminded her of all that?" Aengus exhaled impatiently. "That's what comes of keeping secrets, Suzannah. She should tell him it's a sore subject, and why. He may not be able to convince her her mother was an angel, but at least he can avoid hurting her feelings over it."

"It's not something he said, exactly."

"It's something one of the gossips said yesterday?"

"Not exactly."

"Well, then, what 'exactly' is it?"

Suzannah swallowed, knowing that this was the perfect time to ask the question she'd been dreading, and so she blurted, "Have you been to bed with loose women?"

"*What*? I've been out rounding up horses—"

"No, no," she blushed. "I didn't mean that. I meant, ever?"

He stared at her as though she had gone mad. "No good can come from questions like that, Suzannah."

"I won't be offended, I promise. And I won't judge, either. I just sincerely need to know. Please?"

Aengus pursed his lips. "If Ben visited such women

before he met Megan, that's no cause for concern. Tell her I said so, and let's be done with this conversation."

Suzannah smiled and patted his arm. "I knew this would be difficult for me, but it never occurred to me you'd be embarrassed too. It makes it easier, Aengus. Won't you just tell me?"

He shook his head, as though certain he was making a terrible mistake. "There were four years, from the time I left Katherine to the time I married you. For most of that time, I was still legally married, but even if I'd been free, the last thing I wanted was any complicated female entanglement. There's only one way to keep such things simple, and so I did."

"Of course you did. It's perfectly reasonable."

"It is?"

"Of course." She smiled encouragingly. "They were very experienced women, weren't they? I mean, compared to me, for example."

He nodded warily.

"Well, then." She took a deep breath. "All I'm really asking is for you to tell me what you did with them that you wouldn't dream of doing with me."

Aengus considered it for a moment, then shrugged. "I paid them. Did you want some money, Suzy?"

"Aengus Yates!" She pushed hard against his shoulder, disgusted by the burst of laughter that was rattling the porch boards beneath them. "Can you not be serious for even five minutes? This is important."

"I agree." He patted her cheek. "Tell Megan this: the only real whore I ever slept with was Katherine. Those other women, they were just doing the best they could with the only life they had, and no one with any sense would say otherwise."

"That's sweet, Aengus, but ..." She broke off,

annoyed at the sound of beating hooves in the distance. It hadn't occurred to her that Tom Whalen might be coming to watch the horse-taming, and it wouldn't do for her to be rude or unwelcoming to *him*, of all persons, but she was in no mood to be anything else.

Aengus squinted at the distant figure. "It's Ben Steele. Maybe now I'll find out what all this is really about."

"Don't say a word," Suzannah pleaded, grabbing his arm as he moved to greet their guest. "Let's hear what he knows first. If he really knows, we'll know. But if he doesn't know, we need to know that first."

"You're talking nonsense again," Aengus chuckled. "Settle down and we'll see what he wants." Raising his hand in a gesture of welcome, he added teasingly to his bride, "You're not going to ask him how many whores he's slept with, are you?"

"Don't make me slap your face, Aengus Yates," she blushed. Then she forced herself to smile sweetly at Ben as he swung himself out of his saddle. "Good morning, Mr. Steele. What a lovely surprise."

"Suzannah, don't try my patience," the gambler growled. "What happened at that damned tea party yesterday?"

His fancy coat was dusty; his expensive boots scuffed; his handsome face unshaven; his satin eyes bloodshot. All in all, Suzannah had never felt so fond of him, nor so sure of his love for her friend. "There's fresh coffee, Ben. And I'm guessing you haven't eaten in a while. Shall we go inside and talk?"

Ben sent Aengus a blistering glare. "I don't suppose there's any way you can force her to just spit it out?"

Aengus grinned and clapped him roughly on the back. "Do yourself a favor, Steele. Drink the coffee, eat the breakfast, and don't try to hurry her. If I've learned anything about this female, it's that she needs to do things in her own time. And," he winked toward his bride, "it's usually worth the wait."

As Ben rambled on, Suzannah and Aengus exchanged amused glances, despite the pure distress in their visitor's voice. It was fundamentally comical, seeing so debonair and confident a man reduced to such a miserable state.

"It has something to do with that damned tea party. She was fine when she left, but when she returned, she said she was feeling poorly and wanted to be alone. I should have known something was wrong, but I didn't. Then, when I woke up this morning, there was a note."

"Oh, no! She's left?" Suzannah blanched, ashamed at not having taken the girl's plight more seriously.

"For two days. With the judge and his wife. They've been asking us to go along with them—to visit friends of theirs who moved out here from San Francisco last year. Their housekeeper is a seamstress or some such nonsense, and Dorothy wanted Megan to have a dress made. According to her note, Megan has reconsidered because she wants to have something made for *me* to wear. A surprise, and so she'd appreciate it if I'd be patient until she gets back. What in blazes is that all about?"

Suzannah shrugged. "It's not so unusual. You should have seen her in Chicago. She loves to order shoes and boots and clothes."

"Fine. *I'll* take her shopping. Why go with them and exclude me?"

"Because she needs time alone, just as she said. And do you know what I think?"

He leaned forward eagerly. "What?"

"I think it's sweet of you to honor her wishes. To not run after her. I'm glad you came here instead."

"The only reason I came here, rather than running after her, is because I know she's angry about something, and I know she'll never tell me why."

"Consider yourself fortunate," Aengus drawled. "When Suzannah's angry, she *always* tells me why."

"Aengus, please be quiet," Suzannah scolded. "Ben, you did the right thing, coming here."

"Did I?" The gambler sighed with relief. "You're willing to tell me what happened at the judge's house yesterday? I'm not asking for myself, Suzannah. I'm asking for Megan. She's so miserable."

Aengus arched an eyebrow toward his wife. "Well?"

Suzannah moistened her lips. "I'll gladly explain it, but it's more complicated than you can imagine, so you'll both have to be very, very patient."

"Never mind that," Aengus interrupted, turning his full attention to Ben. "Did you ask her to sing or dance for you? Her mother used to earn a living—"

"Aengus!"

"He's her husband," Aengus reminded her firmly. "He has a right to know. And I have horses to gentle. I don't have all day for this nonsense."

Ben held up his hand to quell the dispute. "Megan's mother used to sing and dance to earn a living? Is that true, Suzannah?"

"Yes. It was before she married Meg's father, of course, but yes."

"Why does that upset her?"

"There were other rumors about her," Aengus explained. "Cruel and baseless ones. No one in our town with any sense paid attention to them, but little Megan took them to heart."

"She thought her mother was a prostitute?" Ben murmured. "Is that it, Suzannah? Is that what's bothering her?" The gambler's jaw tightened. "Did the women say something to her about her mother yesterday?"

Suzannah shook her head. "No one in Bent Creek knows, outside the four of us."

"Well, then . . ."

"Did they say something about Ben's being a gambler?" Aengus asked helpfully. "I mean no offense, Ben, but—"

"I'm not offended," Ben assured him. "Is that it, Suzannah? Is she sensitive about *my* reputation? Because I earn a living in hotels and saloons, just as her mother once did?"

Suzannah bit her lip under the eager scrutiny of the two self-appointed detectives. "Not exactly. But I suppose that's part of it." Her nerve to proceed disappeared, and she added helplessly, "You'd best just ask Meg."

"She won't talk to me," Ben retorted. "It has to be you, Suzannah. Otherwise, I'm convinced she's going to leave me for good."

"Over being a gambler?" Aengus protested. "She knew that when she married you."

"It's not that!" Suzannah glared. "Honestly, Aengus, I suppose there's no other way, so . . . Ben, excuse us, please. Aengus, may I see you in the bedroom?"

"Is this suddenly *my* fault?" her husband grumbled.

"Shh." She grabbed him by the arm and pulled him into the bedroom, closing the door firmly behind them.

"Well?"

"Sit down, won't you please?"

He eyed her suspiciously. "Are you angry with me?"

"No. I'm embarrassed."

He seemed relieved, and sat down on the edge of the bed, patting the coverlet beside himself.

She joined him quickly. "I know how much you love to tease me, but just this once will you please behave? For Megan's sake?"

"I'll do my best."

She gave him her most grateful smile. "We both know Ben's a rascal, but we also know he sincerely loves Megan. Don't we?"

Aengus nodded.

"He just didn't know any better, because he's a gambler. And it's as you said. He frequents saloons and dance halls and such. He doesn't associate with women of normal sensibilities, and so he's lost all sense of what's right and wrong." She could see from her husband's expression that he was about to lose patience again and so she explained quickly, "On their wedding night, he apparently introduced her to a peculiar and unnatural way of showing affection."

"He did what?"

"I'm sure he didn't mean any disrespect—"

"Don't make excuses for him," Aengus snarled. "The bastard abuses that sweet, innocent child, then comes here, taking advantage of my hospitality?" Rising to his feet on a wave of disgust, he turned toward the door. "Stay here, Suzy. I'll deal with this directly."

"Wait!" She pulled him back down beside her, alarmed by the disgust in his eyes. "It's not as though he hurt her, Aengus. If she had protested, I'm sure he would have stopped, but she enjoyed it at the time. And that's understandable," she added sharply. "It doesn't sound at all unpleasant, just naughty. And I ruly don't believe Ben even knew it was naughty."

"She *enjoyed* it?"

Suzannah nodded warily. "That's what she said."

"And it sounds pleasurable to *you*?"

"I never said it sounded pleasurable," Suzannah lushed. "I said it didn't sound *un*pleasant. That's iardly the same thing."

Aengus chuckled ruefully and settled back beside ier. "I have a feeling we're not talking about the ame unnatural act. What exactly did they do?"

"Don't make light of it, Aengus."

"I apologize. Describe what they did. For Megan's ake," he added quickly.

She studied him to see if he was still mocking her, ut he seemed sincere. "I'm not sure I can."

"Then just show me and be done with it."

Aghast, she tried to jump away, but he grabbed her nd insisted, "Don't be so skittish. I'm your husband, im I not?"

She hesitated, reassured by his no-nonsense expres- ion and firm grasp. She should simply say it straight ut before the situation grew any more absurd, and o she cupped her hands around her mouth and blaced them to his ears, whispering the words Marilyn 'otter had so crudely spoken. If Aengus dared to augh, she would be mortified forever, but at least it vould be out in the open.

But he didn't laugh. He simply murmured, "So? That's what it's about?"

"Meg's so ashamed," she sighed, leaning her head gainst his shoulder in relief over having finally livulged her secret. "And she's angry with Ben for reating her like a wanton woman. But she's mostly angry with her mother, I believe. That's where all the doubts start and end."

"What did you say to her?"

"What *could* I say? I tried to pretend it sounded normal, but she could see that it wasn't something you and I . . ." She winced and finished lamely, "I couldn't say what she wanted to hear."

Aengus grinned sympathetically. "I'll explain it to Ben, and he'll set it all straight. Don't worry any more about it."

"What if he can't?"

"They're in love, Suzannah. They'll work it through."

"I hope so." She smiled gratefully. "You know just what to say."

"And *you* know just what to whisper in my ear."

"That's enough," she warned, slipping to her feet and smoothing her apron haughtily. "Go on now and explain it to Ben."

She thought he might tease her further, but instead he left for the kitchen without wasting any more time. *He cares about Meg's marriage too*, she realized gratefully. She also realized that there was no way she could have explained the problem to Ben, or reassured Megan, without her husband's help. What did a little good-natured embarrassment matter in the face of so important a task?

To her surprise, Aengus hadn't been gone for two minutes when the sounds of hoofbeats announced Ben's hurried departure. Bursting into the kitchen, she demanded, "What in heaven's name did you say to him? I thought it would take hours to explain!"

"Hours?" Aengus scoffed. "I told him the truth. That the good ladies of Bent Creek didn't approve of where he'd been putting his—"

"Aengus!" She stomped her foot in horror. "You didn't just say it right out like that, did you?"

"Why not? *You* did," he teased. "And Ben understood, and now he'll talk to her, and it'll all be fine. I thought you'd show more gratitude than this."

"I'm grateful," she murmured, moving to the doorway to try and catch sight of Ben in the distance, but the gambler had long since ridden out of view. "I'm just not as confident as you are that it can be solved so easily. Meg believes no decent girl would have done such a thing. I'm not sure there's anything Ben can say that will convince her otherwise."

"I suppose it's like you said: the only sure proof would be for her to talk to a fine, decent girl who's done the same thing."

Suzannah nodded, then caught the twinkle in his eye and groaned. "That's enough of your foolishness, Aengus Yates. Go and tame those horses, so Tom can take his mother-in-law to the doctor."

Pulling her soft gray cloak more closely about herself, Megan Steele forced herself to take the last few, fateful footsteps that would place her in the doorway of the Comstock Saloon. She'd been watching the place for more than fifteen minutes, and was convinced that, of the four such establishments this ramshackle little town had to offer, the Comstock was the least nefarious. Cowboys, lumberjacks, and miners came and went, but none seemed overly inebriated. Of course, it was not yet dusk, but the traffic in and out of several of the larger dens of iniquity had already been marked by bleary eyes and excessively foul language.

She wasn't sure what she had expected, but to her

relief, the passing men hadn't paid much attention to her. She was invisible to most of them, although occasionally someone would tip his wide hat respectfully, then hurry past her, as though it was he rather than she that was embarrassed by the encounter. It was reassuring, although she wasn't exactly sure why. She hadn't put enough thought into the plan to even know what she hoped to find.

The most difficult part had been leaving the note for Ben. Lying to him. As angry as she was with him, she knew in her heart he had treated her purely with love, whatever mistakes he'd made. He certainly hadn't lied outright, although he had come perilously close. It was Megan who had intentionally deceived her spouse.

She seemed to have a flair for such prevarications, she grudgingly admitted now. Not only had she deceived Ben, she had completely misled Dorothy and the judge. Even now, the seamstress who was supposedly making a vest for Ben was waiting patiently for Megan in a nearby store, where they were supposed to be ordering fabric. It had been easy to convince the unsuspecting woman that Megan had a close friend who worked in the hotel, and that they wanted just a few minutes to visit alone. "Make some selections, and when I return, we'll decide which suits my husband best," she had suggested, and the seamstress had agreed without the slightest suspicion.

"Are you going to stand out here until dark, Megan Steele?" she chided herself under her breath. "Go on in and see, once and for all, where she did what she did."

She intended to watch the expressions on the men's faces as they watched the performers. Did they appreciate their talent, or simply ogle? And she would ask the women, "Why? Why do you do this? How does it make you feel? Wasn't there another way?"

The piano player had been taking a break but now began again, pounding out a medley of tunes that sounded refreshingly wholesome and quaint. He had some talent, Megan observed wistfully. Was it the same for talented men as for women in these places? Did they love to perform, and simply stomach the environment, or were they attracted to raucous crowds and disreputable living?

It was time for answers, and so she squared her shoulders, then pushed open the doors, stepping into the dimly lit, half-filled establishment. Several men noticed her but quickly averted their eyes, as though her mere presence either shamed them or ruined their fun. She wanted to run away, and had to remind herself repeatedly that this was her only chance to glimpse her mother's old life. Eliza Braddock had entertained men just such as these, although not nearly so far west of the Mississippi.

At least they aren't pawing at you or trying to kiss you, she rebuked herself sharply. *That's what you expected, isn't it? Just go on now and talk to the women.*

The only problem was, there were no women in the entire saloon! Which probably explained the fact that the other establishments were more crowded and rowdy, Megan decided unhappily. Now she'd have to go to one of those!

"Can I help you, miss?"

She spun to see the bartender watching her intently.

"I just wanted to have a look. For just a moment," she explained hesitantly.

"If you're looking for your husband, he's not here."

"My husband?"

"Or your father. Or brother. No one's here today. You should go home. He's probably there by now, wondering where you are."

The fact that the man wanted her to leave was reassuring, and so Megan smiled, just a bit, and asked, "Are you the owner?"

"Why do you want to know?"

"Actually, I want to know something else. Why aren't there any women here? I mean, women to entertain the men."

"Listen, miss," the bartender growled. "If your husband's out looking for entertainment, he isn't going to find it here. You can see that with your own eyes, so just run along."

"I'm not looking for my husband. In a way, I'm looking for my mother."

"Huh?"

"She used to sing and dance. She had a beautiful voice. I'm wondering why you don't have a singer here."

He studied her for a moment, then shrugged. "We have them from time to time. Can't pay well enough to keep one for too long, and most of them won't work just for room and drink, like Harry over there." He gestured toward the piano player. "I'll tell you one thing, miss. If your mother was half as pretty as you, I probably couldn't have afforded her."

"What a lovely thing to say." Megan squinted through a haze of smoke, intrigued by hapless Harry and his wasted talent. He looked to be middle-aged at most, and attractive in a weary sort of way. His striped jacket and starched white shirt contrasted sharply with the worn and dusty outfits of the saloon's patrons. It was almost as though Harry knew he was something special, even if his audience didn't.

Mustering her courage, Megan asked, "Could I sing a song? I mean, if you don't mind, and if your piano player is willing to accompany me."

"You want to sing here? Now?"

Her shoulders slumped in defeat. "Forgive me. I don't know what I was thinking."

"Wait!" A lopsided grin spread over his face. "I can't pay much—"

"I didn't expect you to pay me at all," she assured him quickly. "And perhaps it wasn't a good idea—"

"It's a splendid idea," he corrected. "You won't find a more appreciative audience anywhere in the Sierras, I can promise you that. Hey, Harry! Get over here!"

The music stopped abruptly, and Harry turned toward his employer, only to wince slightly at the sight of Megan. Then he hurried over to join them. "If you're looking for your father, miss, he left hours ago."

Megan giggled. "With my husband and brother?" Extending her hand in greeting, she explained, "I'm Megan Steele. I'm here to sing a song, if you don't mind."

Harry turned disbelieving eyes to the bartender, who nodded in confirmation. "Her mother was a singer, and she wants to give it a try. At no charge to me. Couldn't very well turn that offer down, could I?"

"You want to sing *here*?" The musician eyed her with concern. "Where are you from, miss? What brought you to this eyesore of a town?"

"She's looking for her mother," the bartender

explained. "It doesn't make sense, but let's let her have her fun. What harm can it do?"

"That depends." Belatedly accepting the hand Megan had outstretched, Harry smiled and kissed it lightly. "Harrison Lane at your service, miss. Have you sung for an audience before?"

"No. I haven't sung at all in years. But there was a time when it was like breathing to me. My mother taught me, and she was very accomplished. I'm not promising much—"

"They're looking for help down at the hotel," Harry interrupted sharply. "I know the cook, if you'd like me to put a word in for you there."

"I'd like to sing. Just once. I don't intend to perform for a living, Mr. Lane. I just need to know how it feels. How it felt for her, for all those years. I know it sounds silly—"

"Just one song?" He eyed her sternly for a moment, then visibly relaxed. "If that's all it's about, then I think it's a grand idea. I haven't played for a beautiful woman in far, far too long."

Megan blushed and glanced down at her somber clothing. "I wish I'd thought to wear something more becoming."

"There are dresses in the back," the bartender offered eagerly. "I'm sure there'll be something that fits you."

She wondered if they noticed her flinch, ever so slightly. Given the circumstances, it was an absurd reaction, and her smile as she nodded was rueful. "That sounds fine. Just show me where to change and then . . ."

Harry grinned and took her by the arm. "This way, then. While you're dressing, think about what you'd like to sing. I pride myself on knowing almost every tune around.''

''Oh, dear, I hadn't even thought about that. Couldn't you choose something? Something you think the men would like to hear?''

''I don't know about the others, but I have a personal fondness for 'Beautiful Dreamer.' Do you know it?''

Megan gasped at the unexpected choice—the very song Ben had chosen, more than once, to croon softly to her when they were lying in one another's arms in the dark, exhausted from their lovemaking. Such moments were among the most romantic and intimate they'd shared, and she had yearned, more than once, to join in the haunting refrain with him. Did she dare sing it now to a roomful of strange men?

And it was an amazing choice for another, unrelated but equally bittersweet reason. ''Beautiful Dreamer,'' more than any tune Megan could imagine, would have suited Eliza Braddock's voice, had she lived long enough to enjoy Stephen Foster's masterpiece. Gentle and unassuming, yet powerful in its very innocence. So like the woman herself in so many ways.

Truly grateful to the piano player for his oddly perfect suggestion, Megan squeezed his arm in thanks, then allowed him to lead her to the back room, where she rummaged through a profusion of outlandish castoffs. Mortified yet dazzled by the selection, she settled on the outfit she knew Suzannah would insist that she choose if she were there. Although, of course, it was best that Suzannah was miles away. What would she think of all this?

* * *

Suzannah couldn't remember when she'd been so distracted and confused. It was as though she had so many thoughts competing for attention, she couldn't concentrate on any one of them for more than a minute or two at a time.

First and foremost, there was Megan. Poor, darling, helpless Megan, crying her eyes out somewhere without anyone to comfort her. It was so tragic and unbearable, and yet, at least the girl wasn't all alone. Going to a seamstress wasn't the most conventional way to deal with a problem, but perhaps in Megan's case it would provide some temporary solace. With any luck, Dorothy would chatter nonstop, giving her friend little chance to dwell on her misery. And then, choosing a gift for Ben would remind the girl how much she loved her husband, and how much he adored her in return.

Still, Suzannah could kick herself for not having insisted on speaking to Ben before he galloped away. What had she been thinking, allowing Aengus to handle that delicate task? What if Ben went after Megan and insisted on discussing her mother before the girl was ready? Suzannah could only pray he'd have the good sense to abide by his wife's instructions and patiently await her return.

Patiently? She shook her head in defeat. There was no way the impetuous gambler was going to wait. He was probably bursting into the Donner Lake mansion of Dorothy's friends this very moment, demanding to see his bride. Megan would be mortified at the lapse in propriety, and their problems would multiply right there before their eyes.

If only Suzannah had had the nerve to talk to

Aengus sooner. They could have had better advice for Ben when he'd come to them. They may even have been able to tell him he could carry a certain message to Megan. The one message everyone agreed would soothe her ruffled sensibilities.

Although she was all alone on the porch, Suzannah still flushed wildly at the thought—the thought that had been teasing at her now for almost a day. The thought that the only way she and Aengus could truly reassure Megan was by doing what she and Ben had done. Just once, for a good cause. There'd been no doubt, from the twinkle in Aengus's eyes, that he'd be willing. If only she'd gone to him the night before, in his cozy corner of the stable, and gotten it over with!

As she'd done more than once during the day, she wandered into the yard, seeking a better view of her industrious spouse. He had been working a feisty white mare in the upper paddock for hours without a break, and while his posture was relaxed and his every movement slow and reassuring, she knew it was exhausting in its own way. Constantly gauging the horse's progress. Consistently playing the benevolent yet all-powerful sovereign, winning the steed's allegiance and trust by the sheer force of his talent and will. How she adored watching the masterful performance!

The animal balked and snorted, but there was no doubt Aengus would prevail. He was simply too confident to be denied, coaxing and reassuring, stroking and cajoling, all the while rewarding the animal with treats and compliments.

Suzannah flushed again, aroused for no reason other than the suspicion that he'd used similar tactics on her on their wedding night. The firm, gentle demands. The refusal to accept no for an answer. Aengus had known, long before she did, that she would eventually surrender to his amazing blend of skill and charm that night, and so he had been patient with her, until she'd melted right into his arms.

"That's silly," she scolded herself aloud. "Comparing yourself to a horse? You'd best pull yourself together, Suzannah Yates, and tend to your children."

Johnny was playing with Nugget in the distance, and so she turned her attentions to Luke, who had isolated his gray mustang in the corral and was attempting to bend it to his will. And showing signs of impatience in the process.

Why now? Suzannah asked herself uneasily. It was such strange timing. Aengus was improving, wasn't he? He'd brought the puppy home, and given Luke compliments and a horse of his own. He wasn't perfect by any stretch of reasoning, of course, but he was closer to the old Aengus than he'd been at any other time since her arrival. Why would Luke choose now to be more hostile and unhappy than ever?

Maybe he doesn't trust that it will last, she decided sadly. After all, Aengus had been a wonderful father once before, only to turn his back completely on the boys. Luke still bore the scars from that disillusionment. Perhaps he simply wasn't able to open himself again quite yet, for fear another withdrawal of affection would be more than his little heart could bear.

Give it time, she counseled herself finally. *Perhaps it will all work out. Ben and Megan. Aengus and the boys. And then, when all that's done . . .* She caught her breath before she dared speak aloud, "Perhaps yourself and Aengus as well."

Chapter Eleven

Through a haze of smoke, Megan could feel their eyes on her. Dozens of men. Strangers of every size and age. All looking up at her on the makeshift platform that served as a stage at the Comstock. Looking up at her ankles, to be more precise, she informed herself with nervous disapproval.

The yellow taffeta dress had seemed fairly modest in the dressing room. No more low-cut or revealing in the bodice area than the wedding dress she'd borrowed from Dorothy. And the fact that a mass of starched netting made the calf-length skirt flare out hadn't seemed to matter much until she'd laced up the shiny high-heeled boots and stepped out into the crowd.

And it *was* a crowd, thanks to Harry's spontaneous public announcement that unexpected entertainment had arrived. The word had spread through the seamy end of town a little too rapidly for Megan's taste, and while she tried to take it as a compliment, she feared it would be her downfall. There were simply too many of them, and their expectations were simply too daunting. And it didn't help that an appreciative murmur spread through the rowdy bunch every time her skirts rustled, which they did every time she moved.

At least she hadn't offered to dance! She would never have survived that. And her hair wouldn't have survived either. She had piled it to extravagant heights, secured by pins and bits of gold ribbon, in hopes that it might distract gazes from her bodice, but these men's eyes were everywhere at once.

"Go on, beautiful! We won't bite you," a voice called out from the smoky depths, and an appreciative chuckle rumbled through the throng. Turning her eyes in the stranger's direction, she was surprised to see a clean-shaven, ordinary man with a pleasant smile and a respectful twinkle in his eyes. He could have been Aengus, or her uncle, or any other of a dozen decent men she'd known and admired. He could even have been Ben if he'd had a bit more style and charm.

He certainly wasn't the drunken womanizer or shiftless, no-account beast she'd imagined these patrons might be. Scanning the audience, she could finally see the truth, that they were just a group of men escaping their labors and responsibilities for a few harmless hours. And while there was definitely something devilish in their eyes, she had a feeling that for the most part, it didn't extend to their hearts by any means.

Taking a deep breath, she smiled her brightest smile at the man who had taunted her, and was delighted when he flushed. Then she turned to Harry, and nodded, and an eerie silence settled over the crowd. Then, with one last glance about the room, she drew herself up, filled her lungs with air, and after her accompanist had pounded out a dramatic introduction, she allowed the first line of the song to flow, straight out of her heart and upward toward the rafters.

From a dark, crowded corner at the back, Ben Steele watched, mesmerized and confused, as his quiet, soft-spoken bride filled the room with a voice so clear and true and lovely that it brought a sting of tears to his eyes. "Beautiful Dreamer." Of all songs, why had she chosen that? In tribute to their love or, perhaps, in spite of it? From the far-off look in her sparkling gray eyes, he knew she had been transported. But from what? From whom?

Then he realized he was not the only person in the room affected by the resonating splendor. More than one man was wiping an embarrassed hand across his eyes, while others were audibly sniffing. They had come to see and hear a pretty girl. Nothing more. Instead, they were bearing witness to a timeless, sensuous, beatific cleansing of a talented artist's heart and soul, and their own hearts—their own souls—were responding in kind, as memories and dreams were pulled from them and given new hope.

He almost feared for Megan, wondering if the experience might prove dangerously draining, as her clear, haunting voice continued to fill the air. And so, ignoring the bittersweet ache in his heart, he moved quickly through the throng, not wanting to disturb her performance but anxious to be poised and ready should she collapse. He had almost reached the stage when the final words of the song drifted over them.

Then he, like everyone in the room, stood completely still, waiting for their cue.

And then she smiled, the most brilliant smile he'd ever seen, and the throng of strangers broke into a roar of applause and praise. Two of them handed Megan down to the dirt floor, and then the crowd closed in on her, respectful yet insistent, each man apparently needing to tell her to her face how she'd touched him. And Ben's eyes began to sting again, although he wasn't sure why.

From where he stood, he could see that tears were now beginning to roll down Megan's cheeks as well, and so he hastily shouldered his way to her and murmured her name into her ear. She spun toward him and stared, and for a long, frightening moment he thought she saw only one more stranger. Then she reached out her hand and tenderly, wistfully stroked his cheek. "Ben? You were here? You heard?"

"Yes, darling."

"I'm so glad."

"So am I." He stepped closer and asked in a husky whisper, "What are you doing here, Megan?"

"I'm not quite sure. I just needed to understand, I suppose."

"And do you understand now?"

"Yes, Ben. I believe I do."

"Well, then . . ." He glanced sheepishly at the audience, who seemed to be enjoying this show almost as much as the first. "Could we go outside?"

She touched her fingertip to his lips. "Just a moment, please? There's someone I need to say goodbye to."

He watched as she turned, almost into the arms of the man who had accompanied her on the piano, and they embraced as though they'd known one another forever. Then she leaned across the bar and kissed the bartender's cheek lightly.

When she turned, her eyes were not on Ben but on the rest of the men, and with a shy smile she threw them a collective kiss, then literally threw herself into Ben's arms. Relieved, he scooped her up and carried her through the throng, mindful but not jealous of the way the others were staring at her long, beautiful legs, so tempting in the high-heeled boots and lacy stockings. He was beginning to understand that it was all part of the show—and it was this show that Megan had needed so desperately to understand.

"Put me down, Ben. People are staring," she protested when they'd reached the wooden walkway outside the saloon.

"They were staring inside as well," he teased, lowering her gently to her feet.

"That was different."

"True." He pulled off his coat and draped it carefully around her shoulders.

Megan hugged the warm fabric tightly about herself. "It's all so confusing, isn't it?"

"Yes, darling." He touched her cheek and asked warily, "Are you confused about me? About us?"

"No, Ben. Not anymore." Slipping her arms around his neck, she rested her cheek on his shirt front. "I'll never be confused about us again."

He closed his eyes and exhaled in relief. "Thank God."

"I'm sorry I kept secrets from you, dear. I'll never do that again."

"And I'm sorry too, darling. If I haven't made love to you the way you want to be loved—"

"You love me so much it used to frighten me," Megan agreed. "But it doesn't frighten me anymore.

It makes me proud. And so very, very grateful that we met."

"Thanks to your uncle."

"That's true," she sighed. "If he hadn't arranged for me to marry Dennis Riordain, you and I never would have met."

"That's not exactly what I meant, Megan."

"Pardon?"

"A letter arrived for you today, just before I left Bent Creek." He tilted her face up to his so he could watch her amazing gray eyes widen. "Do you remember how I came to be on the same sailing ship to Panama as you and Suzannah?"

She nodded, puzzled. "You won the ticket in a card game."

"From a fascinating gentleman who predicted that that ticket would change my life."

"It's *so* romantic," she sighed. "I believe Uncle Russ would approve."

"I imagine so, since he's the one who conveniently lost the ticket to me."

"He what? Oh, Ben!" She stared, her lips parted in absolute delight. "That means he knew Suzannah and Dennis Riordain . . . Oh! You don't suppose he actually guessed it was Aengus all along, do you?"

"The letter's a little vague on that point," Ben grinned. "But considering the rest, I wouldn't be at all surprised."

"We should go back to Bent Creek right away! I can't wait for her to hear all this."

Ben grinned mischievously. "I imagine Suzannah's having enough excitement for one day."

"Oh?"

"I got the distinct impression she had plans for Aengus this evening."

"Plans?" Megan frowned. "To do what?"

"To provide proof that you've never done *anything* she herself wouldn't do."

Megan seemed unable to make sense of a word he was saying. Then a glimmer of understanding lit her face and, without further warning, she collapsed against him in a heap of laughter. Aroused beyond endurance by the sound and feel of her, he silently thanked Suzannah, then lifted his bride again into his arms and carried her eagerly toward the nearby hotel.

She didn't know which of the three Yates men was most exhausted—Johnny, from chasing Nugget for hours on end, or Luke and Aengus from their horse taming. Each was quiet during dinner, but Suzannah made up for it by chattering breathlessly about everything and nothing. She was so intent on convincing Aengus she wasn't thinking about later, in the barn, that she knew she'd accomplished just the opposite. As weary as he was, he still had energy enough to arch an eyebrow suggestively at her whenever she was foolish enough to make eye contact with him.

Predictably, the five-year-old was the first to succumb to fatigue, falling asleep right before Suzannah's eyes as she sat on his side of the bed, wishing him pleasant dreams. Pulling his covers up more cozily, she turned to Luke, who was already securely tucked. "Nugget wore your brother out."

"Yeah."

She moved to sit beside the older boy, brushing a lock of soft brown hair from his forehead. "You must be tired too, sweetie. You did good work today."

He shrugged his shoulders as though it didn't matter one way or the other.

"Would you like me to tell you a story?"

"I'm real tired, Suzannah."

"It was a good day though, wasn't it?"

"I guess so." He cocked his head and asked, a little too casually, "Why did Ben come but not Megan? Is she sick or something?"

"No. She went shopping with Dorothy Winston. Ben was lonely, so he came for a visit."

"They must have argued," Luke said. "Do you think they'll stay married?"

"Of course, silly."

"If you hadn't married Pa, would you go live with them in San Francisco? Or would you go home to Adamsville?"

"I don't know," she answered honestly. "I don't think I'd ever go back to Adamsville. I don't think of it as home so much, now that my mother and Megan aren't there, and you and Johnny are out here."

"Yeah. I don't think it's home anymore either. No place is."

"No place is *yet*," she corrected. "It takes time, Luke. You haven't even been here half a year. And you have to admit, this is a perfect place to grow up."

"I'm mostly grown already," he reminded her.

"Well, then, think of it as a good place to raise horses," she smiled.

"It's that," he agreed. "But you can raise horses anywhere."

She couldn't think of anything to say to that, so she pulled him into a warm hug instead. "I love you so much, Luke Yates. Promise me you'll try to be happy?"

"I'm trying, Suzannah," he confided against her shoulder.

"And promise me you'll let me help?"

"You can't help. I gotta do it myself."

She held him at arm's length and smiled sympathetically. "I suppose that's true. But it doesn't seem fair. You make *me* so happy, I wish I could return the favor."

To her surprise, he threw his arms around her neck and embraced her firmly. "We'll all be happy. I promise. It just takes some figuring. And patience."

"Like horse taming?"

"Yeah, only harder."

She watched with tentative hope as he settled back into his pillow and closed his weary eyes. At least he was seeing happiness in the future. He was being cautious, because he was Aengus's son in that way, but he also had the father's patience. Maybe it was time Suzannah tried having some patience too. The family wasn't going to heal in a day, or even a week, but they were making progress, weren't they?

When Luke's steady breathing told her he was asleep, she kissed his cheek, adjusted his covers, and crept out of the room, hoping to find Aengus still slouching against the fireplace, waiting for her return. But he wasn't in the living room, and when she checked their bedroom, he wasn't there either.

So, she told herself cautiously. *He may have been too tired to wait, and he's sound asleep in the stable at this very moment. It would be wrong of you to bother him. Unless he's expecting you to bother him . . .*

With a hopeful smile, she reached for her nightdress, then changed her mind and made a more provocative selection: the plaid flannel shirt in which she'd slept her first night at the ranch. Her first night in Aengus's bed—without Aengus, of course. Wasn't it time to remedy *that*? And she still needed to thank him for the puppy!

There was too much cloud cover for the moon to light her path, so she carried a lantern and walked gingerly, her bare feet sensitive to every pine needle and stone. With any luck, he'd carry her back, as he'd done the last time. When the thought made her tingle, she realized sheepishly that almost *every* thought made her tingle where Aengus was concerned!

Entering the dark structure, so quiet she could hear Midnight's gentle breathing, she found a patchwork quilt carefully laid out in the corner where she and her husband had met before. But there was no sign of Aengus, and so she whispered his name, then jumped when he tapped her on her shoulder.

"You'd better let me take that before you burn the place down." He took the lantern and set it on a nearby bench. "What's that you're wearing?"

She forced herself to stand still as he circled her, chuckling appreciatively. Then she explained, "It's my way of thanking you, Aengus. For helping Meg and Ben."

"That was my pleasure."

"And . . ." She stepped closer to him and admitted, "I've been thinking about what you said this afternoon."

"What was that?"

She eyed him suspiciously. "You don't remember?"

"I remember saying Ben was a lucky man because Megan doesn't berate him when she's angry. She just has a dress or two made."

Suzannah smiled reluctantly. "I know you love to tease, but won't you be serious for a moment?"

"Sure." He cupped her chin in his hand. "What's on your mind?" When she hesitated, he offered playfully, "Would it help to whisper it in my ear again?"

She tried to turn away in disgust, but he grabbed her by the waist and grinned down at her. "Until today, I thought *this* one was going to your grave for sure."

"Stop saying that!" She shook her loose hair unhappily. "I suppose you and Katherine—"

"No."

"No?" She bit her lip, confused by the blunt response. "Because she was a lady and never allowed it? Or because you never suggested it?"

"Katherine wasn't a lady," he reminded her quietly. "Megan's a lady. Her mother was a lady. And you're one too, despite all your sinful thoughts."

She blushed but persisted. "Have you ever done what Ben did?"

"Played cards for money?" He chuckled when she tried to pull free again, then suggested in a noticeably more husky voice, "Shall we give it a try?"

Suzannah stared down at the quilt, wondering if he had any idea how deliciously nervous she felt. Finally she dared to ask, "Does it appeal to you?"

He took her hand and placed it on his crotch. "It's been appealing to me all day."

She stifled a laugh at the hard evidence of arousal. "Feels to me like you'd rather do what we always do. I think I would too, Aengus."

"Too late," he murmured, pulling her close and nuzzling her neck seductively. "I've got my heart set on the other now."

This time, she couldn't help but lean into him and laugh lightly against his chest. "You'll tease me until it's done, so I suppose we'd best just get it over with."

Before his grip could tighten, she jumped away and added daringly, "I'm going to thank you now. For the puppy."

Clearly intrigued, he nodded for her to continue. "You said half naked or less, and so . . ." She worked the top button of the shirt easily, then the next, then the third. Flustered by his silence—where were the teasing remarks when she needed them most?—she fluffed her long golden hair so that it fell over her breasts, then wriggled her shoulders until the shirt began to slide toward the floor.

Losing her nerve completely, she caught it at her waist and smiled apologetically. "Is this enough?"

"Aye." He crossed to stand directly behind her, trailing kisses along the back of her neck and down her spine while she tried not to gasp with delight. His hands caressed her shoulders, then moved around, under her hair, to gently fondle her breasts. Even before his hands moved lower, to grasp the fabric at her waist, she knew what he was going to do and she easily surrendered the flannel shirt to him, enjoying the feel of it along her legs as it slipped into a heap at her feet.

"Suzannah," he moaned, turning her to him and falling to his knees all in one smooth, hungry movement. She wanted to stop him. To run away. But her legs were too weak, and all she could do was lean against his mouth as he covered her with kisses, starting at her waist, then working slowly, methodically downward.

"Aengus, kiss my mouth," she pleaded, dropping to kneel with him, her heart pounding with anticipation and confusion. He obeyed her greedily, as though he too had missed the way their tongues loved to spar as passion built between them. Pushing her back so that she was cushioned by the quilt, he kissed her mouth again, but this time she knew his thoughts were elsewhere, and within seconds he was working his way downward again, pausing to nip at her breasts until she whimpered softly, then tasting and kissing, lower and lower, until his lips were buried in soft, damp hair.

His hands, rough and warm, urged her to give him greater access, and when she didn't comply quickly enough, he forced her thighs apart, then coated them with gentle, reassuring kisses in apology. She wanted to apologize too, and laced her hands in his hair, pressing him closer to his destination. And suddenly she wanted it more than she'd ever wanted anything ever, and when his mouth finally moved to take what they both wanted him to take, the world began to collapse around her, with wave after wave of hedonistic release, until finally she exploded.

Still dazed, she smiled when Aengus stretched out beside her. And when he admitted, ruefully, "I need a favor," she didn't hesitate to slip her hand down to unbutton his work pants, soothing and stroking all the while. Without further permission or ceremony, he rolled atop her as soon as he was free, then pumped gently, again and again and again, until he was fully buried in her wet, hot depths.

"You must be exhausted," she purred, then she rolled him onto his back, pressing gently on his shoulders until it was he that was on the quilt and she that was staring down. Clearly impressed, he chuckled as he placed his hands on her hips. "You're full of surprises tonight, Mrs. Yates. I should bring home a puppy more often."

She smiled confidently, then began to move, slowly and suggestively, until the laughter faded from his eyes, replaced by a blaze of ignited passion. Leaning down so that first one nipple, then the other, grazed his lips, she allowed herself to control the feel of him inside her, and it was magnificent. Such power, she realized suddenly. They had such power, each over the other, as though they truly had been made for one another alone, just as she'd believed as a child.

Then his grasp on her hips tightened and he rolled again, so that he was towering above her, his eyes dark with need. His thrusts became surer and longer and more satisfying, and when he bent his head down to kiss her with deep, demanding thoroughness, her own need burgeoned again. She reveled in the sweet torture, arching and gasping with unrestrained delight, and as her glorious spasms engulfed them both, he climaxed in a burst of power and heat.

Through the lingering haze of lovemaking, she noticed that he was still wearing his unbuttoned shirt, and she pushed it out of her way, covering his hard chest with kisses, then resting her cheek there with a weary, adoring sigh.

"So?"

She laughed lightly and snuggled more completely against him. "It was fine."

"All of it?"

She raised her head and eyed him with feigned disapproval. "It's all fine if you don't care about babies. But I intend to give you a daughter, and so—"

"A daughter?" he interrupted softly.

Suzannah smiled at the confused expression on his face. "Did you think you could only make boys?"

He cleared his throat carefully. "I just never thought about more children, I suppose."

"After what happened with Katherine?" She

grinned impatiently. "It was only one time, and you were a father nine months later. We've been together more than once, Aengus Yates. For all we know . . ." She stopped, alarmed by the true distress in his eyes. "I'm not saying it's happened. I'm fairly certain it hasn't, in fact. But really, Aengus, would it be so terribly terrible?"

Something in his clouded blue eyes told her it would be. But why? Sobered, she reached for the flannel shirt and pulled it over her arms, then sat up and began to braid her hair. "It would be wonderful. Especially a daughter. She'd adore you, and make a fuss over you, and you'd wonder what you ever did without her."

He clearly didn't agree, and as Suzannah watched in fascinated confusion, he dressed and began to pace. Finally he turned to her and insisted, "I can't go through that again, Suzannah. We should have talked about this before we married. I see that now." Dropping to his knees, he took her hands in his and covered them with kisses. "I swore I'd never trust a woman again, but I trust you. I've given my heart to you completely. Can't that be enough, Suzannah? I love you with all my heart, and all my soul for good measure."

She tried to speak, but the words wouldn't come. Only tears, of joy and of relief, because she'd wanted to hear these words for so long.

"I love you too," she managed to blurt out finally. "I've loved you since before I can remember. Is it true, Aengus? Do you truly feel the same for me?"

"I love you more than I've ever loved anyone," he assured her, adding softly, "Except Luke and Johnny. I loved them with a passion once, Suzannah. Don't ask me to give my heart to a child again—"

"Because of the boys?" she gasped. "Is that what you're saying? You gave your heart to Luke and Johnny, and then Katherine betrayed you and ruined it. And you think that will happen again, with me—"

"No, sweetheart." He pulled her into a hearty, reassuring embrace. "I've never thought any such thing."

"When you look at them, you see Katherine—"

"No." He took a deep breath, then sandwiched her face between his hands, forcing her to look into his eyes. "When I look at them, I see Alex Monroe."

She tried her best to see what he was saying, but it honestly made no sense. Alex or Katherine, what did it matter? They both betrayed him, one as a wife and one as a friend. "You see Alex? More than Katherine?"

He nodded, studying her reaction carefully.

"And if you and I had a little girl—"

"If you and I had a little girl, she would be so precious, just like her mother. Every time I looked at her, my heart would burst with joy. I'd be an adoring father to the new one, and a coldhearted bastard to Luke and Johnny. Do you think that would be fair to them?"

"Aengus—"

"It would tear me apart. Tear *us* apart."

"Or it would bring us together! Don't you see that, Aengus? The boys would have a sister. And over time . . ." She felt tears brimming in her eyes. "You aren't a coldhearted bastard to those boys. I don't want to hear you talk that way. I know I said awful things about you when I first got here, but I was wrong. I've seen with my own eyes how hard you try—"

"Suzannah?" He wiped a tear from her cheek with

his thumb. "This might be one of those matters best discussed in daylight. Don't you suppose?"

She smiled at his feeble attempt to tease her, but the anguish in his eyes told her he would be as miserable as she until this was resolved, daylight or not. Still, he'd been taming horses all day, and was clearly exhausted. So it could wait, one night at least. "You promise to talk to me in the morning?"

"I owe you that," he nodded. "And the truth is, I'm tired of having it all to myself. I never wanted to burden you with it, but it's your life now, as well as mine. There's no mistaking that any longer."

She smiled through her tears. He loved her. He wanted to share his life with her. All the wonderful things, and the sad ones too. Things she couldn't even imagine, she was sure. After all, she knew very little of his childhood. Perhaps the roots of all these troubles were there! They would talk those through, and find a way to deal with them, whatever they might be.

Almost as though he'd read her mind, he admitted, "I was critical of Megan for keeping secrets from her husband. But I've kept a secret from you, Suzannah, and that will end in the morning. For better or for worse, as they say."

"Just tell me it doesn't have anything to do with our boys," she said hopefully.

"I should take you back to your bed now."

She sighed loudly, then patted his cheek in dismissal. "I can go myself. Get some rest, Aengus. Things will look better in the morning."

But he scooped her into his arms anyway, his eyes warm with desperation. "Don't let this change things between us, Suzy."

"I won't," she promised, wrapping her arms

around his neck and snuggling against his broad, strong chest. As he strode toward the house, she tried to remember how happy they'd been only moments earlier. Laughing and teasing. Making love, and then proclaiming their love for the very first time. Was it all for naught?

Before she knew it, he was placing her gently in his bed and kissing her cheek. "I love you, Suzy."

"Stay," she pleaded. "I can't bear to be away from you, tonight of all nights."

He seemed tempted, but shook his head. "I have some thinking to do. It's best done alone. Will you be able to sleep?"

"Of course," she assured him, pulling his head down for a kiss that was meant to reassure them both. Then, as soon as he'd left her, she wrapped a blanket around herself and went to sit by the embers of the fire. She had some thinking to do herself, and as Aengus had said, it was best she did it alone.

Try to think like a man, she instructed herself after almost an hour of fruitless misery. *Don't think about Luke's adorable scowl, or Johnny's darling smile. Try to see them through Aengus's eyes.*

It was more than she could ever understand. Here she'd been assuming he was angry with Katherine, but it was Alex! Not that she blamed her husband for feeling that way, but to be so unforgiving that he actually saw his ex-friend when he looked at those boys? Did men really hold each other accountable to that strange an extent?

It doesn't help matters that the boys resemble Alex Monroe, just a bit, she mused silently. *Dark hair and gold-flecked*

es. *They'd gotten all that from Katherine, of course, but
ist the same, they were so like Alex they could be his own*—
"No!" she insisted aloud. But even as she spoke,
powerful wave of certainty was beginning to crash
ver her. *This* was Aengus's secret fear! He honestly
elieved Alex Monroe might be the father of his pre-
ious little sons!

And just as surely as she'd been horrified, she was
ow exuberant, because it could not possibly be so.
Ier poor, darling, tortured Aengus had only to open
is eyes to see that his fears had been in vain. Hadn't
e taken the time to look—really *look*—at Johnny?
'he adorable smile, the mischievous teasing, the
arm, kind heart, the boundless energy. The child
iade her feel loved and treasured, the same way his
ither did. There was simply not a doubt in her mind
bout that.

And Luke? He was nothing less than the father
eborn! If she closed her eyes, she could see him
orking Midnight, and the image filled her with
elight. Aengus himself could not have done it better,
nd no one on earth could convince her that that
oy wasn't a Yates. The stance, the attitude—even
ie scowl! Vintage Aengus, at its worst *and* at its best.

She wanted to run to her husband. To gather him
ito her arms and reassure him. And then scold him,
or having ever imagined that Alex Monroe could
ave fathered their darling boys.

She wanted to run to him, but she could not.
ecause as much as she tried to deny it, she had to
dmit, for all their sakes, that it was possible. Dark,
ich hair; golden eyes; something about the nose,
erhaps. She physically cringed from her own imagi-
ation, but still could plainly see Alex Monroe stand-

ing before her. And in a way, he looked like he
precious little Luke.

"Suzannah?"

"Luke?" she murmured, shifting under her blanke
enough to realize that she had fallen asleep in the
rocking chair in front of the hearth. Then she opened
one eye and tried to smile up into her stepson's concerned face. "Good morning, sweetie."

"You slept out here? Is Pa in the bedroom?"

"I think he's in the stable." She stretched, then
fingered her disheveled braid self-consciously. "It'
still dark."

"It's dawn," the boy corrected. "I was gonna build
up the fire, but I didn't want to disturb you." He
touched her cheek. "Your eyes are red."

"I couldn't sleep." She looked at him, and all she
could see was Aengus Yates's son. With a melancholy
smile, she stood up and gave him a quick hug. "I'l
go get dressed. Don't run off. I'll fix you something
to eat in a few minutes."

"I'm not hungry yet. And I gotta go get some
wood."

She wanted to plead with him to stay, but imagined
he was anxious to run down to the corral and renew
his acquaintance with the feisty mustang. Wasn't tha
for the best? It made the boy happy, it brought him
closer to Aengus during the day, and it furnished
proof that he was the son of a horse tamer.

And from the swollen feel of her eyes, she could
imagine how depressing she must look to the child
That simply wouldn't do. There was still hope for thi
family, wasn't there? Hadn't she convinced herself o

at, again and again, in the dark, lonely hours before he'd finally dozed off?

There was a *slight* possibility one or both of the boys was Alex's. Nothing more. They would never now for certain, and there were just as many signs that they were Aengus's. More signs of that, in fact. And certainly in the eyes of the law, and society, they were Luke and Johnny Yates. Most importantly, they knew *themselves* that way. Suzannah had reminded herself more than once, during the tear-filled, endless night, of Johnny's boasting. His father was tall, his father was strong, his father could tame any horse, his father could kiss . . .

Those kisses were part of what had kept her spirit alive, even in the face of her darkest fears. Her wonderful Aengus, whom she'd loved since childhood. She had thought him irresponsible for turning his back on the boys, but now she saw the truth: even in the face of his belief that they were Alex Monroe's sons, he hadn't been able to walk away when they had no one else to whom to turn.

Of course, that hadn't been purely his responsible nature. Wasn't that what he'd tried to tell her last night? He had loved those boys with such heart-wrenching passion that even after years apart he had been tortured by the memories. Love like that didn't die. Suzannah knew that for a fact. Even when one tried to distance oneself from it, it lurked in every corner of the mind and of the heart. It had been that way with her love for Aengus, and it was that way for her husband's love for the boys. That had been the tragedy of it until now. They had to find a way to change that—to make that love a blessing for him again.

*   *   *

Even after she splashed water on her face, pinched
her cheeks, and put on a cheery pink dress, the mirror
told her she was a dismal sight. It would be days,
she decided, before those swollen, bloodshot eyes
returned to normal. Still, when she smelled coffee
brewing, a genuine smile lit her face, and when she
turned to run to him, she hoped he could see that
she'd put the misery of his revelation behind herself.

Before he could speak, she wrapped her arms
around his neck and smiled up at him. "Good morning, Mr. Yates."

"Poor Suzy." He kissed each of her cheeks. "Did
you cry all night?"

She started to deny it, then asked instead, "Did
you get any sleep?"

"More than yourself, I'm guessing. I should have
known better than to leave you alone, with all that
was on your mind."

She glanced about warily. "Is Johnny up yet?"

"They're both outside."

"Let me make some biscuits, and then when they've
eaten, you and I can go for a walk."

"In the daylight?" He smiled wistfully. "That has
a nice sound to it. Walking with my pretty wife on a
lovely spring morning. Too bad I'll be spoiling it with
my troubles. I'm regretting having told you, Suzy. I
should have known you'd take it too close to your
heart."

"Sit down by the fire and let me serve you." She
patted his cheek fondly. "We'll talk later, as we said."
She almost added a comment about Luke building
the fire, and for the first time, she realized how often
she'd made such remarks since her arrival. Pointing

out how wonderful Luke was. How lucky Aengus was to have such a fine son. Now she knew how those remarks had tortured her husband, and she ached to take them back. Or make them true beyond a doubt.

The boys still hadn't returned when she and Aengus were finishing their meal, and so she fetched her shawl and followed her husband onto the porch to call for them. Johnny and Nugget came running immediately, with assurances that Luke would be there "in a minute."

"Your father and I are going for a walk in the woods," Suzannah told the younger boy. "Keep an eye on Nugget while he's inside. I notice he's been getting into my knitting."

The boy studied her face anxiously. "Are you sick?"

"No, sweetie. I just didn't sleep well."

When he glanced toward Aengus, as though suspecting his father had made her unhappy, she knelt and smiled in reassurance. "Everything's fine, Johnny. Go on in and eat. Maybe later we'll take Nugget into town and see if we can find Megan. How does that sound?"

When he shrugged again and went into the house without another word, she smiled sadly. The loyalty of these boys to her—their determination to protect her from their father's moods—was touching. If only they knew how unnecessary it was—if only they knew the price of Aengus's unselfish dedication to their well-being—they wouldn't judge him so harshly. But of course they were children, and shouldn't be expected to know such things. It was up to her and Aengus to resolve this without burdening them in the process.

Then Aengus took her hand, and they strolled a

well-worn path up behind the ranch house. The cool, clean mountain air on her face made her feel vibrant and rested despite the sleepless night, and she began again to believe the worst was over. Tiny blue wildflowers were poking up through a blanket of pine needles, as eager as Suzannah to enjoy the warmth and promise of the spring sunrise. It was just as Aengus had predicted—a man, walking with his bride. As close to perfect as a moment together could be.

If only they didn't have to talk about Alex Monroe.

Chapter Twelve

It was Aengus who spoke first. "I told you I'd share my secret with you, but now I'm wondering—"

"I already know it." She put her hands on his shoulders and locked gazes with his. "You think they're Alex Monroe's."

A flash of pain registered in his eyes. "I shouldn't have left you to figure it out on your own. Can you forgive me?"

"Can you forgive *me*?" she said in return. "I've made so many thoughtless remarks and heartless accusations, never realizing how much I was hurting you."

He smiled wryly. "You never said anything I haven't said to myself a thousand times."

"But no more," she scolded. "If nothing else good comes of this, you can at least stop blaming yourself. I insist."

He nodded and brushed his lips across hers. "Thanks for that, Suzy."

She summoned her most confident smile. "I've given it a lot of thought, Aengus, and I can't deny that there's a possibility they could be Alex's."

"Suzy—"

"I'm not telling you to put it out of your mind completely. But the truth is, we can never know for sure—"

"We know for sure about Luke." He cupped her chin and grimaced apologetically. "There's no easy way to say it, Suzy, but you need to know it's true. Katherine was carrying Luke before I ever met her. It was a convenient solution for her—to have the child in wedlock and still be near Alex, in hopes the sight of a son would provide the strength he needed to leave Elaine and all her wealth."

She felt the boy slip away from her, and whispered "Luke" without even thinking. Aengus nodded and pulled her against himself. "Forgive me, Suzy. I should have told you sooner, or not at all. It was cruel of me to allow it to go this far."

"I was still a child. I don't remember how it went," she admitted. "You were married in May, I know. And he was born during a snowstorm—"

"It was November."

She remembered her mother braving the near-blizzard to take baskets of food to the new mother and child. Thereafter, Aengus had escorted Mary Hennessy back home to the inn. He'd been bursting with pride, describing how the child was already strong and smart . . .

But tiny, Suzannah's mother had kept repeating. *Such a wee, tiny darling. Born a bit early, I'd say.*

"He was born early," Suzannah repeated loyally

now. "Mama said so at the time. I remember that distinctly."

"And I remember Katherine's words, and there's no doubt."

No doubt? None at all? Suzannah sat herself down on a fallen tree and massaged her tired eyes with her fingertips. *Born a bit early . . .* Her mother had said it again and again, almost as though she were trying to convince someone—herself?—that the child had been conceived within the bounds of the marriage. Had she suspected the truth? Or more likely, just suspected that Katherine and Aengus had been intimate before their wedding day, which of course was true.

She turned to face her husband, who had sat down close beside her. "What about Johnny?"

"He looks like Luke, don't you think?"

"Yes."

Aengus took her hands and explained simply, "My advice to you, as difficult as it seems, is to think of them both as Monroe's sons."

She inhaled deeply, then guessed, "You don't really think that, though. You think Johnny's yours?"

He hesitated, then explained, "Sometimes it seems he's mine. I see someone from my past in him— my mother, or my uncle. But it only lasts for a few moments. And then it hurts, all over again."

She thought back to the day she'd told him she saw a glimmer of love in his eyes when he looked at Johnny, and Aengus had asked her: *Do you think Luke noticed?*

"You think it hurts Luke the same way it hurts you?"

He seemed startled, then profoundly grateful,

brushing his fingertips lightly along her jawline. "Can you imagine what it's like for the poor blameless lad?"

She nodded, her eyes filling with tears. "He wants you back, the way you used to be. He remembers so much. He told me you used to carry him on your shoulders—I think he *really* remembers, Aengus." She draped her arms around his neck. "I'm so, so sorry. I see how it hurts you, but can't you just let it happen? Let yourself adore them again. Let yourself see the reason Luke stands like you, and scowls like you, and handles horses like you—because you're his hero." She was on the verge of sobbing, but smiled nonetheless as she added, "Johnny wants to kiss like you some day. Can you imagine any greater tribute?"

When Aengus's eyes brimmed with tears but his jaw stayed tight, she felt her heart sink in her bosom. Something else was wrong. It didn't seem possible, or fair, or bearable, but there was more to this— she'd come to know that look—and so she asked, "What is it, Aengus? If there's something else, please just tell me quickly."

"You've forgotten about their real father. What will you do when he comes for them?"

"Oh!" Her hand had flown to her mouth to muffle the gasp. "Alex? Here? He wouldn't, would he?"

"Wouldn't he?" Aengus muttered. "I know I would, if I were him. If I knew I had two fine sons somewhere—my own flesh and blood—I'd ride to the ends of the earth for them."

"Then where is he?" she demanded. "He knows where they are. He let them ride away with you—"

"Aye, the selfish bastard let them get away once, for fear they'd come between him and Elaine's wealth. But if and when something happens to her, there's no doubt in my mind that he'll be here with open arms, wanting to bring them home with him. To send them to fancy schools and give them all the advantages his wealth could bring them.''

"And what on earth makes you think they'd go?''

"Huh?''

"For goodness sakes, Aengus, they want *you!* They want you,'' she repeated, her voice gentle yet reproachful. "The way *I* wanted you for all these years. Do you suppose another man could have had me the way you do? Do you suppose riches, or position, or fancy clothes could have made my heart soar the way you do, just by looking at me?''

"He's their flesh and blood—''

"He's no one to them. Less, I think. Ask them who their father is. No matter how much you hurt them, they keep turning to you. Because in their eyes, it's only you. Alex had a chance to be their father, Aengus, and he sent them away. Now it's your chance. Your choice. Your privilege. All you have to do is open your heart, and they'll be yours forever.''

He had been staring, transfixed, but now he slowly shook his head. "It's not that simple—''

"Aye, but it is, Aengus Yates. You said you don't like complications, so I'm telling you the simple truth.'' She caught his face between her hands. "You should hear how Luke talks about Alex Monroe. With simple disgust, same as you. Do you suppose that will vanish when he learns he's the man's flesh and blood, or do you suppose he'll hold him in even greater contempt for conveniently denying the relationship for all these years?''

"I don't want him to hold Alex in contempt,'' Aengus protested. "A boy needs to respect and love his father.''

"Then let that boy respect and love *you*, because

you're all he has in this world." She wiped at her tears with her shawl, then whispered, "It won't be difficult, Aengus. They already love and respect you. But they wonder why you don't return those feelings. If you let them see the truth—that you admire and adore them—it could be . . . it *would* be . . ."

He pulled her gently weeping body against his chest and rubbed her back contritely. "There, there now. I'm listening to you, Suzy. I'm hearing what you say."

"Are you?" she sobbed. "Are you hearing me say that those boys *are* your sons? In every way that could possibly matter. If they aren't yours, they aren't anyone's, and that just can't be so. Because they deserve better than that. They deserve *you*. They need you. Your baby boys need you, Aengus Yates. Just as much as I do."

"I need them too," he confessed, his voice choked with confusion. "I don't know if I can do it, Suzannah."

"You couldn't do it alone," she agreed, wiping her eyes hastily. "No man could. It was more than you could bear alone, but you have *me* now. There's so much love now in this family, Aengus, that I know for certain we can do it."

Tears were spilling again, but only because she could see the last vestiges of doubt melting before her eyes. "I know exactly what you want to do, Aengus. You want to take Luke and hug him until his ribs break. And our little darling Johnny—you'll hoist him up on those shoulders of yours—"

"Suzannah," he groaned, pulling her against his chest as though wanting to both silence and embrace her. "I'll talk to them—"

"You'll grab them and show them how you feel about them," she corrected, her voice muffled but nsistent. "And then you'll grab *me* and show me how ou feel about me too. And then"—she pulled free nd flashed an encouraging smile—"I'll show you ow *I* feel about *you*."

"Show me now."

She jumped to her feet and eyed him with pre- ended disdain. "Here in the outdoors? In the middle of the day? Where our sons could see us?"

"Our sons?" He stood before her and nodded lowly. "I like the sound of that."

"So do I."

He turned to gaze back toward the ranch house. 'I don't suppose there's any reason to wait."

"No. I don't suppose there is."

"So we'll just go take care of it now," he decided loud.

"*You'll* just go take care of it," she corrected gently.

He grimaced but nodded again. "Can I walk you ome first, Mrs. Yates?"

It wouldn't do for the boys to see her face so tear- streaked, and so she rushed to wash away all traces of the heart-wrenching talk. She might cry again when he saw them together, father and sons, but those vould be fresh tears—tears of joy. A few such joyful ears spilled out as soon as she saw the empty bread- basket on the kitchen table. A dozen biscuits, gone n a blink of an eye? No one could tell her those two veren't Aengus Yates's sons!

She would have given anything to witness the eunion, but knew it was something between a father nd his sons. And there would be hundreds more such moments, she knew. Each time Johnny beamed, Aengus would beam back. When Luke sassed, Aengus would correct and instruct him with firm, loving patience. And every night, Aengus would clap Luke on the shoulder and tell him what a good job he'd done, and how much he needed him. Then he'd toss Johnny into the air while the boy squealed with delight. Then Suzannah would force them all to admit, out loud, that they loved each other or there'd be no biscuits.

And then the boys would drift off to sleep, and Aengus would carry her to the bedroom—and occasionally to the stable—and they'd make love to one another and then fall asleep in each other's arms for the entire night.

But for now, she had to keep busy, and so she moved to the table, to clear it and begin preparations for a feast, celebrating the most wonderful day yet in their little family's history. A fold of paper in the breadbasket caught her eye, and she smiled when she saw it had her name on it. A thank-you note? How precious!

She opened it eagerly, then gasped at its contents.

Suzannah,
We don't need Pa or his ranch. We can take care of ourselves. Now you can leave too, so he can't make you cry any more. You can live in Sacramento with us, or in San Francisco with Megan. But don't stay with Pa. He's too mean. And don't go back to Adamsville, cause there's no one good there any more. We love you.

Luke Yates and John Yates

"Not today of all days," she whispered aloud. "Not when his heart is wide open." She cringed to imagine

ow much the note's cold finality would hurt her
usband, after all her insistence that his sons needed
nd loved him. And of course they did. She only
oped Aengus wouldn't feel too disheartened by this
ll-timed setback.

"Suzy?"

She spun toward him, startled by his quick return.
But of course, he had been unable to find them.
And now she had to tell him they'd left him. It was
nbearable.

His confident smile almost broke her heart as he
announced, "Those two must have gone down to the
reek to work on their raft. I'm heading down there
now . . ." He interrupted himself to eye her warily.
"Is something wrong?"

"They took the biscuits, then they ran away. You
know how boys are, Aengus. They do this sort of thing
ll the time. Out on an adventure, playing at being
men, not needing anyone else. You mustn't take it
o heart—"

"You're rambling," he interrupted with a reassur-
ng smile. "And it's true. All boys do this at one time
or another. I took off myself back in Ireland once.
Over some insult from my brother—may he rest in
peace. Did they leave you a note?"

"Aye." She reached up and stroked his cheek. "I
adore you, Aengus Yates. Do you know that?"

He rested his hands on her waist. "Don't worry,
Suzannah. They can't have gotten far. I'll go after
hem, and by dinner, or even sooner, it will be
orgotten."

She considered keeping the letter to herself, but
hey had promised not to have secrets, and so she
eluctantly handed it to him. "Children can be cruel

without even realizing it, Aengus. It sounds harsher than it really is.''

He studied the words carefully. "Sacramento? What's there?"

"Luke has it in his head he can get a job there. I'm not sure why. His friends have talked about it, I suppose."

"He's mentioned this before? Sacramento? Not Coburn's Station or Virginia City?"

She nodded sheepishly. "He talked of going there with me and Johnny. I never dreamed they'd just run off on their own."

"I'll bring them back. Don't worry."

The fact that he didn't seem upset or hurt impressed her. Maybe to a man, the note didn't sound so very cold and unfeeling. Aengus had run away himself. Perhaps he'd left a cruel note too, accusing his poor dead brother of something awful.

Aengus headed into their bedroom, returning quickly with an armload of blankets. "If they come home before I do, tell them to stay put. Tell them I have something important to say to them. And try not to worry," he added as he strode toward the front door.

"Aengus, wait!" She caught up with him and demanded, "What on earth do you need *those* for?"

He seemed about to make some excuse, then admitted instead, "There's no stock missing, Suzy. That means they took that damned raft."

"You think it's not safe? I watched them while you were gone, Aengus, and it floats really well."

"On the creek. But the creek doesn't go to Sacramento." He started backing away from her impatiently. "The sooner I go, the sooner I'll have them back to you, safe and sound."

"Wait! I'm coming too." Ignoring his protests, she
atched her shawl off the back of the rocking chair
d followed him out onto the porch, trying her best
t to remember all she'd heard about the relentless
merican River, with its angry rapids, more swollen
d bone-chilling than ever this time of year as the
erra snow pack melted under the hot new sun.

Aengus readied his stallion quickly, spreading the
tra blankets behind the saddle; then he swung
zannah up easily behind himself. Instructing her
rsely to "Hold on and don't worry," he touched
s heels to the perfectly trained stallion and they
aded up past the upper paddock, where they
cked up a trail that wove its way through the dense
nds of pine, fir, and cedar.

"Shouldn't we check down there first?" she
outed as they bypassed the familiar path leading
wn to Bent Creek.

"Luke's too damned smart to try to get to Sacra-
ento on that creek."

She sighed at the fatherly tone—a perfect blend
pride and annoyance. If only Luke knew. If only
ey could find him and tell him now, before it was
o late. "You warned him about the river. Maybe he
tened."

"He's too angry to think straight. Too angry, and
o intent on saving you from me."

She leaned her cheek against his back. "I'm sorry
e note was so harsh, Aengus."

"It doesn't matter. Nothing matters now except
ding them." He reined in the stallion as they
ached a clearing overlooking the river. "Can you
e any sign of them down there, Suzy?"

She couldn't answer. In all her imagining, she
dn't expected so menacing and ominous a sight.

Even from this height, a good five hundred feet abov
the river, she could feel the raw power of the torren
tial, unforgiving waters. And right before her eye
hapless tree limbs, some of great size, were bein
propelled for short stretches, only to crash and splin
ter against larger logs and boulders.

Aengus pointed downstream and shouted, "Is tha
the dog?"

"Where?" She strained her eyes and ears, and nod
ded eagerly at the sound of distant yapping. "I hea
him! But I don't see him!"

"Hold on!"

She gasped as the powerful stallion responded t
its master's urging and began to gallop down th
slope, heedless of the steep, uneven terrain. Clingin
to her husband's vest for life itself, she tried not t
scream, although she wasn't sure he would have hear
her over the deafening roar of the cascading rapid
By some miracle, the horse kept its footing, an
before she could catch her breath, Aengus had reine
it to a sharp stop and half tossed her off its back
"Get the blankets," he ordered, grabbing a rope he'
slung over the saddle horn. "And follow me."

She had barely managed to get her footing whe
from out of nowhere, Nugget catapulted himself int
her arms, whimpering pitifully as he covered her fac
with frantic kisses. "Oh, poor baby. You're soakin
wet. Aengus! He's soaked through!"

"Here!" He grabbed her and turned her face s
that she was looking downstream to a spot where th
river narrowed into a violent, rocky chute. "That
where I'm headed. Watch your footing, and meet m
there."

'But, Aengus—'' She watched him scramble over
ossy rocks and debris until he reached a narrow
nd of granite where the steep wall met the thunder-
g waters. How could he expect her to follow? She'd
o and break her neck!

Then she saw what he saw, and in an instant she
s scrambling behind him with no thought to the
ety of anyone but the two little boys clinging precar-
usly to one another as the mighty river churned
ound them. For a moment, she thought they were
th still on the raft; then she realized Luke was in
e water, his right arm wrapped around a fallen tree
anch while he clung with his left hand to the raft,
lding it in place despite the diabolical efforts of
e cascading waters to sweep it toward a veritable
ircase of boulder-choked rapids.

'Luke!'' Aengus shouted through cupped hands.
uke! Let go of the raft. I'm here now. I can grab
n.''

The boy stared as though he were hearing and
ing a ghost, but didn't release the raft. And Johnny,
o had also heard the instruction, now grasped at
brother's arm, further securing them one to the
her.

''Luke!'' Aengus's voice took on a resonant, nonsense quality. ''Let it go now! I can't get to you
ere!'' He pulled off his boots and turned to Suzan-
h. ''He can't hold on like that much longer. I'll
ve to try to get to them there.''

''Can you do it?''

''I don't have a choice.''

''Talk to him again,'' she pleaded. ''Just one more
ne.''

He nodded, then yelled through his hands, ''Let

the raft go, son! I give you my word I'll be there
catch him!''

Luke nodded, then yelled something at Johnn
who was apparently unwilling or unable to release h
arm.

"Johnny!" Suzannah screamed. "Listen to yo
brother!''

"No! Suzannah! Pa!''

Desperate, Luke leaned his mouth down to h
brother's hand, burying his teeth in the child's so
skin. Johnny yelped in pain and uncoupled hims
from Luke, who shouted, "Get him, Pa!" just as l
released his own grip on the raft.

Aengus had already plunged into the icy water ar
in three powerful strokes had positioned hims
ahead of the raft. As Suzannah watched in horrifi
amazement, the tiny craft hit a craggy rock and se
its passenger spilling overboard. She shrieked, the
shrieked again, this time with relief, as Aeng
grabbed the boy by his collar and lifted him half o
of the water, then hugged him to his chest and beg
to battle his way back out of the icy torrent.

Suzannah raced to the edge, ready with a blanke
and bursting with gratitude toward Aengus f
returning her little one to her. Then she turned
wave to Luke, her heroic son, so he'd know for certa
that his little brother was safe. But the older boy w
nowhere in sight.

"*Aengus!*" She waded up to her knees in the free
ing, swirling waters, meeting her husband just as l
was gaining his footing. "I can't see Luke!''

Shoving the little one into her arms, Aengus turne
and plunged back into the freezing depths witho
a moment's hesitation, while Suzannah bundle

Johnny onto the narrow riverbank, wrapping him and cooing his name as she searched in vain for any glimpse of either of her heroes.

The child cuddled gratefully. "Suzannah?"

"Hello, sweetie." She cradled him against herself, then searched again for some sign of his father and brother, while Nugget clamored and jumped, trying without success to reach his little master.

"Pa came and saved us."

"Yes, darling, I know." She fought against the tears that had plagued her far too often in the last twenty-four hours.

Johnny stirred again and began to look around. "Where is he? Where's Luke?" The groggy voice disappeared, replaced by panic. *"Where's Luke?"*

"Your father went to—Oh! Oh, Johnny! There they are!"

Her heart pounded with relief at the sight of Aengus emerging once again from the treacherous waters with another son grappled tightly against his chest. She was about to cheer in exhausted delight when she realized Luke's body was too limp. Too still. And much, much too pale. And Aengus's expression—

"No!" she wailed. "Oh, Aengus! No . . ."

He strode onto the bank and lowered the boy quickly to the ground, then knelt over him, shaking him gently and calling his name in a firm, patient voice. Then he put his ear to the child's chest and listened intently.

Clasping Johnny's face to her bosom so that he could be shielded from this tragic drama, Suzannah edged closer in vain hopes of hearing Luke's heartbeat herself. Then Aengus tilted Luke's chin back and reached into his mouth to clear his throat.

"Oh, no . . ." Suzannah murmured. "Oh, no . . . please . . ."

Aengus breathed briskly into the child's mouth, once and then again and again, and then she heard him whisper, "Stay with me, son. I need you. I love you."

"Suzannah?" Johnny wriggled so that he could watch as Aengus again began to breathe into the child. "Is Luke hurt?"

"Shhh . . ." She cuddled him close again, her throat too tight to answer, even if she had an answer.

Then Luke's body convulsed with a jolt, while a spurt of water shot out of his mouth. Yanking him up to a sitting position, Aengus thumped on the boy's back, then pulled him into a hearty bear hug while growling, "Welcome back, son. Damn, you had us worried!"

"Pa?"

"It's fine now. Just breathe. Not too deep, though. Nice and easy."

Luke shifted frantically in his father's arms. "Where's Johnny?"

"Right over there with Suzannah. He's fine, thanks to you." Holding Luke at arm's length, Aengus added fervently, "I've never been so proud of anyone in my life. It's an honor to be your father."

The boy smiled weakly, then twisted to look toward Suzannah and Johnny. It was too much for the little one, who wiggled free and ran to stand at his brother's side, announcing, "Pa saved us."

"Yeah, I know."

"You were almost dead," Johnny continued happily. "Like *this*." Falling prostrate on the ground, he spread out his arms, crossed his eyes, and let his tongue hang out of the side of his mouth.

Luke grinned weakly, then turned his attention to Suzannah, who was draping a blanket around his shoulders. "Did you see Pa save us?"

"Yes, I did." She rubbed his arms vigorously through the fabric. "You gave us quite a scare, sweetheart. But you also made us very proud."

Aengus gave Suzannah's shoulder a quick squeeze, then nudged Johnny with his toe. "Come over here to me, John."

The boy sat up, his expression wary; then he shrugged to his feet and stood before Aengus.

Suzannah smiled as her husband cupped the boy's little chin in his hand, forcing him to look directly into his eyes. "I'm proud of you too, son. You didn't panic, and you showed a lot of courage."

"I did?" He smiled with tentative delight. "You're not gonna yell at us for going on the river?"

"Is it going to happen again?"

"No, sir."

"And are you going to stay with me, and give me a chance to be a good father?"

"Sure, Pa."

"Well, then . . ." Aengus pulled the little one into a hearty, loving embrace.

Luke had been watching intently, and now whispered to Suzannah, "He called *me* 'son,' too. Did you hear him?"

"Yes, Luke. I heard him."

He studied her face, as though expecting her to explain it all to him, and she might have tried, but Aengus reached out a hand at that moment, turning the older boy toward him. "Luke?"

"Aye?"

The simple expression brought tears to the man's eyes, and to Suzannah's amazement, he didn't even try to hide them. "Tonight, after dinner, I'm going to tell you the story of the night you were born. One of the greatest nights of my life. We have memories, you and I. We're going to talk them all through— the good ones, and the bad ones—and by the end, you'll understand. Does that make sense?"

Luke nodded.

"I remember that night," Johnny interrupted.

"You do not," Luke grumbled. "You weren't even born yet."

"I remember it," Johnny insisted. "You cried like a baby, didn't he, Pa?"

Aengus threw back his head and roared with laughter, then grabbed the little one and hoisted him up onto his shoulders. "Do you know who you remind me of, Johnny? My Uncle Denny. He was full of malarkey too."

"Malarkey?"

"Aye." He clamped his arm around Luke's shoulder. "Do you think you can handle my stallion, son? Suzannah needs an escort home, and I'm saddled with this one, so you're elected."

"I can do it, Pa." He hesitated, then asked innocently, "Pa?"

"Aye?"

"You said Johnny reminds you of your uncle. Who do *I* remind you of?"

Suzannah held her breath, knowing somehow that this fragile moment could affect the rest of their lives together. She wanted Aengus to think it through. To name a beloved relative, as he'd done for Johnny. To put aside any lingering bitterness or insecurity, and allow himself to see something in this boy untainted by Katherine and Alex's sin.

But Aengus didn't take even a moment to think before nodding and assuring the boy, "That's a good question, Luke." Then, with a directness that suited them both, he said simply, "You remind me of myself."

CARRIED AWAY

Coming from Zebra Ballad, February 2001

Russell Braddock, proprietor of the Happily Ever After Co., is an expert in matters of the heart. So when he receives a letter from a prim Boston governess, offering herself as a bride "for a proper and well-educated gentleman," he knows how to read between the lines. He's certain that what Erica Lane really needs is to be carried away by passion. And he knows just the man to do it: brash, brawling sea captain Daniel McCullum.

But Erica isn't who she pretends to be, and when she steps onto the pink sands of Captain McCullum's Caribbean hideaway, she realizes she's gotten in way over her head. . . .

ABOUT THE AUTHOR

Kate Donovan was born in Ohio and grew up there and in Rhode Island, then moved to Northern California to attend college at Berkeley and law school at King Hall on the UC Davis campus. Today she divides her time equally among her many loves—a great husband, charming son, and delightful daughter; her love stories; and a career as an attorney in Sacramento, California. This is her sixth book.

COMING IN OCTOBER FROM
ZEBRA BALLAD ROMANCES

___A BROTHER'S HONOR, Shadow Of The Bastille #2
   by Jo Ann Ferguson   0-8217-6729-1 **$5.50US/$7.50CAN**
When French privateer Dominic St. Clair seized a ship outside of England,
he found more than a valuable cache of weapons—he found the captain's
beautiful daughter, Abigail. Now, as fate sweeps them to England's shore,
Dominic must fight for the woman who holds his heart in her hands . . .

___LAST CHANCE RANCH, Titled Texans #2
   by Cynthia Sterling   0-8217-6698-8 **$5.50US/$7.50CAN**
Reg Worthington must prove that he can manage his family's new ranch—
and to do this, he needs the help of his unconventional neighbor, Abigail
Waters. In return, Reg instructs her in the art of the uppercrust. Soon, their
deal throws them together in a new intimacy that just might tempt fate . . .

___ONCE A PIRATE, Jewels Of The Sea #1
   by Tammy Hilz   0-8217-6697-X   **$5.50US/$7.50CAN**
Intent on saving her people, Morgan Fisk transforms herself into a fearsome
lady pirate. Yet one man has vowed to bring her to justice. When passion
flares between the two, Morgan's heart is torn between her duty and the man
who challenges her to become a lady . . . and his countess.

___THE FAIRY TALE BRIDE, Once Upon A Wedding #1
   by Kelly McClymer   0-8217-6699-6 **$5.50US/$7.50CAN**
Miranda Fenster will do anything for true love—even confront the man standing
in the way of her brother's happiness. But when Miranda's meeting with the
Duke of Kerstone leads to a tryst that might compromise her position, the
cynical Duke insists on nothing less than marriage. Now the champion of fairy
tale endings finds herself a most unlikely bride!
